Echo of the Cliffs
A Juniper Sawfeather Novel, Book 3

D. G. Driver

Published by
Fire and Ice
A Young Adult Imprint of Melange Books, LLC
White Bear Lake, MN 55110
www.fireandiceya.com

ISBN: 978-1-68046-482-5

Cover Design by Caroline Andrus

Dedication

To Mom and Dad who have supported me through every adventure.

"A giant, who looked as if the whole of him were made of gray stone, lay stretched out on his belly. He was almost ten feet long. Propped up on one elbow, he was looking into the fire. In his weather-beaten stone face, which seemed strangely small in comparison with his powerful shoulders, his teeth stood out like a row of steel chisels."
Michael Ende, *The Neverending Story*

Chapter One

My birthday cake splattered all over the rocks. Haley and Carter dropped it to chase after me. I was already lowering myself over the side of the rocky cliff, and I heard them shouting after me to stop. I knew my feet weren't healed enough to be attempting this descent. I was still recovering from my week in the tree and didn't have a lot of strength. The rocks were slick with mist and ocean spray, and I had a hard time getting a grip. It didn't matter. I had to get down there before the mermaid swam away.

"June! Stop!" Carter shouted down to me. Haley screeched behind him. I'm not sure if there were words involved.

He was coming after me, but I didn't look up to see his progress. I had to stay focused on where I was placing my hands and feet. This wasn't the steepest of cliffs, nor was it a simple staircase, either. My breathing came hard too quickly. I shouldn't have been winded already, and that just ticked me off. I spit out a curse word or two and kept going.

I was almost close enough to the tide pools to let go and jump when Carter caught up to me. He swung down and put his body around me, pressing me into the rocks like some shield against the wind. His arms were stretched out to both sides of my head, and his feet spread out to both sides of mine. He had me trapped. I tried pulling my legs together and wriggling like I might slip underneath him. That didn't work. He pressed his chest against my back and held me still.

"What are you doing?" He had to yell to be heard above the ocean surf, even though his mouth was buried in my hair.

"I saw her!" I shouted back and pointed behind me as best I could. "Down there! She's down there right now! I have to get to her!"

"You're crazy, June. There's nothing down there."

1

"Her hand took the wreath I made. You missed it because you were at the car." I wiggled as hard as I could. "Just let me go before she gets away."

"I can't. You're going to hurt yourself. You aren't ready for this yet."

"Then help me."

From above us I heard Haley calling out, asking if we were okay. Carter waved at her, and when his hand lifted off the rocks, I slipped out the opening he gave me. I didn't get far, though, because he grabbed my right arm. Good thing too, because my sneakers slipped, and I would've had a hard slide into the ocean. With a groan, Carter yanked me back up to where I had my footing again.

"Please let me go," I said instead of thanking him. "There isn't time. She'll swim away."

Carter glanced down at the tide pools and back at me. "There's nothing there."

"She's there."

He knew by my tone that I wasn't kidding. Carter took a sharp breath and looked me squarely in the eye. "I don't doubt you saw something. I don't think I'll ever doubt that again after what you've been through, but this is dangerous."

"She won't let me drown if I fall."

"You don't know that. You don't even know if it's your girl."

"Of course it is. Who else would it be? Let me go see."

"Fine," he agreed, sounding a bit like my dad on those rare occasions when I'd win an argument by being more stubborn than him. "But let me help you."

Somehow, while keeping a hand on me at all times, he guided me down the remainder of the cliffs until we were crouched on the tide pools where the wreath of Red Cedar tree twigs had been.

I leaned forward as far as Carter would let me. He kept his hands firmly around my waist, anchoring me in place. My feet throbbed inside my wet shoes. My thighs and calves burned from the strain I just put on them. I had no idea how I was going to get back up the cliff, but I couldn't think about that yet. I dipped my hands in the water. The waves slapped at my forearms and spit in my face.

"Come on," I moaned. "I know you're there."

I splashed and slapped the water, trying to draw attention to myself. Then I stilled and waited, allowing a couple minutes to pass.

"I don't know how much longer I can hold you like this," Carter said. "This is an awkward position, and my feet are slipping."

I craned my neck to look back at him. He had his left knee bent up beside my hip, but his right leg was stretched out as far as it could go, his foot wedged between two rocks for balance.

"Just hang on. Give it one more minute."

"Seriously, June, I don't think I can."

"Then let go of me."

He didn't mean to. His left foot slipped backward, and he landed hard on his knee. That threw off his balance, and he rolled backward, away from me. The moment his hands left my body, I lurched forward. I didn't realize how much he was holding me in place. I tumbled head first into the freezing Pacific Ocean.

It wasn't a far drop, but the force of the water flipped me upside down. Water went up my nose and made my sinuses burn. My eyes were closed, and I forced them to open in the salt water. It didn't matter, because I couldn't see anything but froth. The pressure of the ocean banged me up against the tide pools over and over. Even as I struggled to get my bearings, all I could think of was how mad my mom was going to be that I let myself get hurt again so badly less than a week after coming down from that tree.

Then I felt hands. I'm sure they were Carter's hands reaching at me from above, trying to catch mine as I grasped for the rocks, but there were also hands on my ankles, slipped under the cuffs of my jeans and above my socks. Wet, slimy hands that felt almost like they had suckers on them. Strong hands tugged me downward away from Carter. Away from the rocks. Away from air.

I was dragged backward into the deeper water for a moment, and then the hands let go of my ankles. Free, I kicked and tried to swim up. My lungs burned. I hadn't taken a deep breath before I fell. Just as my face broke through the surface and I gulped in a lungful, an arm wrapped firmly around my torso and yanked me under again. My eyes couldn't adjust to the darkness or the speed of the water going past, but I understood what was happening to me. A mermaid had me tucked close to her side like I was nothing more than a football. Her tail pumped up and down to propel us away from the shore at a crazy pace.

I heard screaming, and I imagined it was Haley and Carter. In reality, I knew I couldn't hear them. The screams were mine – inside my head. I managed to twist my head and open my eyes to get a look at the mermaid holding me. Her giant, dark eyes focused straight ahead of her. The gills on her thin neck opened and contracted as she breathed. I was certain at that point the mermaid didn't realize I couldn't breathe under the water like her.

My head swam with dizziness as my lungs struggled to hold on to what oxygen was left in them. I had to get to the surface immediately, or I'd black out. Even if the effort of struggling against her used up the last of my energy, making me drown faster, I had to try. I pushed down on her arm as hard as I could with my hands and stretched my torso. Her grip tightened. I dug my fingernails into her thick-skinned forearm as hard as I could. I didn't want to hurt her, but I had no choice. She made this horrible sound, some kind of underwater screech, and flicked her arm away from my hands.

That was my moment. I kicked as hard as I could and pulled with my arms at the water, feeling like I do in my nightmares when I can't seem to figure out how to propel myself forward, away from the horrifying thing chasing me. What was chasing me now was death.

The mermaid reached for me and grabbed my shoe. It came off in her hands. I lurched upward with all that was left of my strength. At last my face punctured the surface, and I gulped in air. Black dots floated around in front of my eyes, and I fought the urge to faint. From what I could tell, the mermaid had taken me out past the breakers. I could see Carter on the tide pool rocks and Haley up above on the cliff, each no bigger than my pinky fingernail. The mermaid could swim so fast.

She was back. I felt her circling my legs that bicycled to tread water. I couldn't do this for long, especially not in this coat and heavy winter clothes. I remembered the subliminal connection I had with my mermaid friend back in October, but I didn't know if this was the same one. I didn't think it was. I didn't know how to communicate with her. Still, I tried as hard as I could to send my thoughts to her.

I can't breathe under water.

I waited for a response, but nothing came. She hadn't grabbed me yet to pull me back under. I wasn't sure if it was because I hurt her, or she was still fascinated with my shoe. I felt her tug at my other foot and that shoe came off, too.

Where are you taking me?

Still nothing. A giant swell of freezing ocean water went over my head. I gurgled and choked on the salt water.

I can't swim like you. I need to get to land.

I put an image of the beach in my head. Maybe she'd understand a picture more than words.

An image came back to me of the ocean splashing against tall cliffs with caves in them at water level. A forest of trees crowned the tops of the cliffs.

"Is this a place you know? Is it where you're trying to take me?" I said it before I realized how stupid that was. I didn't know how to think this in images, though. I simply pointed toward the shore and pictured it again. I needed to get to land. Wherever she was imagining seemed far away.

Her face rose out of the water, only to the chin, so her gills could stay under and help her breathe. Lucky her. Water kept slapping me in the nose and mouth, and between the struggle to stay afloat and constantly gulping in sea water, I wasn't breathing well at all. Those giant, midnight blue eyes focused on me. Under the water her thick tail slipped behind my thighs and tugged me close to her. The flipper worked rapidly to keep us afloat. With her support, I could lift my face higher out of the water. I said '*thank you*' in my mind, but I'm sure she didn't understand.

Her webbed left hand came up out of the water, and I expected to see my shoe in it. Instead, she held the wreath of twigs. She put it in front of her face and peered at me through it like it was a window. I nodded, expressing that I recognized it or that I made it, not quite knowing what she would understand or want to know.

The other webbed hand came out of the water, my shoe dropping from it as she gestured to the north. Pointing might not be a thing for creatures that have webbed fingers and live under the sea, but I understood she was showing me where those cliffs were located. Somewhere to the north. She pushed the wreath at my face so that it touched my forehead and then brought it back to her again followed by more urgent gestures to the north.

I closed my eyes and pictured the woods and the magical Red Cedar tree I'd saved only a week ago. When I opened my eyes again, her head was cocked like she was struggling to understand.

Then a barrage of images attacked my mind. A waterfall. Not a big gushing one. Small. Trickling over the side of a cliff. A cave in the cliff only approachable by water. A killer whale swimming near the cave. A killer whale dead on a pebbled beach, seen from a distance. Ocean water, brown with murk and filth.

It was awful. When she was done, I felt a deep aching in my chest that made the feeling of suffocating a few minutes back seem like nothing. Something horrible was happening up north. Pollution causing the death of killer whales, I guessed. I'm not sure if that was all her images meant, but I think that was part of it. Had she been looking for me? Had she been waiting for me to show up? Had my mermaid sent scouts out for me, hoping I could help them?

The mermaid grabbed my left arm, and her tail slid away from my body. With a tug, she began swimming again, carrying me along beside her. Not as fast this time, thankfully. I fought the current to get my right hand across my body and peel her hand off me. I didn't want to hurt her again. I think she feared my fingernails, too, because she let go easily.

I pointed to the shore. "I need to go to the shore," I told her. I knew she didn't understand my words. I pointed again with more insistence.

She again gestured toward the north. The mermaid wanted to take me with her right then and there. She didn't understand that I wouldn't survive the trip. All I could do was imagine a vivid picture of me dead at the bottom of the ocean as fully and completely as I was capable. I ran my hands along my throat to show her I didn't have gills like her.

The mermaid stopped swimming, and her eyes grew even larger than I ever thought possible as she began to comprehend. I wasn't like her. I would die before I could help her. She looked at the twig wreath, her brow wrinkled as she tried to decide what to do. My coat was heavy with water and weighing me down. I don't know how long it had been going on, but I realized my teeth were chattering. I would freeze or drown, not sure which first, but very soon. I needed her to make a decision fast. That decision needed to be her helping me swim back to shore. I felt certain I wouldn't make it on my own.

"Please," I croaked out. My strep throat from last week's exposure had just cleared up, and if I survived this, I knew I'd have a relapse. Not to mention hypothermia. Maybe pneumonia. Mom would freak if I had to go to the hospital again. She'd been complaining about the bills already.

Somewhere in the distance, above the sound of the ocean and wind, a horn blasted several times in succession. There was a pause, and then the blasts started again.

The mermaid went rigid. Her face expressed a level of terror I'd never seen before on a real person. Then she sank, like an anchor, straight down. Within a moment, I had no idea where she was under all that dark water. It was January in the Pacific Northwest. I couldn't see through the water at all. I couldn't feel her swimming around my frantically bicycling legs.

The mermaid had been frightened off by that horn, I was sure of it. The horn blasted again, closer this time. That wasn't going to bring the mermaid back, and I needed her desperately to help me swim. I tried not to panic. I reached out my right arm to try to swim on my own. It felt so heavy I could barely move it, and the tide was pulling me away from the beach, not toward it.

The horn blared. I looked around for the source. Coming around the cliffs to the south was a Coast Guard ship. It had a ways to go before it reached me, and I doubted I could make it that long. I was so cold. It made being up in the tree during a winter storm seem like a summer campout. My tongue was dry, my lips numb. My legs barely moved. I couldn't feel my feet.

I sank. My mouth, nose, and eyes going into the blackness.

* * * *

The next thing I remember was throwing up on the deck of the Coast Guard Response Boat. When I finished, I rolled back on the cot and whimpered as I was lifted up and carried. When next I opened my eyes, I

7

noted that I couldn't see the sky. I'd been brought to the Survivor's Compartment where a man in uniform knelt beside me. Another officer wearing a dripping wet rubber jacket and pants passed him a small towel, and he used it to clean my face.

"Can you hear me?"

I nodded.

"Okay. We're taking you to the Aberdeen docks where there is an ambulance waiting. I need to get you out of your wet clothes, or you'll freeze to death. Do you understand?"

All I could do was nod again, barely. I couldn't actually feel my limbs and was unable to move them. I closed my eyes while I endured the embarrassment of having my clothes taken off by a strange man. He immediately covered me in warm blankets, lifted me into the cabin, and placed me on a cot. The heated room instantly soothed me, and I began to doze off again.

I know I was barely conscious, but I swear I heard the wet officer say, "I'm telling you, it was like something was holding her up. She was just bobbing there. She should have sunk."

The officer tucking the blankets tightly around me agreed. "She's lucky to be alive."

When I woke up again, the boat had docked. One of the Coast Guard officers was gently nudging me awake before slipping his arms under me to hoist me off the cot. He carried me all wrapped up in blankets like a burrito off the boat where a stretcher and EMT was waiting for me. I saw the ambulance at the base of the dock. A local police squad car was there, too.

"Please," I told the Coast Guard officer. "I'm okay, really. I don't need go to the hospital."

"You nearly froze to death and drowned in the ocean," he replied, placing me on the stretcher. The EMT strapped me down and wheeled me toward the ambulance. The officer followed. "This is protocol. If you're fine, you won't have to be at the hospital long."

"Please! I'm fine! I promise." I wiggled as much as I could to show how much energy and vigor I had. "I'm not hurt. I just need to get in a car with a heater and go home. That's all. Please, my parents will be so mad if I go to the hospital."

8

My mom was going to have a fit about this. She'd complained so much about how much the last emergency visit cost. This was going to be so much more. I just got things kind of okay between her and me. I didn't want money to be the thing that divided us again. Not to mention the fact that my parents were still working on repairing their reputations in the press as bad parents for "allowing" me to tree-sit in the middle of January to protest the logging of an Old Growth tree. It did not need to get out that their daughter almost drowned a week later.

He squinted at me like he was trying to make a decision about something. After a moment he said, "You're Peter Sawfeather's daughter, aren't you?"

I hesitated to answer. "Yes. Do you know him?"

"Oh, yeah," he nodded vigorously, smiling. "We go way back."

"In a good you-helped-each-other-out way or a bad you've-arrested-him-a-bunch-of-times way?"

"I arrested him once, and we've helped each other more times than I can count since then."

That was a story I'd have to probe out of my dad later. He rarely talked about the times when his protests got him locked up, like he didn't want me to know there was a down side to his exploits. I'd always suspected it had happened a time or two.

"Well, then," I tried, "as a favor to my dad, please don't make him waste all his money on hospital bills when you know I'm fine."

He cocked his head like he was considering it. "What were you doing out there anyway? Looking for more mermaids? Do you have any idea what a mess that whole mermaid event caused us?"

I wondered if he expected an answer to those questions. Thankfully, before my not responding got too awkward, I heard my name being called.

"June!" Haley's voice shot above the noise of the men around me and the few onlookers in the parking lot. Carter's voice called my name, too. Their timing was perfect.

I grabbed the EMT's wrist and pointed with my other hand. "Look! See? My friends are here. They'll take me home."

Carter beat Haley to my side, and she jogged up a second behind him, both out of breath. Carter put his hand on my leg. "I'm so glad you're all right. That was really scary, June."

Tell me about it.

"I couldn't believe how fast you went," Haley said. "That was crazy."

I gave her a sharp look to try to get her to shut up about it. I didn't need these men asking more questions. She made a little "sorry" face and lowered her eyes.

"Carter, tell these guys that you'll take me straight home. I don't need to go to the hospital."

Carter nodded at them. "Oh, yeah. Our car's right over there. We can take care of her."

The Coast Guard officer gestured to the EMT and said, "My job is to deliver her to you. You have to make the decision of what health care she needs." He patted me on the foot and then pulled the EMT away from me for a second. I'm sure he was giving a full report of what he thought happened and how I passed out while on the boat.

While they talked, my friends came closer to me. Carter put his hands on my face. "I thought I lost you," he said. "I thought you were going to drown."

"Me too for a minute," I said.

All three of us were quiet for a second as we let that heavy thought pass.

"I'd kind of like it if you could stop doing terrifying things for a bit," Haley said, and we all laughed to break the uncomfortable feeling.

Carter leaned close to me and whispered. "It was a mermaid, though. Right? Is that what had you? Was it the same one we rescued?"

"It wasn't her," I said, "but I got the impression the mermaid had been looking for me. She was making a big deal about taking me with her to some rocky shoreline up north."

"That could be anywhere," Haley piped in. "It's practically all rocky cliffs from here to Canada."

"That's true, but I have a clear picture of it in my head. Maybe I could figure out where she meant."

The Coast Guard officer walked back up the dock to the Response Boat, and the EMT came back to the stretcher. "I tell you what," he said. "I'll check your vitals in the ambulance and make sure everything is what it should be. If it's not, you're going to the hospital."

"Okay," I said.

He rolled me away from my friends and put me in the back of the ambulance which was nice and heated. My friends waited outside while he took my temperature and blood pressure. The EMT stuck his head out of the back of the ambulance, and I heard him tell Carter to get the heater started in the car. He asked Haley if she had any extra clothes with her. She didn't.

He came back to me. "I'll let you go, but you'll have to head home in this blanket. I hope that motivates you to go straight home and to bed."

"It will," I said.

"It's against my better judgement."

"I know."

He unstrapped me from the stretcher and helped me to my feet. I held the blanket tightly around me. I didn't have a stitch of clothing on underneath it. Not even underwear. I was trying very hard not to think about those Coast Guard officers taking all my clothes off. The EMT handed a bag of my wet clothes to Haley and then helped me down the steps where Carter wrapped his arm protectively around me. Carter nodded thanks to the EMT and guided me to the car, which was idling in the parking lot.

I got in the front passenger seat and aimed all the vents toward me. I was still chilled.

Carter and Haley got in the car, and we drove off.

"Your lips were so blue," Haley said after a minute. "They look a little more normal now."

"Yeah," I said. "I'm actually surprised they didn't take me to the hospital. Pretty sure I was super close to being dead."

"Why didn't they, do you think?"

"I pulled the Dad card."

Carter nodded. He understood. My dad's name had some weight in the right circles.

"Hey, is my phone in the car anywhere?"

Haley dug it out for me. I'd left it in the car while we were hanging out, which was lucky. If I'd had it on me, it would've been ruined.

11

"How did the Coast Guard find me, anyway?" I asked as I scrolled through my contacts.

Carter answered. "I have the number saved on my phone. We had to deal with them a lot when I worked with Dr. Schneider at AMARC."

"Oh."

That was still a sore subject between us. Affron Oil shut down the funding for the Aberdeen Marine Animal Rescue Center after we rescued the mermaids back in October. Carter loved interning there and didn't so much love his job at the pet store selling fish and aquarium parts. I thanked him for his smart thinking and let the subject rest.

I found the phone number for Juarez Peña and hit call. I put him on speaker and told him all about my experience with the mermaid and the vision she shared with me. I figured I could tell him, and thereby Carter and Haley, all at the same time. Juarez was beyond excited. He asked about getting more twigs from the tree and trying again to see if the twigs immersed in the ocean triggered mermaids to appear. I told him instead that I needed him to research places along the Washington coastline that had tall cliffs with forest on top and caves down below. I told him I believed strongly that was where the mermaids were living, and if we could find those cliffs we'd find the mermaids. He was so eager to start on this mission that he hung up while I was still talking to him.

We all laughed. Carter took us through a coffeehouse drive-through and got us some hot drinks for the hour ride home. I was nice and toasty inside and out by the time I got there. When I walked in the door, however, I was attacked by some seriously frozen glares from my parents. Clearly, they had been contacted by that officer from the Coast Guard.

Carter backed out of the door quietly and left me alone with them. I was yelled at for a bit. Fussed and worried over for a second or two. Then grounded.

Yep, not even a week after my eighteenth birthday. Grounded.

I'd never been grounded before and didn't know exactly what that meant at first. I learned quickly it meant no Carter, no Haley, no phone, and no internet. Yay. I found a mermaid and clues to where they were living, and now I could do nothing about it. It was pointless trying to convince my parents of the importance of this, because every argument I gave them added a day to my punishment. Right now, I was looking at two weeks.

Two weeks with that mermaid swimming far away from me before I'd be able to find her again.

Chapter Two

When your internet connection isn't great to begin with, and you don't have any friends, not getting to use the internet or your cell phone isn't so much a punishment as an annoyance. I filled my days with books and TV. Having dropped out of school–or been expelled depending on the point of view–there wasn't much else to do.

There was no possible way for them to prevent me from seeing Haley. She lived next door, and our bedroom windows faced each other. Even though the weather was cold and damp, we simply flung our windows open and talked to each other every afternoon when she came home from school. Honestly, I preferred talking to her face to face like this instead of sitting in our rooms using our phones. That had always been her idea, not mine.

As the days passed, Haley caught me up on all the gossip and goings-on at the high school. Mr. Mains was still on probation, and everyone hated Ms. Slater. Apparently, the woman forced all the teachers to buy these hanging shoe racks–using their own money, of course–that they had to attach to their classroom doors. They were called Cell Hotels, and all students were to drop their phones in the slots before entering the classrooms. She'd do surprise cell phone checks, and if anyone was caught with a cell phone in class, that student got their phone taken away for the week and in school suspension for the rest of the day. If more than five students in a class were caught with phones, the teacher was fined. This was particularly hard on some of the social studies and English teachers who usually let their students use their phones to do research for their projects because there weren't enough classroom computers. Teachers were frantically readjusting their curriculum plans.

"Where are all the ISS kids being put?" I thought of that crammed office and remembered sitting in that folded chair in the corner of it. I had to imagine more than one kid a day was getting caught with a cell phone.

"The library," Haley told me.

I laughed, thinking of old Mrs. Katz having to deal with all those trouble-makers. Although, who knows? She might have been happy about the circumstance. At least her library now had people in it.

After a week of this, Haley told me that several teachers were already threatening to quit. She also said that the Recycling Club we'd started last fall had doubled in members.

"Why?" I asked. Did I miss something, and Haley became really popular? Or did people become super interested in recycling?

"A lot of kids are pissed that you got kicked out of school."

"*Who's* pissed?" I demanded to know. "I didn't have any friends at school except you. I'm sure Regina was thrilled to see me leave, and everyone there follows her."

Haley shrugged and gave me one of those apologetic grimaces she'd mastered over the years when telling me the latest horrible thing people were saying about me. "I mean, it might not just be because you got kicked out as much as they're mad that Ms. Slater did it. You see? They want to get back at her."

That made sense, I guess. What didn't make sense was why they joined the club. "They're getting back at her by *recycling*?"

"No," Haley said, laughing. "We're kind of using the Recycling Club as a cover for a protest group. Can you believe it? Me. I'm a protester. Aren't you proud?"

I smiled at her, truly warmed that she wanted to impress me, but I had to say, "I don't want to go back to school, you know. I'm done."

"Oh, come on. You haven't missed that much. You could make up stuff over Spring Break, I'm sure."

I nodded, knowing that was true. "I just don't want to," I said plainly. "There's no reason for me to go back."

"With the steam we're building under this protest, we could probably get you to be prom queen."

"I'd rather die." And having almost died twice now, I meant that.

She teased me anyway. "Come on. You in a gown. Carter in a tux.

Can't you imagine Carter in a tux?"

I put that image in my head for a moment. It was a good one, I couldn't deny it. My expression must have given me away.

Haley shouted a loud "Ha!" at me.

I laughed and said, "Carter would rather die, too."

This she had to agree with. Carter hated high school stuff with a passion.

"Why don't you focus your protest less on getting me back to school and more on getting Mr. Mains back? Okay?"

"We're doing that, too."

Not getting to see or talk to Carter was the hardest part of being grounded. He had promised never to let a day go by without seeing me after I came down from that tree, and now my parents were forcing us apart. I begged them daily to let me talk to him for at least five minutes, and I really thought that they'd give in after a day or two. In the past, their adoration of Carter kind of irritated me. Now it was the opposite. They seemed furious with him. They were still sore about him leaving me in the woods after our fight on New Year's Eve. Their opinion of him plummeted further when he'd taken me to the beach where I "fell" into the ocean and he failed to rescue me.

Haley is the one that gave me the idea for fixing this horrid situation, so I completely credit her brilliance. I told my parents Sunday night at dinner after my first week of punishment that I should probably think about getting a job now that I wasn't in school anymore. They agreed whole-heartedly, not one lick of an argument. I almost got the sense that they were about to suggest it to me, but I beat them to the punch. Mom offered to have me come work for her at the law office and do clerical stuff. I told her I wanted to do something independent of her, if that was all right. She said a bunch of things like how she could pay me more than minimum wage and how she'd get me some nicer clothes, but she didn't push it any further than that. I didn't let on that I saw my dad gently press his hand on her shoulder, his signal for her to let it rest. Mom obeyed him. She was trying really hard to not be so, what's the nice word? Pushy.

The following morning, I got up and drove to my favorite little pet store, the one not far from the university, where a certain blond handsome boyfriend of mine worked. I applied for a job and got hired before I left the building. Turned out they needed someone to work mornings in the aquarium department while that striking young man was in class. So every single day from that point on, I got to slap hands with Carter as his shift started and mine came to an end.

Okay, we did more than high five. Sometimes we'd steal a kiss or two in the backroom where we kept our coats. I usually changed out of my blue work uniform shirt and stuck around for a while after his shift started. I'd linger and talk with him between customers until our manager, Paul, gave me the "nod" to let me know I needed to get on my way. Paul was a pretty cool guy, though, and that nod didn't usually come until at least an hour had passed. As long as I didn't prevent people from getting their ceramic mermaids or baggies of goldfish, he left us alone.

After I left work each day, I'd hang out at one or another of the local food places until Carter had a dinner break or was off for the evening. The Green Table, the vegetarian restaurant was the most expensive, but they had pretty good appetizers and these delicious garlic knot rolls. I visited the frozen yogurt place a lot for their smoothies. There was also a fast food place with tasty fries, and despite my belated New Year's Resolution to do better with following my parents' vegetarianism, I snuck in a couple of their burgers, too. It didn't take long for me to put back on the weight I'd lost while up in the tree, and then some.

My mom never caught on in the final week remaining of being grounded that I was seeing Carter. I might have fudged a bit about my work schedule. When the grounding came to an end, I kept the same schedule because I came to enjoy it. I got myself a sketchbook and some drawing pencils. I'd never been good at art, but I decided to see if practice could improve my skills a bit. I'd seen a lot of interesting things this past half year, and I wanted to remember them somehow. It took me many tries to get my mermaid's eyes just right, and then there was a lot of crumpled up paper again until I could get her whole face. Clearly, drawing the whole mermaid was outside my abilities. I decided instead to try to draw the landscape from the mermaid's vision. Nature came a lot easier to me, and my drawings of cliffs and caves weren't half bad.

After a couple of weeks, I actually got brave enough to show them to Carter.

It was on Valentine's Day. Carter promised me a great, romantic date to make up for all that went wrong on New Year's Eve. I was to meet him at his parents' house, and he was going to take me out for a nice dinner and maybe a walk on the beach afterward. I'd gone to the forest earlier in the week to gather up some twigs fallen from my Red Cedar tree. I was hopeful that if I tossed them into the ocean it would somehow beckon another mermaid to us.

Only, surprise! It was raining. Storming, in fact. Just driving that hour from my house to his parents' house put my life in jeopardy. My car needed new tires and wipers I learned in a super scary way. By the time I got there, I was a wreck. His mom and dad welcomed me in and set me down in their all white living room in front of a fire, and I soon had a cup of hot chocolate in my hands. Mr. and Mrs. Crowe were pretty upset about the weather, too. Their evening plans had to be canceled as well. Mrs. Crowe was dressed in a beautiful tan suit with a pink blouse and matching pink high heeled shoes. That was definitely not a going-out-in-the-rain kind of outfit.

Ultimately, we all decided to stay in and wait it out. She heated some frozen spinach and cheese quiches and made a big salad for all of us to have for dinner. After we ate, they made their way upstairs and left us alone. Carter was devastated.

"I'm so sorry, June," he said for the tenth time. "I can't get a break with these holidays."

"It's okay," I responded for the tenth time. "I'm just happy to be with you."

He put his arm around my shoulders, and we stared at the fire as it crackled. "I am enjoying this, though," he told me. He nuzzled against my ear and kissed it gently. Whispering, he said, "It's a little romantic, isn't it?"

I giggled, a sound that rarely came out of my body. "Yes, I guess it kind of is."

"I've got something for you."

He walked over to the cabinet under the counter where their landline phone existed along with a very orderly collection of magazines and mail. While he leaned over to pull out what I assumed was a Valentine's present for me, I hurriedly grabbed at my message bag. I didn't own a big purse, so this was all I could find to hide the box of chocolate and corny card I bought for him. I got it out and put it on the coffee table in front of me before he came back. I looked up to find him holding a very large package wrapped in red heart paper with a big bow.

"Wait!" I said. "What's that? I didn't get you anything big."

"You didn't have to," he said, placing the box in my lap. It was heavy. He picked up the candy and card from the table and waved it at me. "This is exactly what I wanted—and a kiss."

I kissed him. Just a quick one.

"I feel guilty."

"Don't. It's mostly from my mom anyway. She helped pick it out and paid for it."

I untied the ribbon and tore off the paper. The box was from a department store I'd never been brave enough to enter because I knew the smallest thing in the store probably cost more than I could ever think to afford. I glanced at him, unsure. "Um, is this really okay?"

"Yep."

I opened the box, not sure what to expect. A beautiful black wool pea coat was folded up inside. I pulled it out and marveled at it. "It's gorgeous."

"You needed a new coat. A good one," he said. "You can't keep borrowing your mom's. Put it on."

I stood up and slipped my arms into it, enjoying the smooth satin lining. They got the size right. The sleeves went down to my hands. The length of the coat reached my hips. It had a wide collar I could flip up. I buttoned it. It was so warm and cozy. With my hands in the deep pockets, I twisted my shoulders back and forth as I modeled it for him.

"I love it. I don't want to take it off."

Carter laughed. "Well, I do! I thought we'd be outside tonight, and you'd get to wear it. Instead we've got this nice fire and a cozy couch. I'm kind of hoping some layers will come *off*." I flicked my eyes to the staircase, and he waved my concerns away. "They're up in their room and won't come out. I promise."

My own smile was so big it hurt. I took off the coat and folded it back into the box. In addition, I took off my cardigan sweater, eliciting an approving wink from him. I tossed it in the box. Then I slid it under the table with my feet as I sat back down, acutely aware of my bare arms and the thin material of my blouse.

Carter ran his fingers down one of my arms. I thought he was about to take my hand, but he reached for a piece of candy from his box instead, teasing me. "Delicious," he said with a mouth full of candy. After he swallowed, he ran his fingers through my hair, spreading it out around my shoulders, exactly the opposite way my mom always did. I wondered if he knew he was doing that. My cheeks were warm. I blamed it on the fire.

"So, what did you want to show me?" he asked.

I reached for my bag on the floor and pulled out my sketchbook. "Don't laugh, okay. I'm really more of a photographer than an artist."

"No laughing, I promise."

I wasn't sure if I totally trusted him on that, but I opened up the book anyway. I flipped the pages to show him the different drawings I'd done of beaches, cliffs, forests, and caves. After I was done, he took it from me and went back to the first page. He looked at each picture much slower, taking his time to really inspect them.

"These are good, June," he said as he came to the last one. "I mean, they're much better than I expected."

I smacked his shoulder. "Nice."

"No, I don't mean that in a bad way. They're really good." He turned to the picture that was most panoramic of the cliffs dropping off into the ocean, the one I tried my hardest to match the image that mermaid had put into my mind. He tapped it with his finger. "Have you tried looking on the internet for any place that looks like this?"

"How would I even do that?"

"What if we reverse-image search?"

"You sound like Haley with your technological fancy-talk," I told him.

Instead of responding to me, he pulled out his phone and took a photo of my drawing. He went on the internet to a site I wasn't familiar with and uploaded the picture. In seconds, he got a screen full of photos and paintings similar to my sketch. I was completely floored. "My world has just expanded."

"That's my goal," he told me with that gorgeous grin spreading across his face. "To expand your world on a daily basis."

We started thumbing our way through the images until I saw a photo fairly similar to my drawing. Not an exact match, of course, but definitely the same kind of landscape of steep cliffs falling into the sea, caves almost hidden at the bottom, and trees sprouting from the tops. "Click on that one," I said.

It took us to a website about Olympic National Park. This stretch of shoreline was captured by a kayaker on vacation. Carter began reading the article when my own phone rang. It was my mom. I didn't want to answer, but I knew she'd keep calling if I didn't.

"Hey."

She got right down to business. "The rain is supposed to head out of here around midnight or so," she told me. "This big of a storm is going to cause a huge run-off. Your dad, Randy and I are all headed up to the San Juan Strait in the morning to get some fresh samples. Would you like to be part of this? We're going to need to leave about four."

"That's early," I said.

"Yes, so you'll need to come home now if you're going to get any rest."

I looked at the clock over the fireplace mantel. It was only nine-thirty. I glanced at Carter who was still reading the article on his phone.

Mom was still talking, I realized. "...work tomorrow?"

"Do I work tomorrow?" I repeated, assuming that was what she was asking. "No. It's a day off for me."

"This will be important data," she reminded me. "Pollution from that construction run-off is causing the extinction of many sea creatures, including the orcas."

I knew this. Mom and Dad had been discussing this issue a lot over the past several weeks. Apparently, a killer whale body had washed up on San Juan Island a couple weeks ago. Testing had been done on its blubber to find that it had toxic levels of poison so bad that they had to bury it in a nuclear waste depository. Dad had learned from his contacts in Canada that the number of orcas in the area was down to only eighty. It was a bad situation, worsening every day.

I wanted to help. Marine Biology was still my favorite subject, and whenever their causes aligned with my love of sea life, I always wanted to participate. I just didn't want to give up my nice evening with Carter. Even though it hadn't turned out the way we'd expected, it was still cozy and kind of romantic. The lights were low and the fire warm. I fully anticipated some great kisses and caresses coming a little later on.

"Are you coming or not?" she asked.

Clearly, I was taking too long to answer.

"Hang on, Mom," I responded, equally impatient. I put my hand over the phone and tapped Carter on the knee. He looked up from his phone. I liked how he immediately turned it over, showing me I had his whole attention. "Mom needs my help on a project tomorrow morning. They've got to head out very early, so that means I'd need to leave now."

His face darkened, his blue eyes flicking over to the fire, and then settling on the back of his phone. Just guessing, but I think he was looking forward to what was going to happen on this couch in front of that fire later on, too. He jutted his chin out like he was about to say something, but then he let it relax and simply nodded. "Sure. Fine. I mean, if you need to."

I hated this. I didn't want to ruin our Valentine's evening. Evenings like this were so rare for us. "Hey," I said, leaning into him so that my long black hair fell over his hands and forced him to look back up at me. "What if you come too? I mean, we're studying ocean pollution to help save killer whales. Maybe that might be interesting to you."

The darkness fled almost as if someone shot a spotlight on him. He grinned. "No trees this time?"

"Ocean, baby," I said with a shimmy. "You love?"

"I love." He said that while looking right into my eyes.

Heat rose to my face, and before I could say or do something stupid, I lifted my cell phone back to my ear. "Mom?"

"Oh, you're back?" she said sarcastically.

"Mom."

She did a little laugh. "I'm just joking with you." Who was this woman? My mom didn't joke with anyone. I didn't think she had the ability. "Yes, Carter can come along. Bring him home with you. Oh, and he'll sleep on the couch downstairs," she said as if that fact needed to be clarified before she hung up.

Carter took the phone from my hand and put it down on the carpet by his feet. Then he brought my hand up to his lips for a lingering kiss.

"The fire is hot," I said, trying to explain the rush of heat going through me.

"Oh, is that it?" he teased. He wrapped his arm around my shoulders and pulled me tightly to him. He kissed my lips, keeping his blue eyes wide open and looking deep into mine. He pulled back only far enough so he could say, "I get to spend the night with you, huh?"

I giggled quietly. "Well, don't get too excited."

"I know. I heard. Wouldn't expect anything different." He ran a finger along my cheek and kissed me again. I wasn't quite done with the kisses when he backed away for real and stood up. "Guess I better pack a couple things so we can get out of here."

Yeah. Right. He needed to do that. I stood up reluctantly as I watched him head toward the stairs. "Hey, don't you have classes tomorrow?" I asked.

He stopped at the foot of the stairs. "Only Environmental Studies 101. All I have to do is tell them I was with Peter and Natalie Sawfeather and explain what we were doing, and I'll probably get extra credit."

"Oh, yeah," I said, nodding, "I guess you would." It's rare, but sometimes I actually do forget my parents are big names in certain circles.

"Are you coming?" he asked and then headed upstairs to his room. I followed him up and watched him throw some clothes and toiletries in his bag.

He told, instead of asking, his parents where he was going. They both shrugged like it was no big deal that he was heading out to spend the night with his girlfriend. I tried not to put too much thought into that. I reminded myself that Carter did have a dorm room on campus, and perhaps, he often visited them and then left in time to go back to his own place to sleep. All his mom said to us before we went back downstairs was to be careful in the rain.

As I gathered up my messenger bag and put on my new coat, Mr. Crowe appeared at the top of the stairs, calling Carter's name. "Carter. Did you say you were collecting run-off samples?"

"Yes," I answered for him. "In the San Juan Strait. There's a lot of housing construction going on there, and the pollution from it is out of control."

Mr. Crowe cocked his head as though he was trying to decipher the nonsense babble I just spouted. "Do you know which construction project? Which island?" he asked.

"They didn't say."

"Carter, can you come back up here for a minute?" He put up one finger toward me. "It'll only take a minute, Juniper, I promise."

Carter shrugged off his duffle bag and slumped back up the stairs. They disappeared down the hall out of sight and earshot. My phone buzzed. A text from Mom asking if we were on our way yet. I wrote *yes*, hoping that would be true enough. Five minutes later Carter came back downstairs and grabbed up his bag without a word. He opened the door for me and then followed me out.

"Everything okay?" I asked him.

"Uh, yeah. It's fine."

That was not his *fine* sounding tone. His dad must've said something he didn't like. Maybe he was admonishing Carter for missing school. Maybe it was about me. Or my parents. Whatever it was, I got the sense his dad had just told him not to go do this job with me, and Carter was going to do it anyway.

"Okay if I follow you?" he asked, pulling out his keys and heading to his car.

I was hoping he'd ride with me, and I'd bring him home after we were done. That way we could spend more time together. He opened his car door before I answered, so that option seemed off the table. "Sure," I said, certain he couldn't hear me.

My car was parked on the curb, and before I even got inside, Carter pulled out of his driveway. By the time I got my ignition on, he was driving down the street. Guess I was following him, then. I wished I knew what was wrong. I wondered when he'd tell me.

Chapter Three

The rain had tapered off a little and was miserable but not murderous like earlier in the evening. I didn't have to drive blindly and hydroplane my way home, but even though I wasn't as tense about surviving the trip, my anxiety over Carter's behavior right before we left his house intensified. I didn't follow him to my house. I never saw his taillights. He drove way faster than me, so it was impossible to keep up with him.

I got to my house about eleven, and he was already there parked along the curb waiting in his car for me. I parked behind him. To my surprise, he was standing beside my car, opening the door for me as soon as I turned off the engine and grabbed my purse. Carter took my hand and walked me quickly to the front door, tucking my head against his chest as if that might help me stay dry. While I fumbled for my keys with my free hand, not daring to let go of him with the other, he leaned over and whispered in my ear.

"Sorry about taking off like that. It wasn't you. Dad said something that upset me is all."

"I thought it might be something like that," I said, replacing the word *hoped* with *thought* before I said it out loud. "So, we're okay then?"

"Oh, yeah," he grumbled into my ear. "I mean, do you have any idea how long I've wanted to spend the night with you?"

I laughed, all my worries evaporating. "I don't think this is going to turn out exactly the way you wish."

On cue, my mom opened the door. "Were you planning to stay out here all night? Oh, hi Carter."

His greeting overlapped me saying, "We were just enjoying our last moment of privacy for the evening," as we entered the house.

Dad was placing a stack of yellowed bedding and a flat, limp pillow on the couch. He looked up at us and smiled warmly. "Hey, kids," he offered, patting the stuff. "Gotcha all set up, Carter. We want to hit the road by four, so don't stay up too late."

"Midnight," mom ruled. She looked pointedly at me. "I want to hear your door closing at midnight."

I knew she'd stay up to listen.

They went upstairs to their room and left us alone. I sat down on the couch next to Carter. My living room didn't have a lovely fireplace with a roaring fire. No, it boasted a collection of mismatched furniture with a bulky entertainment cubby hosting an old-fashioned box TV that rarely ever had anything besides the news or documentaries playing on it. Draped over the couch were a couple handmade quilts my grandmother had made when she was alive, and we threw one over us as we settled down on the couch. It smelled like dust and pepper.

We sat awkwardly for a bit and then did a couple timid kisses. Nothing like what I expected would have happened if I'd been able to stay at his parents' place a bit longer. The master bedroom at his house was bigger than most of my second floor and at the far end of the house from the living room. My house wasn't nearly as expansive as his. Even though my parents were upstairs, the paper-thin walls of this place kept us from having any real alone time. I worried that our kissing kept us too quiet, and Mom or Dad would come raging downstairs soon to stop us. I pulled back and rested my head against the sofa cushion.

I made small talk with him, hoping he'd tell me on his own what his father said to upset him, but he never did. Instead we talked about everything that annoyed us about Paul, our manager at work. We also discussed how skillful I'd been at avoiding Nick Klein who works only five doors down from us. It was helpful that I usually worked weekday mornings at the pet store, and Nick tended to work on the weekends at the hardware store. I'd seen him pull in a few afternoons while I was sketching in one of the restaurants, but so far, he hadn't seen me. We laughed at my stealth. After a little while, Mom appeared at the top of the stairs in a robe I didn't know she owned and said it was time to wind things down so she could get some sleep.

I offered to help Carter make up the couch, but he said he had it covered. I gave him one more quick kiss while my mom stood there waiting for me to leave him. When I got to the top of the stairs, I passed her with a quick, "You don't have to guard me. What did you think was going to happen?"

"Just go to bed, Juniper," she said with exhaustion as if I spent all my time disobeying her. "I'm tired."

I wanted to sleep. I knew I'd only get three and a half hours at best, but it was impossible to sleep at all knowing Carter was right downstairs. If I was really quiet, could I sneak down there and cuddle with him on the couch? No, I was too tall for us both to fit. Maybe I could signal him to sneak upstairs to me, but then what if we didn't wake up before my parents? I could set an alarm. Mom might hear that. Ugh.

My phone buzzed. I snatched it up, hoping it was him. It was Haley.

> Is Carter at your house? I saw his car outside.
> Yes.
> I can't believe it! Are your parents home?
> Yes.
> Oh.
> Yeah.
> What's up?
> The natural world beckons us once again.
> And Carter's tagging along? That's cool.
> Yeah, it is.

She and I texted for a little longer until she got too tired and went to sleep. I stared at the ceiling until my mom tapped on my door at 3:30 and said, "We're leaving in thirty minutes and are not waiting for you to get ready."

Good morning to you too, Mom.

* * * *

Three hours later, Carter nudged me awake. I'd been sleeping in the back seat of my mother's car with my head on his shoulder. "Hey there," he said softly.

"I'm sorry," I said, lifting my head, hoping like hell I hadn't drooled on him.

"Oh, no worries. Pretty sure I slept most of the time, too. That couch wasn't exactly comfortable." He kissed me on the forehead and whispered. "Neither was your proximity to me. So many urges." I crinkled my nose and immediately put my hand up to cover it, hoping I didn't look like a deranged bunny. No one would ever have described me as "cute" or a person who does "cute" things. Carter had this way of making my face and voice do things I'd never done with them before. He gently pushed my hand aside and ran his thumb between my eyebrows like he knew what I was thinking. Maybe I didn't look like a deranged bunny after all.

He pulled my head back to his shoulder, and I didn't mind at all. His tan jacket had a soft, down lining that felt like a pillow against my cheek. I had to resist falling back asleep.

Dad had ridden with Randy in the truck, and Mom had kept her briefcase and the sample test kit in the front seat with her so Carter and I could sit together. That was nice of her.

Coffees, muffins, and ferry tickets were purchased when we arrived in Anacortes. I also gulped down a candy bar to get some adrenaline kicking. The ferry dock was as I remembered it from last October, except much busier and colder. Last time we parked in the lot, and I took a helicopter across the strait. It was much less exciting to wait in the long line of cars for our turn to pay and drive onto the below decks. Once the car and truck were parked, we were able to get out and climb up the stairs to the passenger deck.

I wrapped my new coat tight around me as I stopped at the railing to gaze out at the water before going inside the cabin. Carter sidled up next to me, leaning his elbows on the rail and blowing hot air into his hands. He'd zipped up his jacket to the neck, so all I could see of his button up, red flannel shirt was the tail sticking out at the bottom. The wind was vicious that morning with bits of sleet mixed in slashing at our cheeks. Mom was about to pass us by for the cabin door but stopped and stared at me for an uncomfortably long moment.

"What?" I finally asked her, waiting for the complaint.

"Is that a new coat?"

She finally noticed.

"Carter gave it to me."

"It's nice," she said to Carter. Before he could smile and acknowledge her, she added in true Mom form, "A bit flamboyant for a Valentine's present for kids your age."

I put a hand out, stopping her. "Just because you don't celebrate Valentine's Day—"

"It's a pointless holiday. We should let our significant others know we love them—"

"Every day, I know," I finished for her. I rolled my eyes at Carter. "Don't let her get started on why she hates greeting cards."

"Not even the recycled ones?" Carter asked. Mom didn't answer.

I hugged myself and rubbed the wide collar of my coat with my chin affectionately. "Well, I love my new coat, and I'm glad he gave it to me."

"It's not practical for what we're doing today," Mom said.

"It's super warm."

"You should've worn the ski jacket I put out for you. We're going to be on the water. Now you'll probably be no help at all because you won't want to get wet."

She walked away from me like I'd offended her somehow and went inside the cabin where there were long benches, coffee to purchase, and heat. I guided Carter toward the railing. "I've been wearing this jacket since we left the house. Are you seeing what I live with?"

He patted my head. "All moms are weird like that."

"No, they're not."

He laughed. "You're right. I'm just trying to make you feel better."

The sky stayed gray during the trip across the San Juan Strait, and my nose and cheeks got redder and redder. Despite the blah weather, the views remained gorgeous. Cliffs rose above the winding road on the Washington shoreline, and above them the trees of the Olympic National Park were an impenetrable wall of deep green. So much life and mystery existed beyond that barrier, and it was impossible now for me not to think about that.

The whitecaps on the navy blue ocean mesmerized me. I marveled how each one was different. Some broad, some thin, some curling on themselves, and others spreading away. On a day like this it was impossible to see through the water even right below me where it slapped against the hull of the ship. I tried to imagine what was under that barrier of blue and white, but after my harrowing swim with the mermaid a couple weeks ago, all I could drum up was darkness and fear.

"You sure you're not going to get in trouble for missing class today?" I asked Carter.

"Yep."

"Is it sad that I kind of miss going to school?"

"Not really," Carter said. "It's what you're used to doing with your time. You were an Honors student, too, so I'm sure that went hand in hand with being an overachiever. Am I right?"

"You're not wrong."

He smirked. "I wasn't an overachiever in high school. I did only what I had to for my grades and nothing more."

"You never talk much about high school," I said. "Only that you hate everything about it. Did something bad happen?"

"Maybe another time."

His expression was as gray as the day, and like the forest and the ocean, I could only imagine what was happening inside. He clearly didn't want to talk about it, so I changed the subject. "I found an online class to finish my credits for AP Physics and Government. I can take the AP exams in the spring."

"That's great," he said. "Any progress on getting Washington State to accept you again?"

"Mom's still working on that. She's had a couple meetings with the dean and friends of hers on the Educational Board of Directors. Meanwhile, I've been offered scholarships to two other schools."

He flipped around, his smile huge and his eyes full of excitement. "What? Why didn't you tell me?"

"I don't know. Haven't decided what to do yet."

"What schools? Where?"

"That's the thing," I said. "They're both in California. U.C. Davis and U.C. Santa Cruz. Deepak, one of the climbers—"

"Yeah, I remember him," Carter said, a little darkness creeping in.

"He let me know about a scholarship opportunity at Santa Cruz for

Marine Biology. I applied and got it."

"You still talk to the tree climbers?"

"Just Deepak. He got in touch with me through my parents at first, and now we text sometimes."

"About what?"

My heart started beating hard. He was making me feel guilty for something, and I wasn't sure what I should feel guilty about. "Trees mostly. The school. Stuff going on in the tree hugging community."

"That's all?"

"Yeah, Carter. That's all. What else would we talk about?"

All that happiness from a second ago faded again. He stared out at the ocean. "I don't know. He was pretty chummy with you when you were up in that tree."

"Stop it, Carter," I said. "Seriously. He's like way old."

"He's not that old." I gave him a hard look, and he waved at me to let me know he was done. "Anyway, I was thinking about trying to get a job at the aquarium in Monterey this summer and then moving down to Santa Cruz in September."

Carter gripped the railing with both hands super tight. "That's really soon."

"It is." I took a deep breath and said, "I was wondering if you might be interested in going down there with me. At least for the summer. Maybe you could consider transferring. There's no Marine Biology major at—"

"I don't know if I can," he said abruptly, shutting me off.

I was about to say something else to try to persuade him to think about it, when a big commotion further down the deck caught our attention. A few people started pointing and shouting. Others began to cluster around them. Carter and I rushed over to see what they were all gawking at. It took a moment, but then we saw the black fin and then the tail slap of an orca in the distance. I grabbed at my cell phone to take a picture, but I didn't get it in time. The whale disappeared. When it was clear the whale wouldn't resurface, the crowd broke up.

Carter led me to rejoin our group inside the cabin, away from the cold air and the possibility of more private conversation. Mom and Dad were sitting on a bench, and Randy leaned against a pole supporting the roof. Everything was a dingy white with the ceiling and benches painted a seafoam blue like the waterslides at public swimming pools. The cabin wasn't terribly full. I figured more people left the islands in the morning to get to work in Vancouver or Seattle rather than heading toward them. Mostly the ferry was full of tourists.

"What's going on out there?" Dad asked as we stepped up.

Carter answered, pointing with his thumb over his shoulder. "Orca sighting."

Randy was reading a newspaper. He spoke without looking up. "That's good news."

"Oh, good, you're joining us," Mom said, clicking off her phone. "We were just going over the plan."

Dad nodded at Randy and said to us, "Randy and I are going to fetch us a boat, and while we're doing that, the three of you are going to drive over to the construction site. You're going to the shoreline on the property to take samples from the ocean right there."

"What are you looking for exactly?" Carter asked while biting his fingernail.

I'd never seen him do that before.

Mom explained in her clipped lawyer voice that she usually reserves for hostile witnesses, "The construction company developing that housing community is building so fast they aren't regulating their damage to the soil. An alarming amount of chemical pollution is running off into the strait water. We're looking to get evidence after this last rain when the run-off should be at its highest."

"What can we do to help?" I asked.

Mom flashed a look at Carter and then said to me, "Just do what I ask."

Dad put a hand on my arm. "We may need you two for some distraction. We'll be trespassing to get this done, and I'm hoping the two of you might draw some attention away from your mom. Do you think you could manage that? Maybe you could pose as a young couple looking to buy a house or something."

"Very young," I said.

"You look older than you think," my mom said. Then she had me sit next to her and applied a little makeup to my face to help the issue. She was lightning-quick about it, so I wasn't expecting much. When I looked in the compact mirror after she was done attacking me with shadow, mascara, and lipstick, I was a bit surprised. I'd gained at least five years.

"Wow," Carter said when Mom released me. He put up his hand defensively to ward off my attack. "I mean, don't get me wrong, I like the no makeup look, too, but you should really have your mom teach you how to do that."

"Thank you, Carter," my mom said, snapping her compact closed and putting all her items neatly back into her purse.

My dad leaned into the conversation and said, "No, she should *not* teach you how to do that. Not at all."

We all laughed, except for Mom who remained uncomfortably edgy, and then the horn blew to let us know we were close to the dock. An announcement was made for us to go down to our cars. We arrived at San Juan Island and drove off into the quaint, colorful town built up around Port Friday Harbor. Mom blasted the heat, which felt great on my hands and face. I figured I'd get nice and thawed out just in time to go back into the cold again. I did see some clouds parting in the distance and had hope brewing that the sun would come out and warm this day up a bit.

Chapter Four

San Juan Island is very small on a ferry map, but when you're on it, it's bigger than expected. It took over half an hour to drive past the older, permanent structures of the town to the new construction site. It was vast. A lot of trees had been felled to make room for this bedroom community. Several subdivisions were already complete. From what I could see through the fences surrounding the neighborhoods, the houses were similar in style to Carter's. They were all two stories with more rooms than an average family probably needed. Brick tile roofs were popular, and the houses were painted with the limited variety of shades between cream and coral. They all featured balconies. The yards between them were very small, so clearly these people were more interested in the views than having lots of property. None of the yards had been put in yet. No grass, bushes, or saplings of trees, even though there were cars in driveways and toys on front porches giving evidence that some people had moved in already.

In the construction zone, four houses were being built simultaneously. A herd of workers were already crawling about on the roofs or on scaffolding, drilling and hammering to the strains of a Latin music radio station. Many of them were in short sleeves, so they had to be working pretty hard. I couldn't imagine being in short sleeves in this weather.

Mom drove past the gated entrances of the finished communities and the construction zone across from them until the road dead-ended at the start of a small forest. She turned onto the property of a lone house set far back from the road. This house was made of brick and wood, so I knew it had existed long before the new construction began. Weeds grew in the brown yard, and the front porch was littered with old furniture, pots of dried up plants on metal shelves, and a hose coiled up loosely on the steps like a snake guarding the place. Mom drove down the gravel driveway and pulled around to the back of it. The owners of this house lived on the water's edge. Not a beach, but a ledge that dropped straight down into the water. A rusty old VW van was parked out back, and I had to think how irritated the owners of the construction company must be to have this eyesore of a place right near their beautiful, perfect homes. I also wondered how much they'd offered this homeowner for his land, and how much it would take before he finally gave in and sold.

Mom parked to the side of the van and stopped the car. She was out of her seat and walking up to the back door of the house before Carter and I could finish trading curious looks. A woman stepped out onto the cement slab behind the house before Mom got there. Her gray hair hung long and straight to her hips, and she wore a very loose flower print dress and a crocheted shawl wrapped around her shoulders. Despite the cold weather, her feet were clad in sandals, and I couldn't help notice that her toes were too long and some of the bones on the sides of her feet were too large. I fought back a shudder at the ugly feet and tried to look at something else like the braided ribbons tied around her wrists like bracelets. Clearly this was one of my parents' old hippie friends. I wasn't sure if we were supposed to get out of the car or not, but my curiosity got the better of me. I nodded to Carter, and we both decided to follow my mom. When we joined them, the woman was in the middle of giving directions in a thick French Canadian accent, pointing toward the ocean.

"There's a ladder that'll take you down to the beach, what there is of it, and then you can make your way over to the construction site. No one should notice you." The woman brought her fingers to her mouth as she took in the sight of me. She spoke in that weird tone adults get when they knew you as a baby but now you're not a baby anymore. "Look at you! You're so grown up. Aww. The last time I saw you, you were this tall." She put a hand down by her knee to demonstrate. This woman was fairly short, so that meant the last time she saw me I was less than two feet tall. "I'm sure you don't remember me. I'm your Auntie Vanessa." She opened her arms for a hug, and I went into it hesitantly. Her arms wrapped around me, and the smell of incense coming off that shawl made my nose tickle. She let me go, and I backed up to my mom.

"Auntie?"

My mom had a big, genuine smile, the first one of the day. She must've really liked this lady that I didn't remember her ever mentioning. She took Vanessa's hand and rubbed the back of it with her thumb. "She's not your real aunt, June, but she is a dear friend."

"I'm Carter," my boyfriend said before any of us thought to introduce him, sticking out his hand. Vanessa brushed it aside and, instead, patted his shoulder like he was some kind of pet.

"Well, of course you are. I've heard a lot about you."

"You have?" I eyed my mother for clarification. She gave me nothing in response.

"Yes," Vanessa said. She tucked her chin and crossed her arms like she was about to tell us something she cleverly discovered. "He's the handsome boy dating my friend's daughter who also happens to be the son of the man who is supposed to be in charge of controlling the pollution from this construction zone." She waved her fingers absently at the housing community to her right. "Isn't that right, Mr. Crowe?"

When my brain finished untangling that sentence, my stomach flipped. Is this what he'd been keeping from me all morning? Is this why my mom was being so cold to him? I wasn't sure where to look. At my mom for confirmation? At him to see how he was reading it? I only managed to stare at the ground and take in everything from my peripheral vision. Mom didn't move at all, from what I could tell. Vanessa's ugly feet remained parallel to each other, in a strong stance.

Carter's hands clasped nervously together at his waist, as he said, "Uh, yeah, I guess that's right." He gave a nervous laugh. "Believe it or not, I just found out about it last night when Mrs. Sawfeather called asking June to come with her today."

"That's what he was talking about with you last night?" I asked. "Did he ask you to keep an eye on us or something? Why so secretive?"

"He did, but if you remember I volunteered to come along before I knew. I'm interested in helping because marine biology is important to me. I didn't promise to tell him anything."

I had to look at him then. His face seemed sincere to me, but I was the only one in the group who would know that.

Mom took a sharp breath through her nose. "Is he interested in

36

helping, or is he being paid to hush it up?"

"I don't know that answer," Carter said, his tone defensive, his body tense. I'd never seen him like this before. "It doesn't sound like him to *want* to have pollution. That's not why he was hired."

Vanessa made this funny little sound halfway between a sigh and a squeak. "And yet pollution is happening. I tell you, I go out in the morning to get my paper, and then when I go out in the evening to water the plants, there is another new whole house completed. It's astounding the speed." Based on the health of the plants I saw out front, she went a lot longer than a day between watering them. She pointed toward the ocean. Apparently, she was a big fan of pointing. "Go on down there. I find a new corpse every day. Usually just fish, but some of my precious seals and sea lions have fallen to the poison."

Carter didn't stay to listen to any more blame. He grabbed my hand and marched away from them toward the place where the yard dropped off to the shore. I'm nearly as tall as him, but I had to step double-time to keep up with the fast strides he was taking. All his energy was in his face and his whole body leaned forward as he moved. The drop-off was about seven feet down to a thin sandbar. There weren't enough rocks poking out of the clay to climb down. The ocean must have been eroding this land little by little. I wondered briefly why anyone would build houses where the backyards would vanish bit by bit over time or break off all at once in a major storm.

Carter found the ladder Vanessa had mentioned. It was made of slats of wood wedged into the earth. He climbed down two and jumped the rest. I followed him. By the time my feet hit the rocky sand, Carter was already kneeling over a halibut, dead and stinking. It must have happened recently, because the seagulls hadn't found it yet. He picked up a shell and poked at it and scooped to turn it over.

"It's poisoned, all right. I can tell by the color." He cussed under his breath.

"Do you think your dad knows about this?"

"I don't know, but he sure was insistent that I find out everything I could today."

"Maybe that's so he can do something about it. Maybe the company is keeping him in the dark." These optimistic statements juxtaposed against my darker suspicions.

Carter dropped the shell and stood up. He put his hands on his hips and stared out at the water. "I hope that's true. I *really* hope that's true."

My mom and Vanessa appeared above us. Mom began climbing down the ladder. When she was halfway down, Vanessa handed her the testing kit. Mom, in turn, passed it off to me before finishing her descent.

"We've got to hurry," Mom said. "Randy and your father will be around with the boat soon, and once they show up, people will notice us."

"Good luck," Vanessa said, waving to us. Her smile only went as far as my mom and me, and was gone by the time her gaze reached Carter. It was fast, though, and he wasn't looking at her. I don't think he saw the disdain before she turned and left us.

Mom led the way toward the construction site. We had to walk single file, as there wasn't much space between the drop-off and the water. In some places, we had to climb over some driftwood or rocks. That was when I noticed my mom had some ratty old boots on her feet. I hadn't paid any attention to her wardrobe this morning, aside from that gray blend-in-with-the-weather jacket she wore. Now that I looked, I saw that she also wore a pair of stained and distressed jeans. It had been a while since I'd seen my mom in her junky clothes. I almost forgot sometimes that she used to be more active in the field with my dad and not just in her office or the courtroom. She was nimble, too. Climbing over obstacles seemed a lot easier for her than it was for me. I was winded by the time she suggested we stop and set up our equipment. She merely had rosy cheeks from the wind.

I had no doubt tests of this ocean water would come out positive for toxicity. There was a layer of sticky yellow-white foam on the sand left from when the tide was higher that wasn't evaporating and definitely stuck to my shoes. It was also obvious where to stop and do the testing. Runoff from the construction site had canaled and carved a slide down to the ocean. Water was still trickling down it even though the storm had passed hours ago. The spot was filled with fast food trash from the construction workers' lunches and bits of housing materials like plaster, wood, brick, nails, and so on.

A deep groan erupted from Carter like his soul had just been crushed. He stood on his tip-toes to see over the ledge and shook his head disgustedly. I caught Mom looking askew at Carter as she crouched down beside the debris and opened up the kit. I crouched next to her and whispered as quietly as I could so he wouldn't hear me, "Give him a break, Mom."

She just shrugged and kept working.

"Why do you have to be like this all the time?"

For a split second, she stopped and raised her eyes to me. Then she was back to her task. Funny enough, I knew exactly what that moment of eye contact meant. "This is more important than your boyfriend's feelings." Those were the words she didn't use.

I'd done water testing with my parents before. Or at least, I'd watched them do it. We took this trip to the Salton Sea in California one spring right after the snow on the mountains had started to thaw. It was the perfect time to catch the worst effects of pesticide run-off from the neighboring almond farms. I was about nine at the time. I remember being really disappointed that we couldn't go to Disneyland while we were there. It was so close. I think I whined about it all the way home. We had to pass right by it to get to the airport.

Thing is, I was doing the exact same chore now that I did when I was nine. Mom had Carter and I hold the glass jars. Just stand there and hold them, one in each hand. They had been sterilized beforehand, and we were given explicit instructions not to touch the inside of the jars or the lids.

Mom had to go on and say, "Not like that time when you used two of the lids like castanets."

I sighed. "I was nine."

"Two samples we couldn't get."

"Again, I was nine." I glanced at Carter.

He gave me a comical grimace. "She's serious."

"You have no idea."

Mom took the jars from us one at a time and dipped them into the lapping ocean water. She rinsed them three times, and while the jar was completely submerged, she asked for the cap. Well, she didn't ask. She gestured wildly with her hand until she got it. Then she capped the full jar while it was still under water. After that, Carter and I got to hold full jars of water.

To get Mom to lighten up a bit, and because I could no longer contain my curiosity, I asked, "How do you know Vanessa?"

Mom gave a half smile as memories flooded her brain. "We go way back. She was a teacher of mine in high school. She taught AgriScience, which I took instead of Biology. Basically, it was a class about farming, and we learned about soil and fertilization and stuff like that. After I graduated, we stayed in touch. Her husband was a deep-sea fisherman, and she was home alone a lot. I started having dinners with her when I was in college."

As Mom talked, she dropped chemicals into the jars of sea water and shook each one. "Vanessa wasn't actually that great at gardening, despite teaching the subject." Mom chuckled a bit. "You might have noticed that."

"Yeah," I said. Carter covered his mouth, but his eyes twinkled.

"She loved the ocean, but her husband didn't want to live near the ocean when he wasn't working. That's why they were in Olympia. When he died about twenty years ago, she bought the house here on the island. She likes it because she can watch the seals and sea lions from her backyard. They're her favorite animals. She even jokes with me a lot about how she's really a selkie, and her husband hid her seal clothes from her while he was alive."

"I kind of believe that about her," I said.

"What's a selkie?" Carter asked while my mom put the jars in the kit and grabbed out four new ones to put in our hands.

I told him about the selkie myths of people who were seals when in the water and could shed their skins to be human on land. "Most of those legends come from Ireland, but I know there are French ones as well."

Mom nodded. "There's a famous old French fairy tale called 'Undine' from the 1800s, if I remember correctly. It was about a fisherman who found a selkie and hid her seal skin so she couldn't return to the water."

"Well, then I believe it to," Carter said after a long beat while I'm pretty sure we were all considering the similarity of that story to Vanessa's actual life. "Your friend is a selkie."

Mom smiled warmly at Carter for the first time that day. "She's a good woman. I'm sorry if she gave you a hard time. What your father does is not your fault." I think that was my mom apologizing for her own behavior too. Sort of.

She didn't put chemicals in this second set of jars. "I'm going to save these for the lab," she explained.

A motor could be heard above the tide. Dad and Randy were approaching in a skiff. Randy steered, and Dad stood next to him. They both wore life jackets. They pulled up as close as they could, but we'd still have to wade through the water to get to them. I was hiking up my new coat above my hips and about to take a step into the water, when I heard shouting from behind us.

"Hey! Hey you! Stop where you are! What are you doing here?"

Three men were running toward us. One was wearing a blue hard hat and gripped a cell phone in his hand. I guessed this was the foreman on the job. The other two were construction workers he had brought with him as sidekicks.

"Mom, do you want us to stay and talk to them?"

Mom asked Carter, "Do you think you can send them away?"

"I'll try," Carter said. He shouted up at the men. "I'm Carter Crowe. My father is Elliott Crowe. He is the Director of Environmental Engineering for Oceanside Construction. You know him?"

"No."

"Well, you will," Carter said. "He's busy on a job at the Aberdeen office today, so he sent me to take a look at the pollution situation happening up here." He lifted up a couple pieces of the fast food litter and dropped them again disgustedly. "He's not going to be happy about this report."

Mom was climbing into the boat, and I followed her, thigh deep in the water. Carter still stood on the shore.

"Let me check something," the foreman said. He typed into his phone, and while he was distracted with that, we all gestured for Carter to come on and get in the boat. He waited.

"It's legit," Carter said.

After a couple seconds, the foreman looked up from the phone, his expression much less defiant. "I'm sorry, Mr. Crowe. Please tell your father we'll have this mess cleaned up today." He shouted something in

Spanish back at his two companions. They winced in shame and maybe a touch of guilt as they looked at Carter. I'm certain the thought that they could lose their jobs crossed their minds. The foreman said on behalf of all of them, "We'll be more careful with our trash from now on."

"See that you are," Carter said. He took the foreman's name and pretended to type it into his cell phone. He waved the phone at the foreman and told him he could get back to work. The three men did as they were told.

As soon as the men weren't looking, Carter gave us a bow, and we all applauded for him.

"Nicely done," my dad said when Carter joined us on the boat. He patted my boyfriend hard on the back.

The skiff wasn't quite big enough for all five of us. Mom, Carter, the kit, and I were all crammed together in the back while Dad and Randy sat up front. I still kept my coat hiked up around my waist, because the floor and seats were wet from spray. There were only two remaining life jackets. Mom insisted Carter and I wear them, but Carter was chivalrous and refused to put it on.

"Isn't the rule women and children first?" he asked.

"Only on the Titanic," my mom answered, reluctantly allowing him to help her into it.

"Well, I don't think we're going that far out," Carter told her. "I can swim back if I have to."

Randy hit the gas and motored us deeper into the strait. The plan was to get samples from a variety of distances from the construction run-off to see how far the pollution had spread in the short period of time since the rain stopped. The wind was still very gusty, so we were all expecting positive results with the rapid way the water was moving. Our collective mood was uncomfortable. We were eager to get these results and kind of wanted them to be distressing so we'd have the proof we needed to make a stand. At the same time, we didn't want to find that the water was poisoned to extreme levels. Deep down, all of us wished this work wasn't necessary. This was a feeling we often had doing this line of work, and I found it hard to know if I should be grinning at the prospect of our goal or frowning. Except for talk about what needed to be done, we all remained silent.

At Dad's urging, Randy slowed the boat to a stop. Mom and Dad readied the jars for the water samples. They didn't ask Carter or me to do anything this time. To make more room for them to work, I sat on Carter's lap. He and I both looked in the direction of the island and the housing construction.

"Did you know that there's a mass of plastic garbage the size of Texas in the middle of the Pacific Ocean?" Carter said.

I patted his curly blond hair. "You're so cute trying to tell something like that to the daughter of Peter and Natalie Sawfeather."

"What? You knew?" He acted dumbfounded, and I laughed.

I leaned over so I could drag my hand through the cold water and let it trickle off my fingers. "Actually, the island of plastic trash is a myth. Plastic doesn't biodegrade, but it does slowly break down into small bits, sometimes microscopic, and is spread out all over the ocean. It's estimated that there's 25,000 microscopic pieces of plastic per square mile in the ocean. It's impossible to clean up. The sea animals are eating it. We're eating the sea animals."

"So, we're basically eating our own trash."

"Yep."

"Mind if I use all of that info for my paper in Environmental Studies?"

"You can use my whole essay. I learned all of that for an assignment in school last year."

Carter glared at the construction site. "My dad has to do something about what's happening here. We might not be able to fix the whole ocean, but we don't have to add to the problem."

"I hope this evidence will make a difference for him," I said.

Randy shouted from the front of the boat. "Hey, look!" The rest of us followed the direction of his pointed finger. "A killer whale!" Sure enough, that black dorsal fin popped up out of the ocean a short distance from us. The whale spouted and dove under again.

"I wonder if it's the same one we saw from the ferry," Carter pondered.

Dad said, "I wouldn't doubt it, considering how few of them are left."

My parents got busy working again, but Randy, Carter, and I

watched to see if the orca would surface again. It did, a little closer this time.

"Looks like it might be coming this way," Randy said. "We might get a good show."

Randy was right. A moment later the whale surfaced again, definitely pointed toward us, and much closer. It was moving fast, and we were sitting still. The next time it came up, we could see a little of its white underbelly.

"It's so big," I couldn't help saying out loud. "I mean, you see them on TV, but you never think about how big they are." This time the whale came up close enough to the boat to make it rock.

"We better put everything up until he passes," Dad shouted at Mom. Carter and I helped them put all the jars safely in the kit.

We were all occupied with that when the boat rocked again, from the other direction. Randy called out to us, "He's changing direction! Looks like he's going around us!"

The four of us twisted our bodies to watch the whale slip around the stern of the boat. It wasn't more than ten feet from us. Its body was longer than our boat. I swear that as it glided past us, its eye was focused sharply on us.

It turned again, looping around the other side, definitely closer and definitely interested in our boat. Our boat rocked wildly in the wake the orca created and began to shift direction.

"What's it doing?" I'm not sure if anyone heard me over the wind and water, because I couldn't bring my voice above a whisper as trepidation replaced my wonderment.

"It's too close," I heard my mom say serenely, clearly suffering from the same concerns. And then in answer to her, the whale slid right up next to the boat where I was sitting with Carter and bumped it with the side of its body. It dove under the water.

The bump forced me to fall out of Carter's lap toward the front seats. I landed hard on the kit of jarred samples.

"June!" my parents hollered.

I was pretty sure they weren't checking to see if I was okay. "The jars are fine, I think," I told them. My head wasn't. I bumped it hard on the far edge of the skiff. When I raised my head up above the boat's railing I saw the whale surfacing again as though he'd swum underneath us. A swell of water pushed the boat backward, and I held onto the railing to keep from toppling backward into my parents and Carter. The whale was heading away again. Perhaps we weren't that interesting after all.

"That was scary," Randy said, clearly relieved.

"You think?" I asked. I put a hand to my head. A bump was forming.

"Maybe we should head to a different spot, the opposite direction of that orca," Dad suggested to Randy.

"I'm good with going back to shore," Carter joked.

Mom nodded. "I think we probably have what we need."

Real life has no soundtrack. There is no crescendo of music to let you know something is coming. It just happens. One moment you're sitting in a boat rocking on the water. The next a giant killer whale has come at you like a torpedo. *Bam!* It brings with it a force of water, and as it turns a split second before ramming the boat head on, the force of its body in the waves pushes your craft over.

Before I knew what had happened, I'd been flung backward. The heavy kit box flew at me and knocked me into the water. Like an anchor, it weighed me down and caused me to sink. My mind went frantic, and it was hard to process what to do.

Someone yanked the box away and pushed me upward. My life jacket did the rest of the work, helping me float back up to the surface. My parents and Randy were in the water. The skiff was upside-down. The three adults were holding onto the boat and planning how to get it turned over again. I couldn't see Carter anywhere.

"Mom!" I screamed swimming toward her. "Where's Carter?"

Mom and Dad looked around like it was the first time they'd thought of it. They couldn't see him, either.

"I don't know," Mom said, truly worried. "He had to have been knocked off. He was right on the edge."

"Maybe he's caught underneath," Dad said.

The four of us pushed hard to release the suction the ocean water had on the boat. Finally, it gave, and we were able to lift one side high enough to see under it. Carter wasn't there.

"Oh, God!" I screamed. I turned around, searching the water frantically. "Carter! Carter, where are you?"

My parents and Randy continued to right the boat. I heard them talking through their grunting effort.

"Is the whale gone?"

"I haven't seen it."

"We lost all the samples."

The samples! Someone had freed me from the weight of the samples. It had to have been Carter. He wasn't wearing a life jacket. Surely, he wouldn't be stupid enough to try to swim with that heavy box. It wasn't that important. We could get more samples. I scanned the water as far as I could see.

I noticed I was holding my breath while I looked, like I was subconsciously holding my breath with him. He had to be underwater.

"Come on," I exhaled. "Come up. Swim to me."

A swell of water came at me, splashing me in the face and causing me to gurgle. I got my head above the water again and saw the whale passing so close to me, I could reach out and touch it if I dared. Again, I had the eerie sense that it was looking at me. There was something very strange looking about its eye that I couldn't quite comprehend in the state I was in. I returned the gaze, trying to look deep into its eye. It was a blip of a reaction, but I swear it happened. Was it possible the killer whale recognized me? Had it been looking for me? Was it trying to contact me? Maybe on behalf of the mermaids?

I heard my mother screaming behind me and my dad trying to shush her. I dared to peek behind me and saw the three of them in the boat, my mom with her hands over her mouth, terrified for me. That whale could flip and bite me in half in an instant, and she knew it. Yet, I didn't feel afraid for that reason. I didn't fear the killer whale had come to kill me. It came to fetch me. At least that's what I thought.

When I brought my eyes forward again, the tail of the whale was gliding past. The killer whale was pointed away from us, and I hoped this time it wasn't coming back again. When the view in front of me was clear of the giant black whale, my heart leapt. Carter had surfaced. Terror was written all over his face as he watched the whale go by. When the path between us was clear, I saw the expression fade.

He mouthed, "I'm okay!" to me, clearly not wanting to make any noise and attract the whale's attention once more. As soon as it seemed safe, he began swimming toward me.

He was almost where I could touch him, when he was yanked backward. I saw his arms reaching toward me, his face rising up in panic, and then he was skidding backward, pulled by an unseen force that seemed to have caught him by his feet.

"Carter!" I screamed. My scream echoed, and I guessed my parents and Randy were screaming, too. In a second that I would relive in my brain over and over again, Carter disappeared under the water. There was a flip of a long silver tail, and I knew what happened. A mermaid had him, just like the one who had pulled me out to sea weeks ago. She would carry him far away before we could attempt to catch her. I could only pray that she allowed him to breathe, or she would have a dead captive before she got where she was taking him.

Chapter Five

Dad dove into the water to grab me and pull me back to the boat. I was still screaming. I couldn't get myself to stop. I lurched out of my father's arms, but he caught me and carried me back. It took both him and Randy to get me back on board because I was fighting them so hard. Dad held me down by my shoulders on the back seat until I calmed down.

"June!" It was probably the twentieth time he'd said my name, but I finally heard him as I quieted to a whimper. Mom and Randy were in the front seats of the boat staring at me with so much gloom and worry, their clothes and hair dripping. Everything was glossy with seawater.

"I'm okay," I said, trying to sit up.

Dad wouldn't let me at first, but then he loosened his grip. I pulled my knees to my chest, and Dad sat down on the far end of the bench near my feet. He kept a protective hand on my knee. It was comforting but also a reminder that he would stop me if I tried to launch away again.

No one said anything, and it pissed me off. I impatiently put out a hand toward Randy and said, "Well?"

"Well what, sweetie?" Mom asked.

"Why aren't we going after him? You saw which direction she took him, didn't you?"

Dad patted my leg. "June."

I didn't want to hear what he was about to say. "He's not dead, Dad. A mermaid has him. She dragged him away just like what happened to me. If we hurry we can catch them."

Randy gestured at the water. "There's nothing to follow, June."

Mom crouched next to me. "He's gone, honey. Carter was pulled under by the whale."

"No, he wasn't!" I shouted. It hurt to shout because I'd screamed my throat raw, but it hurt more to remain silent. "He could be still alive. We have to chase after them."

"How?" Randy asked. "Look!"

He was right. There wasn't any trail to follow. No wake. That mermaid had taken Carter far away by now. We'd never catch them.

"Call the Coast Guard," I said. "Maybe they can find him like they did me. The mermaid might let him go."

Randy turned to flip on the radio. I'm sure they had to call the Coast Guard anyway to report Carter missing. I couldn't hear what Randy said to them because my parents were so busy petting me and telling me to calm down, reminding me that they loved me and were there for me. I appreciated them, but it wasn't what I wanted right then. I *wanted* to go get Carter. I *wanted* to believe with all my heart he was still alive.

The engine was waterlogged and wouldn't start. We had to sit and wait for the Coast Guard to come to us, and it was the longest thirty minutes of my life. No one spoke as we bobbed in the water. The cold wind attacked my wet hair and made me shiver uncontrollably. My chest was heavy. I struggled to breathe through the weight of my despair. My new, wool jacket was so wet and heavy it made me feel worse. I took it off, but that wasn't better. Putting it back on again was like dressing in a wet, smelly blanket. I put my hands in the damp pockets and my fingers wrapped around the small twigs from the Red Cedar tree. I forgot I'd gathered some to take with us to the beach for our Valentine's Day beach walk. I switched them to the new coat before we left the house that morning in case we had a minute to spare while collecting samples for me to toss them in the water and see if I got any response.

I knew it was a silly thing to hope for, that somehow the twigs had some magical quality to them that would act like a beacon for the mermaids. Hadn't it worked once before? I was positive that the wreath I'd made of the tree's twigs was what brought that mermaid to me weeks ago. Maybe it could happen again. Maybe I could call back the mermaid that stole away with Carter.

With twigs in both fists, I dove for the side of the boat. My dad had to lunge after me to keep me from falling into the water again. He held me by my hips even though I didn't need him to. I think he was afraid I was going to jump in. I heard my mom shouting my name and Randy said, "What the...?" Dad was saying something to me about coming back and sitting down. I ignored them.

I plunged my fists into the water and shook them around. I twirled them in circles in the water and then back and forth. Between each change of motion, I glanced up to see if anything was happening on the horizon. The sun had finally broken through the clouds, and the reflection on the water made me squint. I looked for a silver tail, but all I saw were whitecaps. My parents tried to convince me to get back to my seat, but I continued twirling the twigs around in the ocean water, the edge of the boat cutting into my stomach, until I heard the horn of the Coast Guard arriving.

Randy and my parents reported to the Coast Guard officers what happened with the orca and how Carter was pulled under the water. They didn't ask the Coast Guard to look for him, but one of the men said they'd put out an alert in case there was a miracle. I stayed silent. It had been way too long since Carter was taken to find him. I wasn't stupid.

They first tugged us back to Vanessa's. Mom and I got out of the boat and waded to shore. Dad and Randy rode with the Coast Guard back to where they had rented the boat. Vanessa greeted us with hugs and hot tea. She let us borrow some warm, dry clothes. Nothing fit, but it was all loose, flowy stuff so it didn't matter much. I didn't care what my appearance was at the moment. Mom somehow managed to make the clothes work for her, despite being much thinner than Vanessa. She'd dried her hair so her brown curls coiled away from her face again. She'd left her purse in the car while we'd been on this mission, so she was able to touch up her makeup. All I did was wash off all the makeup she'd put on me that morning so I wouldn't come across like a deranged clown and scare kids on the ferry ride back.

"I'm so sorry if I said anything about your friend that upset you," Vanessa said to me at her back door as I was stepping outside to head to the car. "He seemed like a nice boy."

"He is," I responded. I couldn't look at her, keeping my gaze down at her ugly, sandaled feet. That was how I'd remember her. I walked away without saying goodbye. Behind me I heard my mom thanking her again for the clothes and saying something about being back soon to return them and try for more samples. I think they hugged. I don't know. It was quiet for a second. I didn't look back to see what was happening.

The car was cool inside but it blocked out that horrible wind. Mom got in a moment after me and turned on the engine and heat. It felt good, and I put my icy fingers right up to the vents to warm them as the blasting air got hot.

"Are you all right?" Mom asked me.

I didn't answer. She didn't press.

We rode silently past the construction site where the men kept building houses like nothing had happened. Someday soon, people would be living in those houses. They would grill steaks on their back patios while their children played on their perfect little lawns having no idea when they looked out at their ocean view that my boyfriend had been drowned by a mermaid right there.

Tears rolled uncontrollably down my face. I grabbed up tissues from the glove compartment, but there weren't enough to keep my face dry. Mom caressed the back of my head and scooped some of my long black hair forward over my shoulder. It was crunchy and smelled from the salt water. I didn't even care. I left it like that.

We had to wait at a coffee shop near the ferry dock while Dad and Randy dealt with the Coast Guard report, the local police, and the insurance forms through the boat rental service. They finally rolled up in the truck, and we boarded the next available ferry. I followed them up to the cabin for the hour ride back to Anacortes. I didn't want to be on the water again. I went to the absolute center of the cabin where I couldn't see any of the water at all. This ferry was nicer than the one we'd been on this morning. There were booth tables with cushioned bench seats around them, and I scooted up against the barrier wall and kept my eyes focused on my hands in my lap. Dad sat next to me, Mom and Randy on the other side. The conversation was limited to statements about what had to happen once we got back to town, who needed to be called, and stuff like that.

They didn't mention that they needed to call Carter's family. I guessed that the Coast Guard was handling that horrible job. My parents would need to call them personally at some point, though. I'd probably need to talk to them, too. I had no idea how I'd manage it.

After a bit, they all got quiet. The loud humming of the ferry's engine and the chatter of the other passengers took over. It wasn't terribly crowded on the boat. I hadn't looked at the time at all since the accident, but I figured it to be around three or so in the afternoon. It was too early for most tourists to be heading back unless they had evening plans in Seattle. A group of people over by the coffee stand were griping about their trip pretty loudly, and it caught my attention. I sneaked a glance at them and saw it was two couples, probably in their mid-twenties, dressed for a day of hiking. One of the women had her blonde hair in long, messy braids, and the other had a short, pixie cut that showed off her long neck. They were cute, and their boyfriends were rugged and handsome. They all looked like they had stepped out of a R.E.I. catalog. I eavesdropped on their conversation.

"We'll come back in the summer, Dayna, I promise," one of the guys said to the pixie-headed girl who smiled at him without much enthusiasm. "It'll be better."

"The rain ruined the whole trip," the other guy said.

Dayna crossed her arms. "It always rains here. I don't know why you guys wanted to do this in February anyway."

"It was supposed to be romantic," said the first guy, whom I assumed was her boyfriend.

"Hiking in the mud and almost drowning in a kayak is not romantic," said the blonde one. "I don't care if I come back even if it's summer."

But you didn't drown, I couldn't help thinking. They were all still here. So what were they complaining about?

"But look how pretty it is," the one that I guessed was the blonde's boyfriend declared. He pulled out his phone and held it up for her to see some pictures.

"You've shown those to me a hundred times now," the blonde one said. "It didn't look like that in real life."

"You wanted to turn back before we got all the way there."

Yeah, there was some whining involved.

"Because it was awful."

"Look! It's not." He tried to show her a picture again, but she brushed the phone away.

The first guy leaned against his friend and said, "Dude, if the girls don't want to go again, that's fine. You and I can go in June or July and make a weekend of it. It'll be awesome. We'll camp at Neah Bay, kayak into Cape Flattery, and see the Fuca Pillar for ourselves. They can stay home and paint their nails or something if they can't handle going with us to see the furthest west point of the continental United States." He smiled and put a hand out toward the girls, taunting them to say something.

"You suck, Evan," the blonde girl said.

"Fine," Dayna responded heavily. "We'll plan a trip for June. Maybe it'll be dryer. And just so you know, I can have painted nails *and* still like hiking." She waved her red nails in his face.

My mom's phone buzzed, drawing me out of their conversation. She looked at the number, concern crossing her face, and excused herself from the table before answering it.

After she stepped away from us, I asked Randy, "What's the Fuca Pillar?"

Randy, usually sour and quiet, lit up at the mention of the place. "Oh, that is a great spot. It's a giant rock sticking out of the ocean. It's right off the coast of Cape Flattery, which is the—"

"Furthest west point of the continental United States?"

"Yeah." He looked confused that I already knew that answer.

My dad spoke up then, grateful to have something to talk about. "It is in the Makah territory, and there are many legends about the place. Some say wishes are granted there. Some say there are tiny people living there who steal away children. I've heard that is the magic place where the fallen warriors were taken to have their spirits transferred into majestic killer whales."

At the mention of killer whales a deep hush fell over the three of us. We sat in uncomfortable silence for a minute or two before I couldn't take it anymore. I finally said very quietly the thought that was burning inside me, "But it's a rock? A big rock? A rock with possibly magical powers?"

Dad raised his head and looked at me, catching on. "June, do you think—?"

I nodded at my dad. "I do. Maybe it's the rock we've been looking for."

Randy wasn't following. "What?"

"And I bet that's where the mermaid was taking Carter."

"Come on, June," my dad said. "I know you want to believe that, but—"

"It makes sense."

"No, it doesn't."

I got up on my knees on the bench and waved my hand at the hiking couples. "Hey! Excuse me. Did I hear you were trying to kayak to the Fuca Pillar?"

The blonde girl sneered at my intrusion and the obvious rudeness of having overheard their conversation. The guys didn't seem to mind, though, and they both stepped toward us a little.

"Yeah," said one. "It was impossible to get there. We tried using our kayaks, but the water was too rough from the storm. We couldn't even get away from the dock without tipping, so we decided to skip it."

"We were going to hike in from the trail," the other one offered, "but last night's rain was so bad it made it a muddy mess. Think we're going to come back when the weather is better."

"Sounds like a good idea," Dad said to them.

I whispered to my father, "Did you hear them? We've got to go. We need to find out how to get there. Today."

"Did *you* hear them?" Dad responded. "The water is too rough to try something like that. We can't go back out there today."

"Dad! Carter's out there." I couldn't help it, I began to cry. Randy looked away uncomfortably. My father put his arms around me.

"He's not, June. You have to understand that. He's not out there. He's gone."

"He isn't," I croaked. "The mermaid took him. I know where they're going now. You have to believe me. We have to go to that place."

Mom stepped up to us, putting her phone back into her purse. Worry crossed her features at the sight of me crying. She slipped into her seat and put her hands across the table. My father kept his right arm around me and then put his left hand on top of hers.

"I'm not sure what you're talking about," Mom said, "but we can't go anywhere today. That call was Janiece Appell, the attorney for Mr.

Mains. They need all of us at the hearing tomorrow to testify." She looked at me with genuine concern. "I know this is horrible timing, but it's very important that you be there. The man's job and reputation are at stake. You need to tell the school board committee that he didn't support or encourage you to stay up in that tree."

I nodded. I wanted Mr. Mains back at West Olympia High even though I wasn't there anymore. And I desperately wanted Mrs. Slater, who had usurped his position, fired. It was my fault he got suspended, and I was going to try to make it right.

I had to be able to do *something* to help *someone*.

Chapter Six

Despite the fact that my mom was this bigshot environmental lawyer, I'd never been in a courtroom before. My parents had never invited me to watch her do her thing. It wasn't because they didn't want me supporting her or anything like that. Environmental trials are especially boring, I'm told. Lots of scientists and charts. It isn't anything like a trial seen on TV, just long and drawn out. So, I never went and never wanted to go. Today I had no choice.

We arrived at the county courthouse early the following morning. It was a daunting building, all gray and square. The original courthouse for Thurston County looked like a castle, and I felt like that would be more fun to be inside. Decades ago it became the capitol building, and this ugly cinderblock of a building became the new place of legal business. Normally the school board held its hearings at their own administrative building, but they anticipated a big showing from the community and needed a room to accommodate the crowd.

Mom insisted that we all look as professional as possible. "People are more likely to trust witnesses that look impressive," she explained like I had planned to show up in jeans and a sweatshirt. The pants, collared shirt, and sweater I thought were appropriate turned out to still fall far below her standards.

She wore an immaculate navy blue suit, the pencil skirt stopping just above her knees, and her jacket buttoned over a white blouse made of something soft and shiny. Every hair was in place and the navy blue pumps on her feet were free of scuffs. Dad wore his only suit and slicked back his long, black hair into a tight braid down his back. Randy still hadn't figured out how to trim his beard, but his gray-brown hair was a little less shaggy than usual, and he'd managed to wear a tie and jacket, although the jacket didn't match his pants. Hopefully he wouldn't have to testify. I didn't have anything dressy in my closet, so Mom put me in a pretty gold blouse that tucked into a brown skirt from her wardrobe. She said the skirt was long on her which made it hang right below my knees. None of her nylons would fit me. As a solution, she slathered up my legs with lotion to get them shiny, and then she stuck me in a pair of her shoes that were way too tight.

I limped from the car toward the building and right into a group of students from the high school on both sides of the walkway. They were wearing lime green T-shirts with the words "Mr. Mains is our REAL principal" emblazoned across the front. I recognized some of them as original members of the Recycling Club, but there were so many more kids than I remembered being in the club, probably twenty or so of them. There were a number of faces I didn't recall ever seeing before. When we approached, they cheered for us.

Mom smiled and raised her eyebrows at me. "Look at this," she said. "You're popular."

"No, I'm not," I groused. I was glad for the support, but I still couldn't bring myself to smile. I wanted to get out of these stupid shoes, wipe off the makeup, and go back to crying in my bed.

Haley, also wearing one of those shirts, squeezed out from the group and stopped in front of me. She put her hands on my elbows and took a dramatic deep breath like she was trying to help me *center* or something. Her eyebrows lifted in the middle sincerely. "We're here for you, June. I'm here if you need me, okay. If you need to take a break or whatever."

I had told her about Carter as soon as I got home the night before. I went to her house and sat with her in her room for a couple hours crying while she braided and unbraided my hair because she didn't know what to do with herself. She believed that a mermaid took him, because she'd seen what happened to me a few weeks earlier. Haley didn't believe he'd survived, though. The mermaids don't talk. They live and breathe underwater. He didn't have the telepathic communication with them that I did. There was no way for him to tell them to stop and let him breathe. Haley had tried to console me, but it didn't work. I finally went home and to bed. My face had been cried raw by this morning, and it hurt when Mom applied make-up to my ruddy skin.

I whispered to my only friend, "Are you going to get in trouble for this?" I gestured to her shirt and her friends. A guy with long, black bangs over half his face but buzz cut on the other side, stepped up close behind Haley. He smiled at me with the half of a mouth I could see. I thought he was pretty for a guy, but I had no idea who he was. Who were these people? How had Haley collected them?

"Probably," she said. "I kind of hope so."

"You're a rebel."

"You're my idol," she told me.

"Poor choice," I told her back.

She took the boy's hand and brought him to her side. "Have you met Leon yet?"

I shook my head. I noticed she wasn't just holding his hand. Her fingers were laced with his. He wore purple nail polish.

"June, this is Leon Roh, he just moved here from Oregon. He's a junior, so I've been showing him around."

"Hi, Leon," I said awkwardly. It was an uncomfortable time to meet someone new, especially someone who looked like he might start figuring prominently in Haley's life. My blood began to boil a bit at the thought of Haley getting a boyfriend right now, right when I'd lost mine. How dare she?

I immediately felt guilty for that thought. She'd never had anyone genuinely interested in her before. I never counted Ted. She deserved happiness even if mine had been cut short. I consciously softened my expression and gave them the warmest smile I was capable of making. I'm sure it failed to look genuine.

Saving me from saying something I'd probably regret, Mom said we had to get going and tugged me away by my elbow. Haley waved at me and then went back to chanting, "Let Mr. Mains Run the School Again!" with the other kids.

The courthouse had several different courtrooms. Mom led our group expertly through the building to one toward the end of the hall. My first impression of the room was about how much wood was used in the décor. A lot of trees gave their lives for this place of judgement. The walls were wood paneled. There was this giant wooden art design on the wall behind the judge's chair. Of course, the judge's bench and witness stands were made of wood. There was a fence barrier and tables for the lawyers made of wood. I was surprised at all the different levels in the room, too. The judge's bench was up pretty high, and then the jury box to the right of it was three levels. This case didn't have a jury, so all those seats were empty. The seats in the gallery were nice vinyl seats, though, not hard wooden pews like I'd expected.

As Mom predicted, the place was packed with parents and some teachers who were either skipping school or being character witnesses. Mrs. Slater, our vice principal, sat on the prosecution side of the room with the school board members. Right behind her, like a personal guard, were the members of the Student Council. Regina had knotted up her blonde hair into a bun. I assumed that was supposed to make her look more professional and adultish, but I thought it made her look like an angry ballet dancer. She didn't spare one glance for me as I passed down the center aisle. Marlee edged forward in her seat on the far side of Regina. Her big brown eyes met mine, and did I detect some kind of sympathy in them? From Marlee? The same girl who treated both Haley and me so miserably? I saw her bite her lip to keep from saying anything to me before Regina leaned forward just enough to prevent me from any further eye contact with her. Did Regina block my view of Marlee on purpose? She didn't inch her face toward either of us, but when she sat straight again, Marlee was sitting upright, eyes straight ahead and focused on nothing. Ted and Gary, next to them, were oblivious to everything, engaged in some conversation that had them both laughing and snorting so hard a man in front of them told them to hush.

A number of the press were in the back rows. Not being a real trial, cameras were allowed. Standing behind a video camera against the back wall was a familiar person. I waved subtly at Chuck Emory. He nodded at me and gave a slight grin, trying not to let on too much that we were pals. I wondered which of the reporters was the guy who had taken Juarez's position at the news station. I imagined he was here to cover the case.

As we walked down the center aisle, a few of the reporters shot questions at us. They were all rude, attacking my parents for allowing me to be in that tree and setting poor examples. Mom had warned me ahead of time that this might happen and told me to not respond to anything.

Mom kept her head high but her mouth shut. Dad and Randy both literally bit their lips to keep from spouting off. Janiece stood up in front and gestured to the seats she'd saved for us in the first row. We scooted in, my parents allowing me to sit closest to the aisle in case I needed to get up quickly. I was told if I felt my emotions taking over at any point during the day to sneak out and cry in the bathroom furthest from the courtroom, the basement if possible.

I felt a warm hand on my shoulder and twisted around to see who it was. Deepak was sitting right behind me next to Kyle. The tree climbers were dressed up as much as outdoor types like them ever get. Dockers pants and button-up shirts. They weren't tie-wearing kind of guys. Kyle's shirt was open enough to reveal a T-shirt underneath, and Deepak's beard had grown a bit shaggier since I'd last seen him. I didn't care for the way it looked, less handsome than I remembered. I felt a smile inside me, although I'm certain it didn't make it to my face, as I thought about how glad Carter would be to know that I wasn't attracted to Deepak at all.

"We heard about Carter," Deepak said in his lovely Indian accent. "I'm so sorry."

Kyle nodded and cleared his throat, clearly not knowing what to say.

I didn't know what to say, either, so I just patted Deepak's hand and faced front again. I leaned into my Dad and whispered, "Why are Deepak and Kyle here?" The tree climbers lived in California. This was a bit of a haul to come for a school board hearing.

"We paid for them to come in case we needed them to testify that we hired them to help get you out of the tree. They are also witnesses to what happened with your principal that day."

"You guys are serious about winning, huh?" I said.

"Your mom and Janiece are going to be a formidable team," he replied.

I had to agree. I'd never met Janiece before, but she was impressive to look at. She had to be at least six-foot-three. I'm a tall girl myself, and her height in addition to her full, natural hair made me feel small. I was glad she'd be standing a lot of the time, because sitting behind her prevented me from seeing anything at all.

The case against Mr. Mains began after it was agreed that the president of the board would sit in the judge's seat. He seemed a little too comfortable up there, I thought. He even used the gavel occasionally, which I thought was obnoxious. There was a brief explanation about why Mr. Mains was on probation from being principal at West Olympia High School. Basically, he hadn't been at work, and he'd encouraged a student to risk her life while truant from school. They had Mrs. Slater speak first. The spiky-haired woman waddled up to the witness stand and barked out her whole interpretation of the events.

Janiece didn't interrupt Mrs. Slater's ranting one time. When it was over, the lawyer stood up calmly and simply clarified, "So you were with Mr. Mains in the forest at this time instead of being at the high school. Is that correct?"

"Of course I was," Mrs. Slater said huffily. "How else would I have witnessed all of this?"

Janiece switched her focus to the president of the school board and said, "Then one of the charges against Mr. Mains should be dropped or Mrs. Slater should also be on probation."

"How dare you!" Mrs. Slater said.

The president frowned for a moment, glanced at the rest of the school board while a murmur spread through the crowd. He banged the gavel for no particular reason and said, "We will keep that under consideration."

A grumbling Mrs. Slater was led back to her seat. She shot me a nasty look at she sat down and hissed at me, "This is all your fault. You've ruined a good man's career."

"No, *you* did," I said plainly.

The only other person to speak against Mr. Mains was a teacher from the school that I didn't know. He complained that he had been having a problem with one of the troubled students in his classroom that afternoon, and not having the principal there to help with the situation made it impossible to get the child under control. Again, Janiece pointed out that *neither* the principal nor vice principal were available. She also questioned him about the protocols and training in place for teachers to handle students like this and if he'd understood them correctly. Shamed, that teacher left the courtroom when he was released from testimony.

Now the defense began. Mr. Mains told his version of the story first, followed by both of my parents. The tree climbers and Randy were mentioned, but none of them were called to speak. To my surprise, it was Wilson, the twitchy bird-watcher that had helped with the tree protest that was asked to speak. He snuck up to the witness stand from where he'd been hidden a few rows back. He held a manila envelope in his hands.

Janiece had Wilson tell the school board who he was and his relationship to the family. He told them how he loaned me the camera to take pictures of any birds I might see from up high and shared printed photos of the Golden Eagle I'd captured.

"Did Mr. Mains ask her to go into the tree to take these pictures for a school project?" Janiece asked him.

"No-ooo," Wilson replied with his peculiar talent for stretching out one syllable words. His shoulder and neck twitched. "She'd already taken these pictures for me before they all showed up. She didn't take any more pictures after this." He looked at my parents. "I'm sorry. It's my fault she went higher up in the tree. I asked her to do that, not her school principal."

Neither of my parents said anything, but my mom lifted her right hand just slightly off her lap and made a little wiping motion like she was telling him that it was all over and done with. Wilson was released, and he shuffled back to his seat. Now it was my turn.

I didn't have to get sworn in or anything because it wasn't a real trial. I wanted to be, so all those faces staring at me would more likely believe me when I answered. Waves of judgement came at me, especially from the side of the room with Mrs. Slater and the school board. I did my best to keep my vision focused on my allies. Clearly and concisely, I answered all the questions from both sides. I was told to speak up a few times, that clog of grief in my throat was making it hard for me to speak above a mumble. Janiece made sure I reiterated in several different ways that it was *all my fault* – not that of Mr. Mains or my parents – that I had been up in that tree.

After I said it one more time, "It was my fault," a sharp looking young reporter stood up from the back row. He had his cell phone in his hand and looked up at me after double-checking something he'd read on it. "Is it your fault or the fault of your parents that Carter Crowe is dead?

Says in this police report here he drowned in a boating accident while with all of you on some environmental expedition yesterday." He pointed to his phone where he'd received the little tip. The other reporters in the room exploded to their feet and hailed follow-up questions at me.

I think someone shouted, "Out of order." Probably the president of the school board. There was a ton of noise and commotion happening. For me, a cyclone came down out of the ceiling and encircled me. I couldn't breathe in its vacuum. I couldn't see anything but gray. The courtroom whirled violently. I might have fallen out of my chair. All I knew was that I was on the floor, and my father was on his knees, leaning over me when I opened my eyes.

"Are you okay?" he asked.

"My head hurts."

"You hit it pretty hard, I think."

"It might be a concussion," I heard Randy's voice say, but I couldn't see him.

Dad helped me stand up and walked me to the door that led to the judge's chambers. People were on their feet everywhere. The president of the school board was shouting and banging that gavel incessantly. My head ached, and the pain intensified with every slam. We entered the small office, and Dad helped me into a nice leather chair where I slumped with my head in my hands. Randy, Mom and Janiece entered the room a minute or two later and closed the door behind them.

"They're going to stop the hearing for today," Janiece told us. "It's gone crazy out there."

Mom came right to my side and rubbed her hands along my face and head. "You have a pretty big bump," she said as her fingers passed over it. It was tender to her touch.

"Oh, God, Mom. They think we killed Carter." I crumbled and began sobbing.

She stroked my back. "That's ridiculous," she said as tenderly as she could. "I'm going out there in a minute, and I'll give a full statement about what happened. I've just got to think through how to say it best." Her hand left my back, and I looked up enough to see her join Janiece in the far corner where they conspired about what to do next.

Dad asked me if I thought I needed to go to the hospital, but I told him I just wanted to go home and to bed. He helped me to my feet, and with Randy flanking my other side, they led me back out to the courtroom. It had emptied a fair bit already, the parents and school board eager to get on their way. The press had lingered, hoping one of us would come out and appease their curiosity. I was led through them while my dad announced that my mom would be out to speak to them shortly. Deepak and Kyle stepped behind us to prevent any press from following too closely. We were about to head through the door to the hallway when that reporter who had started the whole ruckus stepped in our way.

"How did it all happen, June? Was it some kind of payback against Elliott Crowe and Oceanside Construction for not keeping the water clean? Was it—" A hand reached out from behind him, grabbed his shoulder, and yanked him out of the way. I looked up enough to see my buddy, Chuck Emory, standing in the reporter's place, his camera down at his hip.

"I told you he was a jerk," he whispered in my ear before I passed.

From behind me, I heard the reporter fire up at him, and I hoped Chuck didn't get in too much trouble for protecting me. Dad and the guys led me out of the building. More news vans were pulling up outside in the parking lot, so the word of Carter's disappearance must have spread. The kids from school weren't chanting anymore. They all stood silently, with their bright poster boards hanging limply in front of their legs. I heard the tree climbers say something about catching up with us later. I don't think I responded. All my attention went to Haley who was stepping out of the group toward me.

"What happened in there?"

"They found out about…" I couldn't finish.

"Carter?"

I only nodded and covered my mouth as I felt the rush of tears again.

She squeezed between Randy and me and put her arm around me. "It's going to be okay. I'm here for you."

Leon was still hovering pretty close to her. Did he have trouble holding his head straight up with his hair like that? He did a small, uncomfortable wave without lifting his hand higher than his waist. I squinted into the late morning sun. How dare it be a pretty day?

"I just want to go home."

A horrible, shrieking voice came toward us from where Mrs. Slater burst through the front door of the courthouse. "All of you kids get back to school! Now! I'm writing you all up as truant! You will have in school suspension if you don't get back to class right now!"

"I think they should all get ISS anyway," said a voice I detested almost as much as Mrs. Slater's. Regina stepped up next to the teacher, with Marlee, Ted, and Gary flanking her. None of them wore the green Mr. Mains T-shirts. "They *are* skipping school on purpose."

"*You're* skipping school, too!" Haley shouted at Regina.

Wait. What? Haley shouting at Regina? In front of all these kids from school? What was happening?

"We are the Student Council, and we're here to help Mrs. Slater," Regina said, all puffed up.

"Help her with what?" Leon asked, brave for a new kid.

Haley crossed her arms and sneered. "Sounds like you think the same way as her. 'I wasn't at work, but Mr. Mains should lose his job because he was with me. I'm not at school, but the other kids who are at the same place as me should get punished,'" she said in the dopiest voice I'd ever heard her use. "Do you people even hear yourselves?"

"Haley, you are on very thin ice," Mrs. Slater said.

"I don't care."

Mrs. Slater pointed a finger at her so hard you'd think she was willing it to grow into a spike and pierce Haley's heart. "Tell your friends they will not be able to make up the work they missed this morning, and they will all report to the office when they get back to school." She didn't wait for any response and walked on toward the parking lot.

Randy whistled, and Dad said, "I'm so glad you're out of that school."

"Me, too," I said.

Regina pushed her way through to cut between Haley and me, because walking around us was out of the question, her hands clasped in front of her and her nose in the air. Just as she was about to pass, Haley leaned in and shouted "Boo!" right in her ear. Regina shrieked, recovered, and then gave Haley the dirtiest look she could manage while all the kids laughed at her. Even Marlee, Ted, and Gary covered their snickers with their hands or by looking at the ground.

"You're so not worth my time," Regina said to all of us.

"Oh, yeah?" Haley asked. "Then why are you here?"

Regina snarled at me. "I'm making sure that people who are failures stop being part of our high school. That includes lame principals and murderers."

Everyone gasped. I might have. I don't know. I might have become a speck on the sidewalk for all I could register about my own feelings at the moment, and she wasn't even done.

She kept spewing. "I shouldn't have come back to West Olympia. If I'd stayed at WU, Carter would've been *my* boyfriend, and he'd be alive right now."

Someone said, "Oh my God," in a low voice.

It might have been Haley. I'm not sure. The world was really fuzzy at that moment.

"That's enough!" my dad shouted. He put his hand between Regina's shoulder blades and pushed her away from us. He stuck with her all the way to the parking lot so she couldn't turn around and let anything else fly off of her forked tongue. I hoped he was telling her what an awful human being she was and how she should be ashamed, but I couldn't hear them. There was this awful buzz in my brain blocking out all other noise. I noticed that Randy had taken a step away from us, like he was ready to help my dad if necessary.

Regina seemed to realize that being so bold in front of my father had been a bad idea, and she didn't fight his escorting her or try to come back when he left her at the asphalt. She got all the way to her car before she realized that Marlee and the boys hadn't followed. They were still standing next to us, I think in shock.

"Come on!" she screamed at them from her car.

The three of them shared an unspoken deliberation of what to do. Gary took a couple steps toward the parking lot, and Randy gestured like an usher which direction he thought the high school boy should go. Ted grabbed his friend by the elbow, and Marlee shook her head slowly at him. Gary shoved his hands in his pockets and came back with his head lowered, disappearing behind his friends. After a beat, Marlee shouted at Regina. "No! We're staying!"

"You've got to be kidding me!" Regina raged. Her friends didn't respond. "Fine!" She got in her car and slammed the door.

In an instant, she was gone. I was half-surprised she didn't back into any cars, certain she hadn't taken the time to look.

Randy put his hands on his hips, lowered his head and shook it. "Kids."

My dad patted him on the back a couple times as he returned to my side.

Marlee pulled a hair band out of her pocket and tied up her thick brown hair in a ponytail as she said to Haley and me, "I'm sick of Regina. I'm sick of Mrs. Slater. We all are. If you came back to school, you would so be prom queen instead of her this year." She put a hand to her mouth so fast, I worried she'd slapped herself. "I mean, if Carter hadn't... Oh, God, I'm so sorry. I promise, none of us think you murdered him."

I was pleased to hear that the worst people I knew didn't think I'd killed my boyfriend, but that didn't mean I had to respond to her.

Haley caught Leon's attention and pointed to the box of T-shirts. Her new friend led the Student Council members over and got them hooked up. Ted and Gary took off the shirts they were wearing right there in front of the courthouse and changed into the new ones. I think I heard some girls titter at their pecks and abs. Haley stared at the grass so as not to see Ted's abs. Marlee folded her new T-shirt over her arm while some of the protesters began to gather around her like peasants approaching a princess.

"What is happening?" I asked my dear friend.

"I've decided to stand for something," Haley said. "Right now, I'm standing up for you, and it seems that other people want to help. It's about time, don't you think?"

I gave her a big hug so tight the tears I'd been trying so hard to keep inside me finally leaked out. When I pulled away she wiped my tears away with her thumbs and said quietly, just to me, "You need me to come home with you?"

"No, I'm good. You shouldn't get in any more trouble than you already are. There isn't anything else to be done here today, so you should all go back to school."

Marlee stuck her chin over Haley's shoulder. "Um, we're gonna need a ride."

I said goodbye and let them work out their carpooling situation. Dad told Randy he could leave, too.

"Thank you," Randy sighed in relief, "because I was seriously about to stab myself in the eyeballs if I had to watch any more of this."

We went to wait in the car for Mom. I stuck buds in my ears and turned up the music on my iPod so I wouldn't have to talk to my dad about what just happened. It took a few minutes, but Mom finally came out, walking as coolly as she could to the car so the handful of press outside didn't make anything of it. When she sat down in the front seat, though, I could tell she was frazzled.

"I hate reporters," she said. Without saying anything else, she gestured for Dad to get the car moving. Silently we rode home, hoping that the accusations from the press would be the worst of it.

They weren't.

Chapter Seven

Two news vans awaited us when we got home. They were parked against the curb along with several other cars. One of them I recognized. As we pulled into our driveway a red-headed girl popped out of that car. Tracy Klein, the girl who pretended to be part of our tree protest when she was actually a reporter trying to get an exclusive story on my strange family. Well, she got one all right.

"Natalie! Peter! June!" she shouted after us as we got out of the car and walked to the front door. How dare she call us by our first names like we were still friends? My parents ignored her. Other reporters called after us, but they were more polite and formal. I almost turned to acknowledge them just to spite Nick's horrid older sister, but I had nothing to say. Mom had Dad and I go into the house, and then she stopped to say to all of them, "You can sit out here all night, but we've got nothing for you. Carter Crowe's death was a terrible accident, and we are mortified at his loss. That is all."

A car came careening down the street and skidded as it turned into our driveway, nearly rear-ending Mom's car. It was a gold Lexus in sharp condition, and I knew that car, too.

"Oh, no," I moaned. "It's Carter's dad."

Elliott Crowe stepped out of his car wearing a golf shirt and slacks. His white blond hair, usually neatly parted on the left and combed was sticking up like he'd been running his fingers through it. His face, normally kind and friendly, an older version of Carter's, was drawn and his eyes rimmed with red. "Peter and Natalie Sawfeather, I have something to say to you!" he shouted as he approached the door.

The reporters gathered on our lawn, microphones and cameras at the ready. I heard them verifying Mr. Crowe's identity with each other. This was going to be good for them, and they were all excited.

"Yes, Mr. Crowe," Mom said. "Please come inside. Juniper, get something for everyone to drink." She gestured for Carter's dad to come quickly, her eyes nervously darting to the reporters.

"I don't want to come inside," Mr. Crowe said. He stood on our front porch, one hand on his hip and the other hand gripping his car keys in front of him like they were some kind of weapon.

"Please, Mr. Crowe. The reporters."

Dad stepped next to my mom, and I stood behind them on my toes to see over Mom's fluffy hair. "Elliott. We'd like to talk to you about what happened."

"I know what happened," he said. "I read the police report."

"Then you know it was an accident." Mom kept her voice very low. I'm sure she was hoping Mr. Crowe would follow her example, but he didn't. He was too mad and heartbroken for volume control.

"Yes. I'm aware it was reported as an accident, but it was an accident that didn't have to happen. My son shouldn't have been on that boat. He should not have been with you at all."

"Mr. Crowe, I—"

"And to make it worse, he was the only member of the team not wearing a life jacket. Can you explain that to me? Can you tell me why you, Peter, and your friend, Randall Harris, both grown men, had life jackets on, and my nineteen-year-old son did not?"

Dad cleared his throat. "There weren't enough, and he volunteered—"

"He was a *child*. You should have insisted!"

"Nineteen is not a child," Mom said plainly.

She shouldn't have. I had the same thought, but I bit it back. He locked his hateful gaze on her and would have bored holes in her skull if he'd had the power.

"He was *my* child," Mr. Crowe seethed.

Mom swallowed hard. She knew she'd made a mistake. "Please, Mr. Crowe, Elliott, please come in the house."

"No. I'm not here to be sociable or hear your excuses. I'm letting you know that I tried to press charges, but the police said it was an accident, and you couldn't be held responsible. I disagree, and I will be suing you. Expect to hear from my lawyer."

He turned around and five cameras snapped the moment. He waved an angry arm at all of them and walked toward his car.

I pushed through my parents to chase after him. "Mr. Crowe! Mr. Crowe, wait!"

Mr. Crowe opened his car door and paused to look at me as I approached. "What is it, Juniper?" The anger fled as he looked at me, replaced with so much sadness, a sadness I shared.

"I know how terrible you feel. I feel it, too. I can barely breathe it hurts so bad, but something helps me. I want you to know."

"What?"

"I don't think Carter's dead."

He shook his head, as if to clear the static and hear me better. "What do you mean?"

I swallowed hard before asking, "Has Carter told you much about how we met? What we were doing?"

"You mean all that mermaid hogwash?"

"It wasn't hogwash." I leaned in and spoke to guarantee the reporters couldn't hear me. "It was all true. The mermaids are real, and I'm positive they have Carter. It's the only thing that gives me hope."

His lips closed to a thin line, and he took a deep inhale through his nose. "I wanted to respect your family, what they stand for. Carter and I were fans of your father's work in particular. He was a fan of yours, but frankly, after that tree sitting mess and now this, I think we were both wrong about the Sawfeather family. You're all crazy. Especially you."

Mr. Crowe got in his car and slammed the door shut. He drove away, leaving me standing in the driveway. Tracy sauntered up to me, writing that last comment down on her notepad. "Nice, June. That went really well."

"Go away, Tracy." I started back to the front door.

"What did you say to piss him off like that?"

I spun around and knocked the pad out of her hand. Her pencil rolled down the driveway to the gutter. Cameras snapped pictures of me red-faced and her snickering. "Leave us alone!" I shouted at all of them.

I saw my mom's arm reaching toward me from the door and Dad hugging her shoulder. I dashed for them like I was running for the trap door during a tornado. They pulled me into them and shut the world outside. I let them hold me like that for a long time.

"He's not dead," I sobbed. "He's not. I know he's not."

They patted my head but didn't say anything about me being right or wrong.

After a minute, my mom pulled away. She wiped the tears of my cheeks with her thumbs and put her hands on my shoulders with that "buck up" expression I knew so well on her face. Thankfully, she was aware enough of my distress to not actually command me to buck up. I might have spit on her. Instead, she let me know that she and dad had some work to get done.

"We're going to need to head back up to San Juan Island to get those samples again. If Mr. Crowe is serious about this lawsuit, litigation is going to clamp down on us, and we won't have the time or access. We'll need to be there first thing in the morning, before the construction crews start working. I'm thinking we might even drive down tonight and stay in Anacortes overnight."

My mom, always able to stay focused. I both hated and loved this about her. Dad snapped to attention, taking his arm away from me and starting for his office.

"That's right. June, go rest up. It's been a hard day. Your mom and I have stuff to do." He looked at my mom and then grimaced toward the front window where the reporters lingered on the far side of our closed blinds. "I'll have to go out at some point to get some more supplies."

"I'll get them," I offered.

"No, I don't want you out there," Mom said.

I supposed she was worried I'd slip up and say something to the press about their plans, so I offered lamely, "I'll tell the press I'm going to work. They'll give me a hard time about it, but they'll leave me alone because going to work is a boring story. I mean, they might wind up at the pet store after they do their investigations and find out Carter and I work at the same place. That'd be good, though, because they won't be here, and I won't be there. A little wild goose chase for them. Then I'll come back and get ready to go with you."

My parents shared an unspoken moment before sharing their concern with me. "We don't need you to come with us," Dad said. "It'll be too hard for you. We'll grab Randy and take care of it on our own."

I understood what they were saying to me, but they were wrong. I wanted to help, because if Carter really was dead at least something good could come of that like raking Oceanside Construction over the coals for pollution. That would've been important to him. And if he wasn't dead, like I suspected, then I needed desperately to get back up there where I could find him.

"I can handle it," I told them as earnestly as I could. "If you don't let me go with you, I'm going up there on my own anyway. I'm going to find him."

"June—" Mom started.

"Don't tell me I can't. I know I can. I know the mermaids have him. All I have to do is find one of them and get her to show me."

"That's crazy."

There. She finally said it plain. No more sugar-coating. Dad didn't soften it, either. The way he shook his head and scratched his scalp let me know he was harboring some doubts about my sanity, too.

"How can you still not believe me after everything we've been through?"

My dad sighed. "I want to, but we saw him disappear under the water, June."

This time Mom was nodding next to him. Their bobbling heads got on my nerves. I put up my hands to block out the sight of them. "Fine! Don't believe me." I ran upstairs to my room and slammed the door so I couldn't hear them discussing how worried they were about me for the next ten minutes.

I turned on my computer and checked my emails. Still no word from Juarez. I really thought the death of Carter hitting the news would bring some sort of response out of him. Where was he? I went to his blog, ???SCIENCE or FICTION???. There hadn't been a new blog post in ages. I checked the message boards. He hadn't been on there either. I typed in a query.

Anyone heard from TruthBeKnown?

A few slow responses popped up basically saying they hadn't seen anything from him lately. Then people began to recognize my SilverScales username, and the questions flooded about Carter going missing and if I was okay. I wanted to tell these people my theory that that the mermaids had him. I knew they would believe me and comfort me. Heck, half of them would have come out here to search with me if I asked. I seriously thought about asking.

In the end, I kept my secret and continued to press about Juarez. Finally, one person who went by BigfootBeliever wrote that he remembered the last post from TruthBeKnown being about a month ago when he was asking if anyone knew any myths about "rock people". I scrolled back through the nonsense about alien sightings and strange telekinesis powers to find the conversation.

Not very many people responded to the rock people question. It wasn't high up on the list of mythical creature interests amongst these people who firmly believed in stuff other people joked about. One person told him there was no such thing. Another person just referenced fictional characters from *The Neverending Story*, *Fantastic Four* and *Frozen*. Juarez called all of them useless and vanished from the board. And life, apparently.

I threw my head back and bit my upper lip. No one in the world would be more helpful to me right now than Juarez Peña. He believed the mermaids were still out there. He would help me look, but maybe... I stood up and paced around my room. Maybe he was already looking. Maybe he'd found them. Maybe they had him trapped, too.

Why, though? Why would the mermaids take Carter or Juarez? What would they want with them?

I had to know. I opened my closet and grabbed my new coat off the floor. The wool had finally dried, but it smelled of sea water. Mom told me not to wear it again until we could get it cleaned. I didn't care about that. Carter gave it to me, and I would wear it fish smell or not. I slipped my right arm into the sleeve, and as I opened it to put my left arm through I noticed there was an inside pocket I hadn't observed before. It bulged ever so slightly, like something was in it. I finished putting the jacket on and then dug my fingers into the pocket and pulled out a heart-shaped piece of chocolate wrapped in red foil. Taped to it was a square elementary school Valentine with a silly mermaid girl in the arms of a little sailor boy. In a heart above them were the words, "You *mermaid* for me". So corny, but down at the bottom, in Carter's scratchy handwriting were his own words, "I love you."

I sucked in a breath. Carter had only told me he loved me once, and honestly, I wasn't sure if I counted it. I was up in a tree and things were a little desperate. He hadn't said it since then, I'd noticed. We'd been a lot closer lately, and I believed he loved me as much as I loved him. Why was it hard for him to say it? Was this the beginning of him breaking down that wall? He knew I'd find this note. Were the words from his lips going to be next?

Would I ever hear them now?

I wanted to collapse on my bed and cry for hours again. The urge was so overwhelming, but I didn't have time for that. Every minute was precious. I had to get back up north. I had to find where the mermaids had taken him. I flung the candy to my bed and stuck the note back in the lining pocket before buttoning up my coat. I grabbed my keys and purse, sniffed away the desire to sob, and headed downstairs. Mom saw me leaving and shouted something about how Randy was going to get the supplies for them, and I didn't need to go. I acknowledged that I heard her and went outside anyway without another word. I still didn't have a cell phone, so she'd just have to worry until I got back.

Something about the way I held my head up high, or maybe it was the smell of my coat, kept the press at a distance as I walked out to my silvery-blue car that Carter had delivered to me just over a month ago. Even Tracy stayed back. A feeble "where are you going?" came from the crowd just as I sat down in the driver's seat.

"Nowhere" I answered. Then I drove away, and none of them followed me.

* * * *

I drove to the forest. It was quiet up there now that the timber company had moved out. Spring was still a month away, so the barren swath of land that once was home to hundreds of trees still looked bleak, even in the late afternoon glow. In a month, when the rain would pour a little less and the air warmed, maybe some saplings might start their reach for Washington's elusive sunlight. I'd never see them reach their potential height in my lifetime. My children's children would never see them reach the heights the trees that used to be here had achieved. I pushed the thought away and continued on to where the wall of trees began again.

I parked my car where we used to have a protest camp and strode past the long burned-out fire pit. I had only returned once since the giant Red Cedar tree came alive and almost killed my uncle and me. That had been earlier this week, and I only stayed long enough to gather twigs, the same as I planned to do right now. I had promised to come back and visit but was waiting until warmer weather. I didn't figure a 1,000 year old tree would notice the time passing if it were only a few weeks or months. Amelia, my aunt, whose spirit was trapped in the tree, didn't seem to know time had passed at all from the day she'd disappeared thirty years ago. Seeing her brothers' aged faces did little to impress upon her that the world was continuing on without her.

Remembering the way to the tree wasn't difficult. Even though I'd only made my way through the forest twice on my own, someone else clearly had been trekking through here. A path in the dirt was formed now, shoe prints evident in the soil. From what I could tell, mostly the same prints. It was one person going back and forth regularly.

I passed between two large trees and entered the ten-foot clearing in front of the Red Cedar tree. My eyes fell on the massive trunk first, so wide and forbidding, more like a wall or a barrier. A chill ran up my spine as I remembered being stuck up in its branches. I couldn't bring myself to look up at them. I tore my eyes away, focusing on the ground to see if any twigs from the tree were scattered about. That was what I'd come for. I believed strongly that it was the wreath I'd made of the twigs that somehow attracted the mermaid to me at Grayland Beach back in January. If I took more of them with me to the strait, maybe they would act as a beacon for another mermaid. It was all I had to go on.

The rain from Valentine's Day had been strong, and it served to knock some weaker branches and twigs down. I crouched beside the tree and began gathering them up. As I came around the base I smelled cigarette smoke. I took a few steps and found my uncle leaning against the tree, smoking, and staring off into the forest.

"Uncle Nathan?"

"Oh, Juniper." He nervously dropped his cigarette and stubbed it out under his what-once-was-a-nice deck shoe but was now splattered with mud. "Please don't tell my wife. She thinks I quit."

I promised I wouldn't, an easy promise to make. I couldn't remember the last time I'd seen my aunt and had no plans to see her soon. This did remind me that I should head over to the reservation sometime and check in on Cousin Ronnie and my grandfather.

"Is Ronnie doing any better?" I asked, willing myself not to look up at the branch over our heads that had come alive and beaten the crap out of him.

"He's still in casts and stuck at home," Nathan said. "His friends are bringing his schoolwork home, and we got him a tutor so he won't fall behind. Last semester, you know."

"Yeah, I know."

"Well, I guess not for you, huh? How's freedom treating you?"

I squinted at him, thinking it an odd question if he'd been following the news at all. "How long have you been out here?" I asked.

He hesitated before answering, unconsciously playing with the zipper on his jacket. I noticed he didn't wear a tie with his collared shirt. I also noticed his usually slick hair, was sans product. I liked it soft and feathery. Even though he wore it short, the natural style made him look more like my dad. "I've been coming out here every day since... since..."

"Every day?"

"I take a long lunch," he admitted.

"It's about four o'clock," I told him with a gentle smile.

"Is it?" He rubbed his face with his hands and dug his fingers into his eye sockets before gesturing with his thumb. "I walked over from the clearing site. I have a team doing some re-seeding."

I put my sticks on the ground, turned around, and pressed my hands to the tree trunk. "Has she visited you?"

"I keep hoping," he said, "but I don't have whatever power you have. She won't speak to me. The tree is just a tree when I'm here."

"But you come anyway?"

"I want her to know I'm here."

The hitch in his voice caused me to glance up at him. A tear formed in his eye, and he quickly wiped it away with his knuckle. He took a sharp breath to control himself and asked, "What are you here for?"

"I'm guessing you haven't seen or heard the news today?"

"No, I've been avoiding the news since that girl wrote that article calling me out as crazy because I thought a tree was attacking me. It's been hard to convince people on the reservation that she was making that all up, and I have to start thinking about campaigning for reelection as Tribal Chief Executive. Why? What's going on?"

I struggled to answer. "My... *friend*... Carter... went missing... yesterday. The press is blaming Mom and Dad because he was with us when it happened." Now it was my turn to wipe away a tear. I refused to start blubbering again. Not in front of my uncle.

"I'm so sorry, June. Is there anything I can do?"

I shook my head. "No one believes me. They think he drowned, but I think the mermaids have him. I came to see if Amelia and the tree knew anything more that I could use to find them."

My uncle cupped my elbow with his hand, his eyes eager as they looked into mine. "Do you think you can contact her again?"

"I'm going to try. I need it quiet for a minute, though. Okay? I need to concentrate."

He hushed up and nodded. His days of not believing me were over. I closed my eyes and pressed my forehead against the bark between my splayed hands. *Are you there?* I thought. *Can you answer me?*

It took a long moment, long enough that I almost pulled away in defeat, before I heard the faintest whisper.

Yes.

"Do you hear anything?" Uncle Nathan asked.

"Shhh!" I hissed at him.

I concentrated again. I pulled up the image of the cliffs leading into the ocean that the mermaid had shared with me. *Do you know this place?*

Yes.

Where is it?

Far.

A slideshow of images passed through my brain. A journey up a mountain and through a giant forest that ended with a breathtaking view of the ocean. I understood that in his lifetime, the warrior had made this

78

trek at least once.

Where the world ends.

I think this is where your brothers went after they left you here.

Brothers. Not *brothers.* Like *brothers.*

A new image came to me of two American Indian warriors sitting on the far side of a campfire. It was as if I were part the scene, sharing the memory. They were laughing and drinking water from hides, and yet the feeling coursing from the tree into me was mournful. The larger warrior pointed at me to drink up. I did. The world became dark.

Left me here.

I whispered for Uncle Nathan to hear, "Something happened to him. I think they left him here because he died."

My uncle leaned in and asked, "Who?" I shushed him again.

How did you become the tree? Did the sun really turn you into a tree?

The tree didn't answer. Finally, after a long silence, I heard Amelia's familiar giggle. It was faint at first and then grew louder like she was laughing right beside me. "He doesn't know," she said. "I'm sure it wasn't the sun, though. Where did you hear such a weird idea?"

"Amelia?" I asked aloud. "Are you here?"

"Of course, I'm here."

Uncle Nathan flipped around. He put his hands flat on the tree, his left hand overlapping my right a bit. He copied me and pressed his forehead hard against the bark. "Amelia? Amelia? Can you hear me?"

"Tell him I can hear him."

I did.

"Can I see her? Can you do what you did last time and help me see her?" He was so desperate. I ached for him. "Please."

This time the tree answered, not Amelia.

No!

He wasn't allowing her to separate herself from him again. Maybe he was afraid she'd escape. What would happen if she did get away from the tree? Could she become a real, living person again or would she vanish? She was just a spirit or a ghost, something without substance.

Amelia whispered weakly, "I'm sorry, Junie. Tell Nate I'm sorry."

I turned my hand over and squeezed his hand. "She can't."

He took a ragged breath. "Okay. Okay. I understand. Just let her know I love her. I'm thinking of her. I won't forget her. I'm keeping my promise."

"She hears you," I assured him.

He nodded that he understood. I pressed my forehead against the tree again. "I'm still looking for your friend that became a rock in the old legend. I think it's where that cliff is. Would that make sense to you?"

Far. Long journey. Several days.

I suppose to a man living a thousand years ago the miles between this forest and the western-most point of Washington State would seem far. To me, it was a few hours by car. Yet I felt certain these cliffs from the mermaid's image were connected to this story. I knew they were important. That was where I'd find the brother/friend who became the rock, and somehow it was all connected to Carter's disappearance. I was sure of it.

"Amelia?" I asked. "Are you still there?"

"Yes."

"I have to go now, but I'll be back."

"I know. I trust you, but tell Nate he doesn't have to come so much. He seems too sad. Tell him not to be sad. I'm not sad."

I caressed the tree bark like it was a horse's hide. "Why don't you tell him?" I asked as innocently as I could.

"Tell me what?"

I put my finger to my lips.

I felt the tree groan, like a parent frustrated with his child. Then, beneath the hands that Uncle Nathan and I still had twined together, the bark began to pulse. We moved our hands aside and watched as the rough bark became smooth and an oval shape bubbled out of it. Then it took on the definition of a forehead, nose, lips, and chin. The eyes opened, and there was Amelia's face comprised of wood and yet animated.

"Amelia!" Nathan cried.

"It's okay, Nate," she said. "I only have a second."

He touched her hard cheek and lips.

"Stop it," she giggled. "That tickles."

He couldn't take his fingers away, continuing to trace the shape of her face with his fingers. "I miss you."

"I know," she said, "but you have to stop. I'm fine. I'm happy."

"But—"

"Come back *sometimes*, like Junie. Bring Peter with you. Not all the time, though. I'll be here."

"Will I see you again? Like this?"

No.

That was the tree. He was done sharing. The trunk began to encroach on her face again, closing over her. She managed to sneak in a wink, before her eyes were covered.

"Don't forget me," Amelia said before she vanished. "I love you."

Then she was gone. Uncle Nathan rubbed his hands frantically over the space where her face had been a moment ago. "No. Come back. Please. I love you, too. Come back."

"She's gone, Uncle Nathan," I said, gently tugging at his elbow.

He turned to me and put his arms around me, burying his face into my thick hair. "Thank you, June. Thank you for what you can do."

I let him work out his sadness for a moment, uncomfortably patting him on the shoulder while he cried. When he lifted his head again, I said, "I don't know if I can bring her out again. You know that, right?"

"I do."

"My parents are waiting for me." I crouched down and gathered up the twigs I'd dropped and a few more. "You should get home, too, and take care of Ronnie." His cigarette butt flipped out of the pile of sticks I gathered. "And no more smoking, okay?"

"Okay, I'll be good," he agreed, accompanied by the softest chuckle. "I bet Amelia hates it."

"I'm positive she does."

As he started away, I said to him, "I, um, I'm glad I saw you." I honestly hadn't thought about my uncle since the whole tree event had ended. I'd been preoccupied with my new job, finding the mermaids, scouting out the rock, and now—Carter. I wondered if my dad was hurting about Amelia as much as my uncle. Did he ever come here? I didn't think so. It seemed like he was handling it a lot better than his brother from what I could tell. How selfish of me not to check in on him.

Giving me one last long look at the tree before waving and walking away, Uncle Nathan said, "You can't imagine how glad I am that I saw you." In this, he was wrong. I had a very clear idea how glad he was. It was a feeling I hoped to match when I saw Carter again.

I *knew* I would see Carter again.

Somehow.

Chapter Eight

Needless to say, my parents were furious with me when I got back to the house after dark. They didn't have much time to yell at me because they were fielding constant phone calls. The reporters had left our house, but stories about the court case and Carter's disappearance were on the local news. My mom was getting bashed pretty hard about it. Headlines like "Environmental Lawyer's Investigation Leads to the Drowning of a Local Teen" and "Environmental Activists in Court the Day After Local Teen Goes Missing" like the two events were somehow connected. After the Channel 4 News team shared one of these stories, the female anchor shook her head, and offered, "It's just so sad, isn't it?" I wondered which part she was referring to, the teenager going missing, the high school principal losing his job, or my parents being vilified.

I heard my mom telling someone on her cell phone, "Can we at least get them to say what the investigation was for so we'll get some positive spin out of this?"

My dad yelled into his phone at someone, "Obviously, the orca was aggravated! It's being poisoned!" He pressed his thumb hard on the call end button. "God, I miss being able to slam a phone to hang up."

"Me, too," Mom said, slipping her cell phone into her pocket and hugging his shoulders with her other arm. They both focused on me. "We're heading out as soon as you grab some clothes," Mom explained. "We'll stay overnight in Anacortes so we can catch the earliest ferry in the morning and be first in line. The boat rental company on San Juan Island won't rent to us again, so Vanessa is going to help us out and have one waiting for us at her place."

"The selkie?" I asked.

Mom gave me a good smile, the kind that let me know she needed to remember how to do it. "Yes, sweetie, the selkie."

A few minutes later we were in the car. I told them about seeing Uncle Nathan and how I got Amelia to talk to us again.

"I wish I'd known you were going to do that," Dad sighed heavily. "I would have come with you."

"You were kind of busy," I reminded him.

"Do you think I'll ever have the chance to see her again?"

"I honestly don't know."

We rode in silence all the way up to Anacortes. My parents were avoiding the whole "search for mermaids and Carter" topic, I knew, and we were all done with talking about the fiasco with the press and the school board hearing. We were starving when we finally stopped. Mom miraculously found this tiny café that had lots of vegetarian options, and it had a tiny, 8-room inn above it. I swear the hotel was a billion years old. We had to get three rooms, because none of them had more than one bed, and there was one bathroom in the hall to be shared by all four residents on the second floor. Luckily, three of those four rooms were my family and Randy who met us there after he stopped for a better, more filling dinner than lentil soup and rolls, so it wasn't too awkward.

Not surprisingly, there was no free Wi-Fi or TVs in the rooms. I caught up briefly with Haley on the room's telephone before settling down to a night of drawing. I wound up sleeping in my clothes on top of the bedding, because the sheets were a mysterious shade of yellow, and the bedspread kind of scared me with its fraying edges and faded pattern. Mom assured me the place was on the up and up, but I couldn't decide if the place was either haunted or once used as a brothel.

We woke very early, grabbed some coffee and croissants from the diner before catching the first ferry across to San Juan Island. I swear two new houses had been built in the community beside Vanessa's house in the past day. She greeted all of us with hugs, and my mom returned the clothes we'd borrowed, washed and folded. Vanessa tossed them onto her sofa as we passed through her house. I caught her giving Randy a once-over, and it brought a tiny amount of joy to my heart. Odd, hippy widow and shaggy, grumpy bachelor would be an interesting match. I was for it. Although, I didn't see Randy even glance her way, so it might take a little work to get this all up and happening.

Mom didn't want to waste any time socializing, so we headed straight out to the ladder that led to the water's edge. A small motorized fishing boat waited for us, tied to a stake.

"It was my husband's," Vanessa said, mostly for Randy and me, because I assumed my parents knew this already.

Randy bobbed his head. "Looks in decent shape."

She smiled with a hint of pride, or was it pleasure, that he'd responded to her. "It is. I store it at a friend's slip and take it out once in a while to go seal watching. I thought it might come in handy today."

Randy didn't say anything to that. He started down the ladder.

I gave Vanessa an apologetic look on his behalf. She returned a humble smile and waved my apology away.

"Thank you," Dad said, following his friend. "We won't be long."

Mom put a hand on my shoulder. "Why don't you stay here? We can do this without you. I didn't even think until now what it will be like to be out there where Carter…" She didn't finish, putting her hand to her mouth as if to stop the words.

"I need to go," I told her. "I need to be in that place again so I can try to contact the mermaids."

Vanessa stepped up beside me, taking my hand into her own as she peeked into the canvas grocery bag hanging from my shoulder and saw all the twigs. She whispered in my ear, "Stay here with me. We'll sit by the water and call for your mermaids together. Maybe my seals will help." Then she winked at me.

My first thought was that she was mocking me and my belief in the mermaids or that I could call them to me. Then again, why would she do such a thing? My parents had to have told her the kind of agony I was suffering. Being a widow herself, she had to understand at least a little bit what I was going through.

"It's the same water here as it is over by the construction site, just a touch further away," Vanessa added.

"I guess so," I said, not completely agreeing.

Mom shared a grateful look with Vanessa before climbing down the ladder and wading out to join Randy and my dad in the boat. I saw them share a couple words, probably Dad asking why I wasn't coming. Then Randy started up the motor, and they putted off.

I instantly regretted not going with them and launched myself down the ladder. I jumped the last two rungs into the hard sand and was up to my knees in the freezing water before I stopped. They whizzed away quickly, making no effort to slow down or come back for me. I turned around to find Vanessa almost at the bottom of the ladder, her flouncy clothing and long silver hair blowing in the breeze that was so much stronger down here at the water's edge.

"I should've gone with them."

"Nonsense," she said, clapping some sand off her hands. "I promise it'll be better to stay with me."

She took my hand and led me in the opposite direction of the housing construction. The wall of dirt curved ahead of us and blocked my view of anything beyond it. We came around the corner, and a thick forest of trees coming all the way down to the water's edge came into view.

"Does your property go all the way to the woods?" I asked her.

"No," she said. "It stops just before it, but I go in there all the time. There's a spot I'm taking you to that you'll really enjoy."

It was a bit of a walk. The water came almost all the way up to the wall sometimes, and there were plenty of large rocks or driftwood in the way. Finally, the land evened out, and instead of a wall of dirt beside us, we were walking between the elegant arching branches of madrone trees. The forest here wasn't nearly as dense as the one on the mainland, and the trees weren't as tall. I felt peacefulness from the trees as I moved through them. Their ochre-colored limbs curled and twined about, as though they were dancing to the music of the morning birdsong. They seemed unaware of the threat from the construction nearby, that they could soon be gone and replaced by new homes. I wondered if I should warn them and how do it. I also wondered if I should leave them with their naïve beliefs that they would live forever.

Vanessa pointed to a spot up ahead where the trees formed a semi-circle around a smooth patch of sand. Not a single rock or shell marred its perfect surface. A few feet out in the water a flat slab of stone stuck out above the tide. We'd rounded the island enough that the breeze blew a different direction and without the same strong force. The water was calm here, almost like a bay, lapping quietly against the stone and the sand. This little beach was in the shade, as the sun hadn't quite made it up and over the treetops yet.

"It's so beautiful," I whispered, afraid that if I spoke too loudly I'd ruin it somehow.

"It's my favorite place," she said in a normal volume. "I come here every day."

The sand showed no evidence of her footprints. They had been wiped clean by the tide. I almost didn't want to step into the area and mar the perfection.

"Go ahead," she urged me, gesturing for me to enter this peaceful place.

I took off my boots like I was entering a house with white carpeting and stepped onto the smooth sand in my bare feet. It felt mysteriously warm on my feet despite the cold winter water from the Strait de Fuca and the lack of sunlight. I walked all the way to the middle and turned in a full circle to appreciate the majesty of the trees and the ocean. "You are so lucky," I told Vanessa. "I wish I lived here."

She smiled without showing her teeth. She knew what she had.

Vanessa took off her ugly sandals and put her shawl on the ground beside them. "Get your sticks," she told me as she walked to the water. I grabbed a few of them and joined her where she stood with her toes being lapped by the water. It was probably my imagination, but I swear her toes elongated and the bottom half of her feet below the water turned brown. The water was pretty dark and murky, and it was hard to see clearly. All the same, my feet didn't look any different when I stepped ankle deep into the water.

I leaned over and put the ends of the sticks in the water, drawing with them in circles, squiggles, cross marks, and zigzags. I wrote Carter's name in cursive. I wrote my own name. The whole time I meditated on the image of my mermaid's face. Nothing happened.

"This isn't working," I said. "Maybe I should make them into a wreath. When that mermaid came to me last month, she took the wreath I made and wore it like a crown. Do you think that will work?"

Vanessa didn't look impressed by the idea. "How would a mermaid sense the difference between sticks as sticks or sticks twined as a wreath? Aren't they still sticks?"

I groaned at her logic. "I don't know. I'm just guessing here. I mean, maybe the thing is that the mermaids like jewelry. The one I saved last year wore a necklace of shells, and several of her friends in the Affron experiment tank had them, too."

"You could try it," Vanessa said. "There's no harm in that."

I twisted the two flexible twigs together and brought them to a circle. Connecting the ends was the tricky part, and I couldn't quite figure it out. "Carter did this for me last time," I said, my voice cracking unexpectedly as I said his name. "I don't know how…"

Vanessa undid the leather string around her neck and slid the charm off. I only noticed then that the charm was a seal made out of bone. She put it in her pocket, and then wrapped the string around the ends of the wreath and knotted it into place. "That should do it."

"Thank you," I said. "I'll get you a new string."

"Not necessary."

Then before I could blink, she flung the wreath into the water. "Wait!" I called out too late, but the wreath already pulled out to sea too far for me to get it without diving after it. I turned to Vanessa. "What if it doesn't work?"

"I have a strong feeling we'll get some help," she said.

We stood and stared at the water. I wanted to feel as sure as her, but I didn't. My wreath floated away until I couldn't see it anymore.

"We should probably head back," I said. "My parents won't take that long to get those samples and will be mad if they have to wait on us."

Vanessa put up a finger, signaling to wait a bit longer, her eyes focused on the water. I hushed and waited. Only a moment later, I saw something in the water coming toward us. It was smooth and dark and moving quickly. My heart began to race. Could I be this lucky? Was I right about the wreath?

The creature came closer, and my excitement escalated until I realized the smooth head of this creature was brown and had a snout. What I saw was a seal not a mermaid.

It climbed up on that smooth stone in the water and bleated at us. Then it snorted through its whiskers and shook its head. Around its neck was the wreath of Red Cedar twigs.

"Great," I groused.

Without a glance at me, she put a hand gently on mine. I think it was her message to be still and quiet so I wouldn't scare the animal away. "There's my baby," she said sweetly to the seal. On the rock, the seal bobbed its head like it was doing a show at a theme park. I half expected Vanessa to toss a fish at it. What she did instead was walk further into the water toward the seal. Her long dress went into the water and billowed up around her. Either the sandbar dropped off quickly, or she had lowered herself to her knees, but she quickly dropped a couple feet in height. I couldn't see below her dress or through the water to see what happened. She glided easily, her head not even bobbing as she approached the stone.

Vanessa reached out a hand and petted the seal. It allowed her to, no flinching or any obvious signal that it was going to flee. She got close to it, and I thought she was going to kiss the seal on its small head. Instead, she began whispering into one of its earholes. The seal bobbed its head some more, like it was telling her it understood. When she was done, she gave one long stroke along the animal's back and a gentle pat. The seal snorted in my direction and then flipped backward off the stone. In a moment, the seal was out of sight.

Vanessa rose back out of the water as she came back to me. I swear as her feet emerged from the water a dark brown stain slipped away from her toes. She walked over to her belongings and put her ugly sandals back on her feet. "Time to go," she said, as if nothing weird had just happened.

I marched over to her and grabbed up my boots. "Is that it? We're done?"

"You said we didn't have a lot of time, and you're right."

"I needed those twigs," I told her. "I only have a couple little ones left."

"The seal will help us," Vanessa assured me, her eyes sincere as they locked on mine. "If your mermaids are out there, she will find them."

I stared at her. After what I'd been through over the past half year, I found it a lot easier to believe things I would have found impossible in the past. "Can you talk to seals?"

She only nodded, not wanting to share more. She was used to keeping her secret.

"I won't tell anyone," I promised.

Vanessa cupped my chin with her fingers sweetly and winked. "No one would believe you anyway."

"Maybe not." Right then I knew my mom's friend really was a magical creature, a seal trapped in a woman's body.

I chewed on my lip, unsure if I should say anything else. Vanessa pointed over my shoulder, the signal that we should get going. Before the trees blocked the view again, I looked back one more time at the secret beach. Even though we'd just been standing on it, the sand was perfectly smooth again as if someone had come and wiped it clean of our prints. I wondered how that could happen so quickly.

"It must have been hard for you, living in Olympia, far from the beach."

"It was dreadful," she said from behind me as we walked. "My husband kept me there. If he could have moved me to Kansas, in the middle of the country, he would have, but he made a living as a deep-sea fisherman and needed to be here. Olympia was as far from the water as he could take for the commutes to work."

"But he'd be at sea for a while with a job like that, right?" I asked. I glanced back at her and saw a secret smile cross her face.

"For weeks at a time," she confirmed. "I would come here. I bought it with my own money. Lonnie never knew about it."

"I hope you get to keep it," I said, nodding in the direction of the construction that we could hear but couldn't see from where we were.

She laughed, but it sounded strained. "I own this land, and I have no intention of selling."

I hoped the stretch of her land included that tiny, magical beach. It seemed like a source for her power.

"How did your husband pass away?" I dared to ask.

"Fishing accident." She didn't elaborate. I didn't press.

My parents and Randy were waiting for us when we got back. Randy was still in the boat, and my dad was tying the rope to a stake in the ground, so I figured they hadn't been there long. That was good. My mom wasn't the most patient person, and she especially hated waiting for me. It's one of the reasons I'd become so low maintenance over the years. When I was in middle school and learning how to do makeup and braids, my mom constantly shouted at me for taking too much time. This from a woman who could somehow do her face magazine cover perfect in five seconds using only a compact mirror and a tube of lipstick. I finally just gave up trying and decided to live with my makeup free face and straight, often scraggly, long hair most of the time. Lucky for me, my natural appearance was one of the things Carter liked most about me.

I swallowed hard at the thought of him and willed myself not to cry again.

"You were quick," I told my mom.

Randy stepped into the water and came toward us with the box of jars in his hands. "They had security right there at the shore."

My dad took the box from Randy, so his friend could climb the ladder. It was an unnecessary move, because my dad could have climbed the ladder first. I think he did it to keep his hands busy and not have to look at me while he said, "They also had police dragging the water for Carter's body. We had to stay pretty far back so they could do their work."

"And to keep from being recognized," Mom added. "So we were much further out to sea than we should have been, and we had to work fast. I know these samples won't be as potent as they could be, but I imagine they'll still show something."

Dad handed the box up to Randy and then climbed the ladder himself. Vanessa stepped up to my mom. "I'll keep the boat here for a bit longer. If all the business over there settles down, I'll get you some more samples on my own. Would that help?"

Mom sighed so deeply and put a hand on her friend's shoulder with such gratitude, you'd think Vanessa had just offered to pay our mortgage for the next year. "Yes, thank you. I know how you hate to go out on the water."

I stifled a laugh, and Vanessa pinched me. "You're right," she said, mostly for me I think. "I don't like to ride in boats much, especially since Lonnie passed."

Mom nodded solemnly. She squeezed her friend's hand and then started up the ladder.

Randy leaned over the edge and asked, "Do you have a kit for testing the samples?"

"I do, actually," Vanessa said. "Would you like to stay and use mine?"

"That would be handy," Randy said. "Then I could stick around and see if you're able to sneak back over there and get us some more samples before the day is over. I could keep them all together. That is, if you don't mind, and you don't mind driving me back to the ferry."

I was climbing up the ladder now, but I took a moment to glance back and see some color rising in Vanessa's cheeks as she answered, "Oh, I don't mind at all." Her French-Canadian accent made that seem so much more romantic than just a politeness. I winked at her, and she waved me away like I was an annoying fly.

A few minutes later we were back in Vanessa's house. She insisted we all stay for a cup of tea to warm up. It was some kind of herbal tea, and right after I politely told her it was delicious, she let me know it was a homemade concoction of kelp and lavender with some raw honey failing to sweeten it. Ew. I didn't finish it. Neither did anyone else, I noticed.

Mom double-checked that Vanessa had everything Randy would need for the samples. When she was sure, she gave her friend a final hug. "We'll see you again soon, I hope."

Now it was Vanessa's turn to wink at me, "Very soon, I hope."

"I'll see you back at home later today," Randy said, already unpacking jars of water onto Vanessa's small kitchen table in the other room.

I crossed my arms and announced, "Not me. I'm not going home."

Both my parents rounded on me. "What?"

"When we get to the dock, I'm going to take the ferry back to Washington and catch a bus to Neah Bay. I brought money I've been saving. There are some cabins I can rent on the reservation there, and then tomorrow morning I'm going to Cape Flattery to look for Carter."

Mom shook her head and waved her hands by her ears like she was hearing nothing but static. Dad stepped closer to me and took my hand. He rubbed the back of it with his thumb and kept his eyes on the movement while he said in a low, calm voice, "When are you going to let this go, June?"

I yanked my hand away and shoved it deep into my coat pocket. "I'm not. Stop trying to make me." Before any of the adults in the room could say anything, I went on. "I've seen things no one would ever believe, and my mind is open to anything being possible. I saw how Carter was dragged away from me by mermaids. If the orca had killed him, there would have been blood. He was dragged not eaten. I don't know why you guys don't agree with me. You were there. The mermaids have him. I'm taking a wild stab that the mermaids are at the place where I will also find a magical rock or stone or cliff of some kind. I believe with all my heart that place is at Cape Flattery, and I'm going there. I'm eighteen, and you can't stop me."

There was a long silence amongst the adults. The clock in the corner ticked. The cat prowling in the hallway mewed softly. The wind whistled past the front window. Randy faced away, trying to stay out of it, probably super tired of being around during all of our family struggles. Vanessa had a hint of a smile in the corner of her lips like she was holding back her opinion, but her eyes were calm and steady. My dad's thick eyebrows raised in the middle showing a mix of concern and mournfulness I'd never seen in him before. Mom's eyes were as hard and determined as ever. She locked her gaze on mine for so long I swore she was reading a scrolling message in them. Finally, she gave a short, curt nod.

"Okay. You can go," she said. "But your father and I are going with you."

"What?"

This was an unexpected turn. Even my dad looked baffled.

"Natalie, we have to get back—"

"Everything will wait," Mom said. "My daughter has been almost killed in a tree and drowned in the ocean in just the past month. If she's

93

determined to put herself in danger again, I'm damn well going to be there if she needs me. I'm not sitting on the sidelines. I'm not going to hear about it later. I will be at her side." She ran her hand down my hair and then flicked it back behind my shoulder. "Besides, I still haven't seen a mermaid. I was promised."

"Yes, you were, Mom," I said, reaching out an arm and pulling her to me for a very rare hug. "Yes, you were."

Chapter Nine

My parents were serious about participating. They got on the phone with one of Mom's interns at the law firm, and he went to our house to pick up a whole bunch of camping gear from our shed out back. After the wait for the ferry, the ride across the strait, and then another drive that actually took us back south of Seattle a bit, we found Ernie waiting for us outside a diner in his old beat up Ford with all the stuff. He even helped my parents cram it all into the trunk and back seat of our car. Mom offered him gas money, and then some, for the favor. Ernie, a cute guy around twenty-two and on the softer side of fit, acted like he wasn't going to take it, like doing this massive favor for my mom was enough for him. I wondered what kind of secret serum Mom put in the water cooler at her office to make her staff so willing to work for her.

We ate a quick lunch at the diner after Ernie got on his way, and then headed back north again by a highway on the western side of the Puget Sound. It was another couple hours before we hit Port Angeles, the last biggish town before the end of the world, and someplace I marked in my mind to come back and visit when I had time because it was so quaint and beautiful. I was told it would still be close to another two-hour drive from there. Dad drove as fast as he could, because we needed to get to the Makah Heritage Museum before five o'clock or we wouldn't get passes for camping. It was going to be close.

I rode all day squished against the door, my cheek pressed against the window. The view along the two-lane highway was incredible, what I could see of it. To my left I only saw sleeping bags, and if I could have seen through them there would be a rocky cliff. To my right was the Strait of San Juan de Fuca on a remarkably clear day for the Pacific Northwest. I could see the forested shore of Vancouver Island in the distance and the gorgeous deep blue water separating me from it. Occasionally I saw a large splash in the water, and I searched to see if I could catch a whale tail, or maybe a mermaid one, but I was never fast enough.

Between the heat of the car, the stress of the day, and now the sun lowering below the place where the window shades could block it, my eyelids lost the battle and drooped. My dad had some American Indian flute music playing for atmosphere, which didn't help. Mom's droning voice through relentless phone conversations about issues with the different cases she was working on was worse than taking sleeping pills. Good thing she had remembered to bring her charger, because she had the only cell phone. I fought the urge to sleep, even though I probably needed it. I listened to them discuss options about what to do if we didn't get to the campground in time, ultimately grateful they'd decided to come with me. I'd had no idea how far it was from the port at Anacortes to this campground, and it would have been miserable on a bus, if a bus even traversed this skinny highway. I hadn't thought it all out, obviously.

Even though we'd been on this journey for seven hours since leaving Vanessa's house, my parents hadn't said one more disparaging thing to me about my goal of finding the mermaids and Carter. I could tell they were kind of skirting around it but held back the discouraging comments. Mom didn't even give Ernie a good explanation for why we were going on this spontaneous camping trip. She stammered about trying to observe patterns of some killer whales, and my dad offered up a vague thing about visiting friends at the reservation while they were up here.

Neah Bay was just across the Makah Reservation line. We definitely knew we had entered reservation land, because the road immediately became rough and full of potholes. Neah Bay was a notch in the shoreline where the Pacific Ocean met the Strait of San Juan. It had a nice, calm beach surrounded by docks for fishing boats. There were a few stores along the main road and a neighborhood off to the distance. A swath of land between the beach and the woods was for camping, with room for tents, campers, and a variety of cabins. We pulled into the parking lot in front of the Museum of Makah Cultural History at four-fifty as the sun was dipping toward the horizon, my parents audibly sighing as the wheels crunched over the gravel. Dad dashed inside while Mom fixed her lipstick, and I got out to stretch. My tall body isn't designed for small spaces like that. Several times I'd thought about asking my much shorter mom to switch places with me during the drive, but I held my tongue, figuring she was doing enough by skipping work to be with me.

Two giant, wooden totem poles guarded the parking lot, and a wood-plank sign listed all of the fun things to do while visiting. I nodded at the totems respectfully as I passed by. When we stepped inside, we found Dad already at the counter beside the gift shop offering his debit card to the cashier. The entrance to the museum section was to the right of us. From the photos on the wall of the whale skeleton and some of the artifacts we'd see if we bought a ticket, I could tell it was a well-managed exhibit. I wished we'd arrived earlier, and I made another note in my mind to come back here someday. Mom immediately headed to the restroom while I wandered toward the gifts.

"You're lucky," the cashier was saying to my dad. "I was just about to close up. It's slow this time of year, and we don't usually get people this late."

If he was upset, he didn't show it. The man sported a friendly grin, his teeth a little big for his mouth. His manner was very at ease. He had his dark brown hair pulled back in a short ponytail at his neck, with the flyaway pieces flopping around his sharp cheekbones.

"I appreciate you waiting for us," Dad responded.

They got to talking about how the cashier lived on the reservation with his wife and kids, making him older than I originally thought. Dad asked about the campgrounds and amenities, and the small talk began in earnest. I guessed it bought us some time to relax for a moment. I poked around the displays of souvenirs, enjoying the clay pots with bold black paintings of some of the legendary symbols of the area. Ponchos hung from racks, and I assumed the expensive ones were made locally and the cheaper ones were imported in from Arizona or maybe Mexico. There were toys for the kids that were what tourists would expect, such as tom toms, tambourines, sucker-cup-ended, plastic arrows with bows, and dolls in faux-leather fringed outfits. That kind of stuff was sold at every American Indian gift shop in the country. Next to the toys were some picture books about the mythology of the region. I flipped through the pages quickly, looking for anything about the 'Three Warriors and the Sun'. Nothing.

Beside the children's books were some titles for adults. I didn't have the patience or time to skim through the thick tome about local history that I was certain had been there untouched and unwanted by tourists for a decade or more. My eyes were drawn to the sexy cover of a paperback romance novel featuring a white woman being seduced by a shirtless American Indian man. The title was something ridiculous with a super obvious double entendre, and the author's name, Naomi DeSilba, was scrolled in cursive across the bottom. There were too many copies of this book compared to the others. It looked like at least a dozen, so I wondered if the author was local. My fingers itched to read the back cover and see what it was about, but I didn't want my parents to catch me looking at it so I moved on to a rack of postcards featuring pictures from the area and some guidebooks for the hiking trails.

There were some gorgeous photos of the Fuca Pillar, a tall rectangular rock sticking out of the ocean and staring off to the west. Yes, staring, because at the angle of every picture I saw, it looked a lot like a giant head with a high forehead, flat nose and a prominent chin. I was holding two of the postcards in my hands when my dad called my name. I raised my head to see him and the cashier both looking at me expectantly.

"You want those?" the cashier asked. "I need to close up my register now. So hurry."

"Uh, yeah," I answered, grabbing one of the hiking trail guides as well and scuttling over to them. At some point, Mom had emerged from the restroom, looking refreshed and not at all like she just spent the majority of the day in a car. She made her way over to the racks of tourist T-shirts. Her hand lingered on one like she was thinking about it, and then she let it go and joined the rest of us at the counter empty-handed. I handed the postcards to the man.

I cleared my throat as I worked up the words I wanted to ask. "Have you ever... I mean, do you know... any legends, or whatever, that go with this area?"

A glint formed in the cashier's eyes. He liked this question and had a ready answer, one that was well-practiced for tourist children. "Long, long ago there was fear of Sxwayok, the Basket Woman. She was known to kidnap little children and carry them away in her basket. One time she dared to sneak into a village at night and take several children at once. She took them to her house in the woods." His voice lowered to just above a whisper, probably the way he'd rehearsed it. My parents and I leaned forward to hear him. "She lit a fire and then pulled the children out of her basket one at a time. She was going to cook them and eat them. The smartest of the children, a little girl, grabbed a pitchfork and charged toward Sxwayok, causing the wicked woman to back into her own fire. The children held the monster down in the fire until she died." He was quiet and waited for our response.

I shivered. "That's pretty gross."

"You tell that to children?" Mom asked.

"I tell them that if they don't behave the Sxwayok will come for them. It's pretty common around here."

"Eek," Mom said. She patted me on the head. "I thought I was a tough parent."

We all laughed and the cashier went back to ringing up my order. I handed him some money from my pocket, and then tried again. "That was a cool story, but, um, do you know any that are more specifically about Cape Flattery or Fuca Pillar? Something more nature oriented?"

The cashier lifted his head and stared at the wood paneled ceiling above him for a moment, tapping my postcards on his lips as he considered my question. I kind of wanted to go get other copies of the cards, but I didn't.

"There are two stories that come to mind. One is kind of silly and not much to it, and the other has been proven to be real. Sort of."

Dad nodded enthusiastically. "I'd be interested in hearing both if you have the time."

The cashier looked at his watch and then shrugged. "I mean, it's not like I live far from here, so…" He leaned on his elbows on the counter and began his show again, his eyes bright and his face eager. "There are caves in the cliffs near Cape Flattery, and in those caves, are mysterious drawings. They are too high to have been done by normal people. Legend says there were tiny, full grown people, no larger than children, called the Wah-tee-tahs who lived in the caves. They only came out at sunrise and sunset. They sought out the smooth places in the stone for their drawings and handprints. No one knows how they got up so high, but some say they lived in the rock itself and only came alive at those times." He shrugged. "That's all I really know of that story."

"I'm guessing that was the silly one, right?" Dad asked.

I didn't think it was that silly, but I held my tongue. If the warrior who turned into a merman could eventually spawn more of his kind, why couldn't a man who had been turned into stone somehow have more of his kind, too? Maybe the Wah-tee-tahs were the evolutionary version of the warrior from the legend. It wasn't the time to push my parents on this wacky logic, though.

"Yes," the cashier said. "The other one is about a tsunami." He stood up and raised an arm as if magically erasing the wall behind him so that we could see straight to the ocean beyond. "It was the great battle of Thunderbird and the Killer Whale."

I took a sharp breath. Mom reached out and held my hand as we all listened to the story.

"The killer whale had been eating all the food and frightening away all the other whales so the people were starving and had no oil. They prayed for help, and the great Thunderbird came to help them. He snatched the giant killer whale out of the ocean in his great talons and carried him to the top of the mountain and dropped him to his death. Then he flew back to the ocean and found the killer whale's son and had no mercy on him, either. When the ocean was free from the tyranny, it rejoiced with giant waves that crashed over the land. The people saved themselves by climbing onto their roofs or getting into their canoes. The waters finally receded, but a piece of the land was forever separated from the rest, and a new island was formed – Tatoosh Island. After that, the fish and oil were plentiful again." He turned back to us, the big story over, and shrugged. "There are a few different versions of that one."

I cocked my head. "What part about that is true?"

He nodded with the whole upper half of his body and put up his hands as if to prepare us for the best part. "Oh, there really was a tidal wave. Geologists have proven that there has been a major earthquake in this area about every 500 years, and they believe there was a major tidal wave around the year 1700. Pretty cool, huh?"

"Yeah," Dad said. "I'm going to have look that one up. It's interesting how coincidental it is."

The cashier reached under the counter and grabbed up a jacket he stored there. He slipped his arms into it as he said, his eyes darting back and forth to my dad and I as he made his point, "Don't discount our legends. A lot of them have truth to them."

Mom reached out and grabbed the paper bag with my postcards and guidebook. With an inflection that clearly showed that she knew she wasn't being included, she said, "Oh, trust me, they know."

The cashier gawked at her for a moment as if trying to make sense of my mom's words, and then his eyes widened with recognition. It all dawned on him at once–my dad, my mom, and me and who we were.

"Oh! You! You're them!" He gestured to my father, palm up. "You're Peter Sawfeather! And you're…" He gestured to my mom the same way. Then he focused on me. "And you. You're the one who saved the trees. Juniper, right? You're a hero around here. Did you know that?"

"Me?"

It was never me. My parents were the heroes. I was their shadow. They were in the news for saving habitats and endangered animals. My name only got in the news when I was being called a liar and fake. I was the one who tarnished their reputations. I was the one who got our school principal fired from his job. I was the one who brought my boyfriend along to one of our missions and watched him fall overboard during a killer whale attack and get pulled away to his possible death.

"Yes, you," the cashier said. He extended his hand to me, and I shook it hesitantly. "A large part of our land is forest. It is connected to the Olympic National Forest, but it isn't protected by the government. We maintain it, and we use a lot of the wood from the Red Cedar trees for our crafts." He flicked his fingers toward the gift shop. Ornate sculptures topped all the souvenir stands. "We have a huge wood-working community here, and we sell our products all over the world. But when Nathan Clark convinced the people of your tribal nation to sell off some of the forest for logging, that same discussion began in earnest here. We could use the money to fix up our roads and get some computers in our school. A lot of us were against it. When your tree-sit stopped the logging down there, we decided to let the idea rest here as well. I'm so glad I get to thank you personally for that."

I stammered through my astonishment. "It didn't go exactly the way I planned. There was a—"

Mom didn't let me finish. She was so used to controlling the interviews. "We're pleased that our efforts had a ripple effect over here, and thank you for caring about the Old Growth trees."

The cashier opened his mouth like he was going to say something else about that and then stopped. He came out from behind the counter, keys in hand, and led us to the front door of the museum, reminding us that he was running late and his wife would be missing him.

"She'll be awfully excited that I met you," he said as he locked up behind us.

It was dark out now, only a strip of orange at the horizon. No street lights lined the roads. Some lit signs or lamps above shop windows offered the only illumination.

"Do you think you'll come back by in the morning and enjoy the museum exhibit? I bet she'll swing by here just to meet you." He swiped some of his straggly brown hair away from his forehead. "My name's Greig by the way, Greig DeSilba." He shook Mom and Dad's hands.

"Wait!" I blurted. "DeSilba? Is your wife an author? I just saw these books over there…"

He rolled his eyes and shook his head, but the friendly grin stayed on his cheeks. It reminded me of Carter so much my stomach flipped. "Yeah, she writes these romance novel interpretations of Native mythology. They're a little embarrassing, but they sell like hotcakes."

Mom grinned. "Looks like you're both storytellers, huh?"

He snorted playfully. "I guess so."

I tapped the guidebook in my dad's hand, trying to get things back on track. "Does this show how to get to the Fuca Pillar? That's why we're here."

"The trail to Cape Flattery is nice, and it gives a great view of the Pillar."

"I want to touch it," I said.

"*Touch* it?" He looked at my parents for clarification, but they didn't offer any. This was my mission, and they were letting me make the decisions about where we were headed.

"Yes. Is there a way to walk down to the shore and wade across? Or do we need to come back here and rent kayaks in the morning?"

He shook his head, a doubtful expression crossing his face. "You would need a canoe or kayak for what you want to do, and they rent them down at the slip." He pointed the general direction. "It's not the season, though. They don't usually open up rentals until April, sometimes not even until May depending on the weather. It's too rough and cold out there right now. And then there was this kid that drowned the other day, so…"

All of our heads dropped at once, signaling him to audibly choke on his words. "Oh. Crap," Greig said slowly under his breath. "He was a friend of yours, wasn't he? I remember them saying your names in the news report. I'm so sorry."

"It's okay," my dad grumbled. He lifted up his guidebook and pointed it toward the campgrounds in the distance. "This has a map of the campground and how to get to our spot?"

"Oh, yeah. Yeah, it's easy. Let me show you." Greig gave Dad some quick directions while Mom led me to the car without saying goodbye to the well-meaning guy.

A minute later, Dad got in the car and turned on the engine. I saw Greig shuffle over to his rusty old car. He fiddled with his keys, because the car was too old to have an automatic lock. As Dad backed our car out of the spot, Greig stared at us, frozen in the motion of opening his door. Across his face was the question he burned to ask us. *Why are you here?*

Chapter Ten

The campground was deserted. Not a big destination in the middle of February. We were given a specific spot, but honestly, we could have chosen whatever we wanted. It was freezing out, and a bitter wind blew in from the north. Rain clouds were building up again, and the wind pushed them along so that the moon played peek-a-boo all evening. I hoped Mom's supply list for Ernie-the-intern included some long underwear and fleece pajamas, because it was going to be a chilly night. Dad insisted the cabins were pretty rustic and didn't have heat. I didn't care. Being inside a cabin with no heat had to be warmer than being inside a tent if for no other reason than because there would be no wind chill. We weren't *that* poor. Surely, we could've afforded one night's lodging.

There was a nice facility in the area that was more resort-like on a nice stretch of beach. I knew that would've been out of the question, so I didn't bother to mention it. I didn't offer any complaint. I kept my mouth shut about it and helped pull everything out of the car. My parents were doing all of this on my whim, so I had no business being a butt about it. Without them, I wouldn't even be here.

We'd gone camping quite a few times throughout my childhood, and I know at least half of my parents' dates before they got married were centered around hiking and camping. Putting up tents and starting a fire were second nature to them. There was no Chevy Chase slapstick *Vacation* comedy about them at all. *Zip Zat*! Both tents were up. *Zip Zat*! Full fire blazing.

Before most people would finish getting the first stake into the ground, my parents were already relaxing in folding chairs in front of a fire, flipping grilled cheese sandwiches on a portable gas grill. I asked if

I could borrow the phone and call Haley, but it didn't get any service. So, we sat in silence, blankets over our legs and hats pulled down over our ears, alternately staring at the fire or out at the ocean while we ate our sandwiches and drank hot chocolate.

Dad broke the silence. "I've always wanted to come up here."

"I can't believe you never have," I said.

"Sometimes it's the places in your own backyard that you never get around to visiting. The forest is well protected by the federal government, so we've never had any cause to get involved with it. The reservation up here is small and just inconvenient enough to make it a weekend trip I never got around to planning."

Mom stuck a marshmallow on one of the aluminum kabob rods that were in the cooking gear. She poked it toward the fire and let it get nice and brown. "I'm eager to see what it looks like in the daylight. It's a little bleak right now."

"Everything is bleak right now," I mumbled.

Mom brought the marshmallow out of the fire and blew on it to cool it off, but she didn't eat it. Dad dragged his toes around in the dirt. After enough of an awkward silence, he said, "We should all get some rest. It's been a long day, and tomorrow might be longer."

Mom flicked the marshmallow into the fire, got up, and cleaned up our mess. We didn't use any throwaway items like paper plates or plastic forks. My parents had a full picnic kit, and they stacked everything back together, ready to be washed tomorrow night when we were home again.

Dad continued talking as he poured out the dregs of hot chocolate from the pot and rinsed it with some bottled water. "We'll get up and have some breakfast in town. Then we'll head up to the outpost and hike down to the beach. There's a trail—"

"We have to get all the way to the water, Dad."

"I'm aware," he said, this time not as sweetly. I attributed his lack of patience with being tired. "We'll have to see how it goes." He strolled off to the bathrooms.

Once Mom had everything in order the way she wanted it, she made for her own tent. She looked back at me before going inside. "Get some sleep, June."

"I will," I told her. "I just like the fire."

Mom nodded and a beat later a lantern flashlight lit up the interior of their tent. I needed to sleep. I was exhausted from the day. It's weird how a car ride can be so tiring when all you do is sit. I yawned deeply as I stared at the orange fire and fixated on the black shapes between the flames. They looked like demons and monsters doing a tribal dance. Dad came back and kissed the top of my head. He said something about putting out the fire before going to bed and then joined Mom in the tent.

I pulled out the remaining twigs from the Red Cedar tree from the canvas bag near my feet. They were very small and thin, which was why I hadn't twined them into the wreath I'd made. I thought about flinging them into the fire because they were so useless. My grip tightened around them, protecting them from my destructive urge. I wore mittens to keep my hands warm and pieces of the twigs poked through the yarn to my skin, one of them caused a snag. The twigs were determined to be noticed.

I stood up and let my blanket fall to the ground. I wandered away from the fire down toward the beach. My parents didn't pitch the camp too close to the water. Their logic was that it would be colder near the shore. I'm not sure what difference a couple degrees would make at this point. It had to be in the thirties at least. As soon as I was away from the fire, I immediately missed it. The warmth it had been sending to my cheeks was replaced by icy wind, which I'm sure felt even colder than it was in contrast to the heat waves from the fire. I pulled my collar tighter and wrapped my scarf so it covered my nose. I breathed warm, moist air into the material, uncaring if I got chapped lips from it.

The beach was full of rocks and driftwood. I wondered in the summer months if they had a crew to clean some of it up, because right now there was no hope for anyone who wanted to sunbathe or play in the water barefoot. Any inflatable raft or toy would pop. I sat on a log, one of many I could see on the shore. Hunched over to keep warm, I watched the water lap at the sand a few feet from my boots. The sound of the surf usually soothed me, but on that night it got under my skin. Its constant rhythm needled me like a timer on a bomb. The fizzle of the foam reminded me of a burning fuse. The roar of the waves far out at the break line were the explosions I couldn't prevent. The sea was reminding me that I didn't have a lot of time to find the mermaids or Carter. Even taking time to sleep tonight seemed like more precious hours I shouldn't waste, even if there was nothing I could do in the dark.

I got on my knees as close to the water line as possible, allowing my jeans to get moist from the sand but not drenched by the water. I'd need these pants again in the morning. I took off my mittens, leaned forward, and put my weight on my left hand while I twirled one of the tiny sticks around in the shallow water.

"Please," I whispered. "I need to talk to you. I'm near you, I'm sure. Come find me."

I closed my eyes and breathed in and out slowly, trying to focus all my energy on the stick and the magical power I believed lived within it. The memories of being inside that tree with Amelia still made me shiver, but I couldn't think of how terrifying that had been now. I concentrated on the time I spent inside that hot space too large to be real, 170 feet up inside the tree, and how I pressed my hands and face up against the smooth wooden wall to speak to the spirit that lived in the fibers of it. The aching loneliness of the tree snuck back into my veins like I'd been given a shot, and it raced from my mind down my face and neck through my shoulders and out to the stick dipping in the water. The sadness of the warrior who missed his brothers, or friends, and wondered where they had gone and why they had left him oiled its way through my body as well. The tree wanted answers. I wanted answers.

"I beg you to tell me where you are hiding. I need to know. Please. It's not like I haven't helped you. It's time to return the favor."

I heard a crunch nearby and opened my eyes hopefully. The water before me revealed no secrets. No mermaid had pulled herself to my side. Had I really expected that would happen? Did I really think a mermaid would show up so quickly? It takes time to swim, even if there's a magical beacon calling you.

Keeping the twig in the water, I twisted around and saw my mother stepping up behind me. I let out a sharp exhale through my nose, trying not to vent out loud that I didn't appreciate her interruption. I also hoped she hadn't heard me talking to myself.

"It's freezing over here," Mom said, stating the obvious. I didn't respond, only turning back to look at the empty ocean. "What are you doing?"

"Nothing," I lied.

"You need to go to bed. It'll be a long day tomorrow, and you don't want to wake up with a cold."

"I'll be fine."

Mom sat, uninvited, next to me on the log. "Do you know why all these logs are here? They're the ones that spill of the logging ships. Dozens, maybe hundreds of trees along this coastline, wasted. Chopped down for no reason, because now this wood is waterlogged and unusable. You'd think the companies could find a better way to ship their cargo."

"Why are you here, Mom?" I asked. Maybe I wasn't just asking why she came down to find me at the shoreline. Maybe I was wondering why she was helping me at all.

"Do you really think those sticks can call the mermaids?" Mom asked instead of answering. "You were doing that on the boat, too."

I shrugged, although between the coat and scarf she probably couldn't see me doing that. "It's all I have to go on. The mermaid showed up at Grayland Beach when I threw the wreath of sticks into the ocean, so…"

"I see."

Mom was quiet and stared out at the elusive moon while I twirled the stick around in circles.

"I might be doing this for a little bit," I finally told her. "You don't have to stay here with me."

"I don't mind."

"I kind of do." I hadn't meant to say that. It slipped out, and I felt very ungrateful for saying it. Still, I'd been with them all day, and a moment of alone time didn't seem like a lot to ask.

Mom slapped her thighs decisively. "Look, I won't stay. I just wanted to check on you. Make sure you weren't running off or something."

She said it jokingly, but I knew she wasn't joking. "I promise I won't run off. I'll come back to the tent in a minute."

She squeezed my shoulders and rubbed my arms like she was trying to create some warmth. "You know what else you promised me? Magic."

"You might see some tomorrow," I said. "If I'm right."

"I really hope you are."

Mom wanted to believe me. I could feel it. She was just an adult, and her world was full of provable facts. It had to be. She was an environmental lawyer. Her job was to prove to the world that bad things were happening to endangered animals and natural resources. Having a belief or an idea wasn't enough in a courtroom. The people she fought against had lots of money and power, and her emotions or opinions made no difference against them. Evidence, testimony, studies, charts, and photos were all necessary to make her causes. So it went against everything she was as a person to buy into my claims that my boyfriend wasn't dead at the bottom of the ocean or inside a killer whale's stomach and was instead being held captive somewhere by mermaids for some unknown reason.

I wish I had a reason for her. That would help. All I really had was hope and a vision in my head of an ocean cliff with caves. I stared off at the horizon. Across the sea from us was the outline of an island. I asked my mom. "Do you think that's the Tatoosh Island the museum guy mentioned in his story of the great tidal wave?"

"No, that's still Vancouver Island. We'll be able to see Tatoosh from Cape Flattery tomorrow."

"How horrible that must have been for the native people back in 1700 or whenever the tidal wave happened. To not understand why the water pulled so quickly away from the shore and came back with such vengeance. No wonder they made up a story about the Thunderbird and Killer Whale having a battle."

"You sound like your father," she said with a chuckle. Then she got quiet and said in a very serene tone, "Why do you think some of the legends are just stories while other ones appear to be real?"

"I'm not sure," I said. "I've thought about that. You can't even imagine how much. I think all the legends are based on something real. Like Dad is always teaching, right? Sometimes, like with the tidal wave, it was to explain a phenomenon they couldn't understand. So, I wonder if the legend of 'The Three Warriors and the Sun' came from a real time when three young men went missing from their tribe. Over time, rumors about what happened were created and grew into a fantastic story."

"Okay," Mom said. "That makes perfect sense except for one thing.

The magic is real in this particular story. Why is that the case?"

I shook my head and chewed on my lip a moment. "I want to know that, too. Surely, the sun didn't do it like the story says. We know the sun is not a god, so that's not believable. Where did the magic stem from? Who cast the spell or curse? How did the man become a tree? How did the other man become a merman? What happened to the third one? Is he really a rock? What really happened?"

"Some kind of magician or witch?" Mom suggested. "Maybe the witch that was going to eat the children in the story we heard today?"

I laughed. "Ew, that was gross, right? Like an American Indian 'Hansel and Gretel'."

"That's what I thought, too. Funny how similar stories show up in different cultures."

"Like mermaids," I offered.

"Like mermaids," she agreed.

We both stared at the water again, and then I noticed something. It was so far away I almost couldn't see it, but still it flickered over the tops of the black silhouette of Vancouver Island. "You wanted to see some magic, Mom? Look!" I sat back on my knees and pointed in the distance with the twig.

She leaned forward so that her face was right next to mine, our cheeks almost touching, and studied the horizon until she saw the swirling purple, blue, green and yellow lights. "Ah! I see it!"

"That's Auroras Borealis, isn't it?"

"I didn't know you could see it from here," Mom mused.

"When I was learning about Cape Flattery, I read that sometimes it could be seen from here if the weather was right." I looked straight up and shouted, "Thank you wind for clearing away the clouds for us."

Mom shouted as well. "At least you're good for something."

We both laughed. She put her arm around me and held me while we watched the lights dance so far away. In that moment, I remembered the way I loved my mom as a little girl, when I doted on her and couldn't wait for her to get home in the evenings. Sitting on her lap while she braided my hair or making her six different cards for each Mother's Day. I wondered if she still had them somewhere or if she remembered getting them at all.

"We should go get some sleep," I said quietly, talking through a lump I hadn't expected to form in my throat.

"Are you done here?"

"Yeah, I guess so." I flung the twig into the water and let the current take it away.

We walked back to the tents. The fire was out in the pit, and I wondered if it burned out on its own or if Dad got up and put it out, probably irritated that I hadn't done it when asked. Mom hugged me goodnight and slipped into her tent, zipping it shut behind her. I heard some grumbling from Dad but didn't bother to get close enough to listen to them talk about me. With one last look toward the ocean, followed by a deep sigh, I went into my smaller tent and got dressed for bed. All my layers and the thick sleeping bag did their trick. I fell asleep in seconds and didn't wake until my mom crawled in the following morning and nudged me.

We packed up quickly, my parents as efficient as ever. They managed to get everything into the car with much better precision than Ernie had and left me a lot more room in the back seat. While dad and mom went over the map again, I wandered back down to the ocean one more time to see it in the daylight. The view wasn't much better because a thick fog had rolled in. From what I could see, it really was a messy beach. I hadn't noticed how much trash was caught up amongst the driftwood as well. I made a mental note to talk to Haley about this. Maybe we could organize the Recycling Group to come up here on a mission and do some cleaning.

My parents hollered for me to come on. I swung around, ready to run back, when something caught my eye. On a jagged piece of the broken end of the log where I had sat the night before something rocked in the breeze. I stepped toward it to see what it was, thinking it was probably a piece of seaweed or maybe a plastic grocery bag. My parents shouted again, miffed that I was dilly-dallying when this was my mission, after all. I leaned over and touched a piece of cotton. I tugged on it, but it wouldn't come loose. I came around the side of the log and found that the scrap of material was braided into a wreath made of twigs hooked on that jagged point of the log. I gasped, sliding the wreath free and turning it around and around in my hands.

It was the wreath I'd made yesterday at Vanessa's private cove. The one she'd given to the seal. And the piece of material was from Carter's red plaid shirt.

Chapter Eleven

None of the fishermen at the docks that morning were interested in talking to us. They dodged us, averted their eyes, or simply shook their heads when we asked about where to rent a kayak, canoe, or even a rowboat. One guy said, "Eddie might help you, but I doubt it," and pointed to a guy down at the end of one dock who was smoking a cigarette while loading a small boat with large buckets. We made our way down to him, and as we approached, he turned to the water and flicked his cigarette in. Before we even asked the question, he said to my dad in a voice full of salt and grit, "Sorry, man. I'd like to help you, but I just can't."

Eddie was probably about my dad's age, but the saltwater, wind, and hard life he lived had etched deep lines in his worn, leathery skin and frosted his hair and beard, making him appear older. He picked up a rope and concentrated on coiling it instead of looking at us. The thick fog around us should have been enough explanation, but he went on to tell us, "We got these rules for a reason. We've had a number of local men go missing over the last few years, and we've had to be extra cautious when it comes to tourists." His eyes flicked up to my dad and back down the rope again. "I know you're pretty familiar with boats, Mr. Sawfeather, but still…"

The man knew my dad without an introduction. Had Greig from the museum spread the word, or was my dad's face just that well known? I figured it was probably a little of both.

My dad cocked his head. "Locals are going missing? Who? I haven't heard about it."

"Yeah, when a man from the Makah Res goes missing it probably doesn't make headlines in Olympia." His bitterness was profound.

"No," my dad agreed, knowing what Eddie was complaining about, "but my brother, Nathan, should have been aware of it. He would have told me."

Eddie chewed on his lip for a second as if attempting to stop himself from speaking. The attempt failed. "Rumor has it Nathan Clark doesn't care much about anyone these days but himself."

"That's not exactly true," I mumbled. Defending my uncle was new for me.

Eddie shrugged my comment away.

"How many locals have gone missing?" my mom asked. "Maybe there's something that can be done."

"Usually one a year, as long as I can remember, but since October we've lost one a month. All of them supposedly fell off their boats and drowned, except that all of them were young and strong and should have been able to swim. Some of the elders are telling the children than the Wah-tee-Tahs are to blame. That they are taking our young men into the caves and killing them."

"But why?" I asked.

Probably because I asked that question instead of saying the expected, "That's ridiculous," Eddie raised his face to study mine. "I suppose," he said too slowly, like I was an idiot, "because it's a story the grandparents say to spook the kids into staying away from the water."

Mom put a hand on my shoulder, a gentle warning not to push it. I smiled graciously.

Dad tried again. "If we promise to be careful and stick close to the shore?"

"Got to say no," Eddie said, tossing his coiled rope into the boat beside him. He wiped his hands, and they sounded like sandpaper. "It's not even up to me. We have the boats insured now, and the Coast Guard made new regulations for us after the last time we gave in and let a tourist talk us into renting him a kayak. He disappeared, and we never even found the boat. They'll shut us down if they find out we did it again."

"A month ago?" I asked, my pulse racing. "Do you remember his name? Was it Juarez Peña, by any chance?"

He thought for a second and answered, "Yeah. Yeah, I think that's right. Hispanic guy. Said he was a reporter and had an important story to cover, that's why he needed the kayak. Can't imagine what he was after in January at the Cape." He paused and put his grubby finger to his scruffy chin. "Now that I think about it, he dropped your name, Mr. Sawfeather. Said something about researching something for you. It's what convinced me to let him have a go. Any idea what it was?"

My dad blanched, but Mom was always quick to answer difficult questions.

"Killer whales," she said firmly like it had been waiting to come out. "We had him on a mission to spot and record the movements of killer whales as part of a cause we're working on right now about how pollution is affecting their migration and life expectancy." This wasn't a lie except the part where Juarez was involved. My mom sure could spin. "We were consumed with the press after the tree protest and didn't have the time to do it ourselves, or it would've been Peter out there." She put a hand to her mouth and gasped as the truth hit her. "Poor Juarez." She looked at my dad, tears brimming in her eyes. "I hate to sound heartless, but I'm so glad it wasn't you."

Dad pulled her into a tight hug. It was weird to watch them do this scene. I knew they legitimately cared about Juarez, but I was the one who should be getting the hug. It was my fault Juarez went missing. I was the one who challenged him to find the legendary rock. He must've guessed it was the Fuca Pillar like I did. My eyes burned as I blinked away the tears threatening to fall.

I spoke, barley loud enough to be heard. "I don't suppose it would be too much to hope…"

Mom petted my hair. "No, honey. It's been too long."

I think she meant I shouldn't hope for Carter, either, but I refused to listen to her. Maybe they were together somewhere. Maybe the mermaids took Juarez, too. But why?

"I've got to get back to work," Eddie said, clearly uncomfortable. "Sorry about your friend."

Dad put up a couple fingers as a silent signal of gratitude before Eddie slinked away. All our arms around each other, we headed back to the car. Dad turned it on but didn't start driving. We sat there in a funk, processing the fact that twice in one week we'd lost someone we knew to these cold, dark waters.

"He was a good reporter," Mom said, her voice catching. "It's a tragedy."

"It's my fault," I whispered. It was all the volume I could muster.

Dad turned around so he could see me between the two front seats. He put a hand on my knee. "It's not. You didn't tell him to come here. You didn't know the water would be so rough."

I didn't think it was rough water that killed Juarez or those other fishermen at all. It had to be the mermaids, but I didn't know why. Why would they be snatching men out of the ocean? And that's when it really hit me. If all these local men were missing, then Juarez, and now Carter, then it was possible Carter wasn't being held captive by the mermaids at all. The mermaids might have drowned him just like all the others.

I couldn't hold it back anymore. I sobbed, my face in my hands, breathing in big gulps like I was drowning. I wanted to drown in my own tears. It would serve me right for putting Juarez and Carter in danger. For a guilty moment, I wished I'd left the mermaids in that tank to die.

My parents waited calmly, hoping I would settle down. Mom dabbed at her eyes with a tissue and handed me a couple. I swiped and wiped, but the tears and snot seemed relentless. They had drummed the "don't cry" thing into my head for so many years, and this week I couldn't stop. This time my crying was even worse than the day when it first happened. It wasn't like I had a scraped knee or something stupid. Surely, they understood that grief for a person, or people as it happened to be, carried more weight than crying over a dead bird or forest animal. Dad put the car into gear. Was that a huff I heard from him as he steered the car away from the docks toward the main road? I saw the totem poles of the museum pass by and a flag that probably belonged to a post office or something. After a couple potholes, he pulled into a gravel parking lot and stopped the car.

"What are you doing?" I croaked.

"Your mom and I are going in to get some coffee and breakfast. When you're ready, come in and join us. Then we'll decide what to do next."

"We're going to the Cape Flattery trail," I said without hesitation.

Mom let out a small, sharp sound through her nose, followed by,

"We'll talk about it when you come inside. I'll order you some pancakes, okay?"

"I'm not hungry."

"You should eat anyway."

They got out of the car and left me to get myself together. I watched them walk through the door to the diner and find a seat near the window. I found myself despising them for their chin-up attitudes and having appetites. I know decades of painful experiences trained them to handle things like learning one of your friends has gone missing and is probably dead at the bottom of the ocean, but I resented them forgetting I didn't have that experience. I haven't earned a rough exterior yet. I wasn't ready for this kind of pain.

And so I decided to hang on to the last shred of hope. I picked up the twig wreath I found that morning and held it in my hands. I touched the piece of Carter's shirt knotted into it and closed my eyes tightly.

"This was a message. What does it mean?"

I brought it up to my nose and mouth, took in the fishy stench of it, and tasted the sea salt on my lips.

What does it mean?

Then a vision pushed its way into my mind. Webbed fingers on the cloth, nimbly pushing it through the holes left between the braided twigs. The mermaid that had done this concentrated so hard, fumbling at times because the tips of her fingers where the webbing stopped were short and not good for fine motor skills like this. Finally, the material was secure. She shook it to be sure it wouldn't come loose. Then the mermaid placed it lovingly around the neck of a seal and petted the animal's head. The seal nodded and barked before diving into the water.

My mind fogged over again and I sighed, opening my eyes.

"That didn't tell me much," I said to the wreath. "But I do believe you were sent to me on purpose."

I set the wreath down on the seat next to me and wiped my face again with the damp tissues. After balling them up in my hand, I got out of the car. I dropped them in a trash bin by the front door of the diner and went inside.

The place smelled of coffee and grease. It wasn't big, only ten or so tables. None of the tables were the same, and the chairs didn't match.

117

Everything looked like it had been gathered from a variety of second-hand stores or garage sales. Framed photos of the forest and shoreline were evenly spaced along the light blue walls. In the back of the restaurant was a counter separating the patrons from the fry cook and a door leading to an office and restrooms. My parents had moved from the table by the window to join a couple over against the wall. It was a four-top table, but a chair had been pulled to the end of it for me.

"There you are!" Dad said cheerily, waving me over.

Mom was smiling, too. Across from them sat Greig DeSilba and a woman I assumed was his romance novel writing wife. She was attractive. Her black hair was pulled into a messy bun, with loose tendrils curling purposely around the side of her face and slender neck. She wore a dark green knit sweater that hugged her figure. The startling amount of eye liner and mascara made me guess she got her makeup tips from magazine covers. Even though I wasn't much of a makeup wearer, I felt super self-conscious about my eyes, which were probably red-rimmed and bloodshot.

"You doing okay?" Greig asked. "If not, I tell you, the waffles here will make you feel better." He patted his stomach. "They always help me."

I smiled as politely as I could. "Sure. Yeah. Waffles sound fine."

The waitress came over for my order, which my mom did for me. Waffles, hash browns, and milk. Did they have almond milk? No? Soy? Great. That.

I really only wanted some bacon and hot chocolate, but whatever.

Greig's wife introduced herself in a pleasant voice I could imagine doing a reading at a chain bookstore back home. "I'm Naomi." She offered her hand over her coffee, and I shook it carefully, so as not to knock over any of the cups or water glasses.

"I saw your book at the gift shop," I told her. "It looks interesting."

"You like romance? I'd be happy to sign a copy for you."

I shook my head. "I don't read much, actually."

Naomi wriggled her nose like she was used to that response. "Maybe when you're a little older. It's not really a, what's it called, young adult story anyway. Your mom might not approve."

"Probably not," Mom said with a laugh that I knew was fake, but

Naomi didn't.

Dad cut off the awkward conversation about me reading romance novels, thank goodness, by inserting, "Naomi was just telling us that during the tourist season she works as an interpreter on the Cape Flattery trail." His elbows were on the table with his hands together. He pointed all his fingers at her. "What does that entail exactly?"

She liked being asked that question, I could tell by the way her face lit up. Naomi was a big fan of having the spotlight. "Basically, I guide people along the trail, pointing out the flora and fauna, showing them things they might miss. I also tell them some local history and stories that go along with the area." She touched the top of my hand and leaned into me. "It's not a hard trail to walk. There's a boardwalk for the whole thing. Most people do the trail all by themselves, but some like paying me to come along and share these little tidbits. Down at the bottom is a platform with an amazing view, and we stay there for quite a bit while I talk about the things you can see from there like the lighthouse on Tatoosh Island and the Fuca Pillar."

"Do you know how to get to the Fuca Pillar," I asked. "Is it close enough to wade to?"

"Sometimes in the late summer when the tide is out, you might be able to swim there, but without a kayak or something you couldn't get to it right now. The water's just too rough and deep." She paused and thought for a moment. "There is a place where you can sneak off the trail, though, if you're daring." She wiggled her eyebrows deviously at me. "And I know you are. I can show you on a trail map where it is. It'll take you past this secret waterfall that no one knows about and down to a pebbled beach. From there you can see the Fuca Pillar really well."

"What's the waterfall?" I asked. "Why is it secret?"

My parents seemed interested, too. Greig smiled and leaned back in his chair. "Oh, you've asked for it now." He drank his coffee even while smirking at us.

Naomi shimmied her shoulders as she geared up to tell us something that clearly tickled her. "You'll love this," she told me. Then she addressed all of us like we were sitting around a campfire. "There's this waterfall. It's tall but not very strong, as if from a small stream. Only, what's weird about it is that I've been there hundreds of times, walked all over the area, and I cannot for the life of me figure out where the source of it comes from. It literally comes right out of the rocks. On top of that, it's made of saltwater, not fresh water like it should be."

"Ground water," Dad said simply, kind of ruining it.

"No," she said, undaunted. She'd heard this answer before. "It's saltwater. Ground water would be fresh."

"Well, that is weird, isn't it?" Mom said.

"It is, and I'll tell you what I think."

I began to warm to her enthusiasm. I bet it was fun in their house, the two of them trying to top each other's stories. They had lucky kids who probably never went to bed on time. It made me ache for the days when Dad would tell me these crazy myths at bedtime, even though I never appreciated it when it was happening.

"I think the waterfall is magic. I think it belongs to an old legend that a lot of people have forgotten about."

"What legend?" Dad asked.

I could almost see the little man in his head rifling through the files of American Indian legends about waterfalls and coming up empty.

Greig rolled his eyes playfully. "Here it comes."

Naomi splayed her fingers out on the edge of the table like it was her keyboard. I noticed her wedding ring was a plain band of gold, no diamond. "Well, this is the story my new book is based on, so it's pretty dear to my heart right now."

The waitress returned and plopped plates and bowls of food in front of all the adults. All talk was on pause. As soon as she was finished, she pointed at me and said, "Yours'll be right up, sweetie," before walking away.

The adults laughed at the bad timing, and then Naomi started again. "It's a love story, you see…"

"Well, duh," Greig said.

That almost made me smile, and a laugh gurgled behind the sadness cork stuck in my throat.

She hushed him. "There was a beautiful girl, and her brother was very protective of her. He wouldn't let any of the young men in the village near her. Two of the young warriors loved her terribly, but she had eyes for only one of them. The two men and her brother were all friends. One day, they went on a hunting journey into the woods." She made a grand gesture toward the wall and the woods presumably beyond it. Greig made a big show of ducking, and she brought her hand down and cuffed him on the back of the head. "I have decided that the brother was planning to test his friends and decide which one could court his sister, but I made that part up for the novel. The legends aren't as specific as novels have to be, so I have to add stuff."

We all nodded for her to go on.

"Anyway, the men went deep into the woods and eventually settled down for the night. The man who was not loved by the girl…" She put a hand to her mouth and stopped herself. With apologetic eyes, she said, "I've given all the characters names, and I'm trying not to use them."

"You can use the names if you like," Mom said.

"No," Naomi said. "It's better if I don't. It sounds more authentic without them, I think." She looked at my dad for his opinion.

He just said, "If you say so."

"I mean, you're the anthropologist," she said, a hint of unease breaking her otherwise delightful manner.

I raised my eyebrows at my dad and mouthed *anthropologist*. He flared his nose at me as a response but otherwise said nothing. Mom smirked into her coffee cup to keep from saying anything. I kind of loved that my dad made Naomi nervous. If only she knew that my dad thought he wasn't important because he didn't go to college.

"Keep going," her husband said, looking at his watch. "I've got to get to work eventually."

"O-*kay*," she said to him. She looked back at us, me in particular, and continued. "One night the men were sitting around the campfire, and the two men were talking about their love for the girl. The brother said he would decide who got to be her husband. The man the girl didn't love didn't like that and killed him. The other man, afraid for his life, ran away as fast as he could."

An image launched in my mind, the one from the Red Cedar tree spirit. He had recalled sitting around a campfire with his friends, and then the world went dark. Could it be that he was murdered that night? But that made no sense. How did he become a tree based on that?

I missed a couple things Naomi said and had to focus back in on her story.

"…back in the village. The girl's father was a shaman." She put a hand to the side of her mouth as though sharing a secret only with me, even though my parents could totally hear her. "I know it's not authentic, but I'm making him extra mystical in the book. The readers will love it." She put her hand down. "When the warrior showed up and told her father and her how the brother had been killed, the shaman cast a protective spell on the girl and her lover." The hand again. "I have them as lovers already in the book because it's a romance novel. It's expected." Hand down. "The two of them ran north from the village, up the mountains, into the vast forest. The other warrior chased them all the way to the end of the world. There, on a cliff over-looking the ocean, they fought violently." Hand up. "This is going to be an epic scene. I can't wait to write it." Hand down. "During the fight, both men toppled over the edge of the cliff toward the freezing ocean water and rocks below. The girl screamed and threw herself over the cliff after them, not wanting to live if her lover did not. As she fell, she magically transformed into a waterfall. The waterfall is salty, made of her tears."

The waitress dropped my plate in front of me right then. I kind of wanted to hit her. It did give Naomi a chance to drink a sip of water, which she probably needed.

"Her tears mixed with the ocean water right where the two men fell. Her lover grew a fish tail and gills so he could survive in the water. The other man turned into cold hard stone."

"Stone?" Dad clarified, looking up from the oatmeal he had been endlessly stirring. He shifted uncomfortably in his seat, avoiding my eyes.

"Yes," Naomi said. "Although opinions vary whether he became part of the cliff or if he is one of the sea stacks sticking out in the ocean."

"Like the Fuca Pillar," I said.

"Yes, like that."

My waffles were golden under the melting butter, and I suddenly regained my appetite. I dug in, and through a mouthful of bread, I said, "It's a good story."

"It'll make a great romance novel," Dad said, finally pushing his bowl away only half-eaten. "Especially all the parts you're adding to make it juicier." He drank from his black coffee.

My mom ate a spoonful of blueberries and waved the spoon around to punctuate as she said, "Well, I liked it. Full of adventure and romance. It's got a sad ending, though."

"That's what I've been telling her," Greig said. "No one wants to read a romance that ends tragically."

"Romeo and Juliet ends tragically," she said.

Greig laughed. "They make people read Romeo and Juliet in school. People don't read it for fun."

I bet they'd had this argument before.

I swallowed some of the soy milk and said, "There are a bunch of popular teen romances that end sadly."

Naomi gave Greig a pointed look as if to say *at least someone agrees with me*. Then she sighed dramatically and wafted away the sentiment with her expressive hands. "I'm thinking about fictionalizing the end."

"You haven't done that already?" Dad asked. Mom elbowed him in the side to stop being so bitter.

"Maybe I'll have the merman gather the waterfall of tears into a bowl, and when he drinks it they both come back to life as real people." At all of our scrunched up faces she snickered. "I don't know. I said I'm working on it. I'm only about halfway through the first draft right now, so I have time." She looked at my parents, my dad especially. "I can tell you don't like what I've done with the legend."

Dad wiped his mouth with his napkin, even though it wasn't messy, and put the napkin on top of his bowl, signaling that he was done with his meal. "Look, it's fine what you're doing. I don't even recognize that myth, so have fun with it."

My jaw dropped, and I leaned into the table toward him. "What do you mean you don't recognize a myth like that? 'The Three Warriors and the Sun' is like the first half of her story."

Naomi had pulled out her cell phone, and her thumbs jabbed at the buttons. "The waterfall story is a real legend, I swear. I found it on this website that collects American Indian stories. Ah! The internet in this town! Rachel!" she called to the waitress. "Do you have internet on your computer in the office? Can I look something up real quick?"

123

Rachel nodded at her and pointed a thumb in the direction of the office/kitchen. Dad waved his hands. "It's all right. You don't have to prove it. I know a lot of myths, but I certainly don't know all of them." To me he said grudgingly, "It kind of fits, but you really have to work at it. After all, Naomi's story doesn't say anything about the brother turning into a tree."

Yeah, that's what I was thinking, too, but there had to be more to it that we were all missing.

Naomi gasped. "Wait. You know a story similar to this one where the brother who got killed turns into a tree?"

Mom snorted. "Do we ever."

"Oh, you have to tell me! Although I have no idea how I'd add that into the book."

Greig scooted his chair back from the table and stretched. "Not now, Naomi. I've got to get to work."

"You could come with us to the trail, and we can keep talking," I suggested to Naomi, who was gathering her purse while Greig went over to pay Rachel for the meal. Mom sprang out of her chair to make sure he wasn't paying for ours. As they haggled over whose treat it was, I continued, "Then you could show me where the cut off is to the waterfall." Dad was shaking his head to tell me to stop inviting her.

"Oh, I'd like to, but the kids are with their grandmother right now, and I promised I'd be back. I only came in the hope I might get to see you three this morning. Greig thought you might stop by here since it's the only place open this early."

Dad was standing now, and I was the only one still sitting. I shoved one more giant forkful of food into my mouth and got up as well. I swallowed hard and then asked if she could point things out on my hiking trail map. She followed me out to the car and helped me with that.

A few minutes later, after goodbyes and stilted hugs and Mom bought a couple bottles of water at the convenience shop next door to the diner, we were packed in the car again. Dad started the engine, and I gave the directions to get to the trail head.

"We're not going."

His hands were at ten and two on the steering wheel, and he stared straight ahead at the diner's front window.

"Why?" I nearly launched at him between the two front seats. "There's no reason not to go."

"There's no reason *to* go," he said to me, turning his face so that our noses nearly touched. "We've humored you long enough with this, but you heard what the fisherman said this morning. People are going missing. Juarez is dead. Carter is probably—"

"You don't know that!"

"I do!"

He didn't even blink. His brown eyes stared into mine, and he didn't flinch. I know his purpose was to drill the cold, hard fact into me, but it just felt mean. The waffles I'd eaten turned into lava and threatened to burn their way back up my esophagus.

Mom's soft hands appeared in the corner of my vision. One landed on my dad's shoulder, the other on mine, a referee calming down the fighters. "Take a breath, you two," she said.

I shook her off and flopped back in my seat, my fingers flicking the door latch. I'd listen to her for a minute, but if I didn't hear what I wanted, I was going to bolt. I was certain I could convince Naomi or Greig to take me to that trail.

"This has gone far enough," my dad said to her. "I'm ready to get back home. Work is piling up for both of us, and we don't have time for this. Not to mention we still need to get new phones for June and I. I've been out of pocket too long. So have you."

Mom sighed, and I clenched my jaw. She was going to side with him. It wasn't like her to be away from work this long, and I hadn't seen her check her phone once this morning. I could tell it was burning at her to get back to managing her staff. She wasn't great at delegating, so her staff was probably sitting around the office twiddling their thumbs, waiting for her great return. But then she surprised me.

"Peter, we're already here. Aren't you even a little curious to take a look?"

She stroked his set jaw with her finger. I noticed the nail polish was chipped. A scratchy layer of gray stubble covered his brown cheeks, making him look older than he was. He frowned at her. "Natalie."

"It's a long drive home," she said matter-of-factly. "I'd rather do it after I have a chance to see the most northwestern point of the continental United States. That's a regret that I don't want to carry with me."

I wondered if she also meant that she didn't want to regret not helping me look for clues to the mystery the mermaids had given me.

"It's just up the road a bit, and Naomi says it's about an hour walk. Then we'll get right back in the car and start for home."

Unless we find something, I thought. *Like a waterfall made of tears. Or a cave in a cliff that looked like the one in the vision.*

Dad's posture softened. His hands came off the steering wheel, and he lightly pinched Mom's perfect chin. "The news about Juarez is devastating. I feel like I need to get back home and take care of that matter, let people know what happened. And that woman's silly romanticizing of our culture's mythology…"

I saw the mix of sadness and anger etched in his face, but I didn't care.

"I hate to say this, Dad, but Juarez has been missing for a month. One more day isn't going to make any difference in you letting people know about it. It is, however, going to make a difference if Carter is being held in a cave somewhere and needs to be rescued."

"June." He practically moaned at me.

Mom, who never took her hand off my father for a moment, like she was keeping him under her control somehow, said, "Look, Peter. You know June's going to stay and do this on her own, and it's clearly dangerous down by the water. Last time she went off on her own, voices no one else could hear tricked her into climbing into a tree where she almost died. I won't have her lured by some sirens no one can see except her into the ocean where she will drown. Do you understand? I'm staying with her until she's finished and satisfied with what she's discovered. I expect you to do the same."

I flicked the door latch to emphasize the point. Mom shot me a look to let me know my help wasn't needed, and then she was right back to my dad with her gentle, persuasive tone.

"While we're at it, we'll get to see some phenomenal views. Maybe we can even use some of the empty water bottles to gather up some ocean samples and see if the toxicity of the strait is still potent here."

"You don't have to keep convincing me," Dad said. "I got it. Be a good dad, naturalist, and otherwise patient and decent man, right?"

"Just like you've always been." Mom leaned in and kissed him.

Their faces were perfectly centered between the front seats. I secretly loved the hell out of the scene I was watching, but I couldn't let them know that. I groaned audibly for them to stop. They both turned their faces toward me, their foreheads still touching.

"What? You don't like seeing Mom reminding your father he's a hero?" Mom asked.

"Can we just go now?"

They chuckled, and Dad put the car in reverse. A moment later we were on our way to the next step in this journey.

Chapter Twelve

Getting to the trail wasn't difficult. It was one of the big tourist attractions up here, and there were plenty of signs pointing the way. We had to go up the mountain quite a bit, and my ears popped. I wasn't expecting to go up so high, considering that the trail was supposed to take us close to the ocean. The cliffs here had to be tremendous. We pulled into a nice, paved parking lot. Everything looked well-attended, with empty trash-cans and clean bathroom facilities. From what the pinned note at the trailhead sign read, this walkway was relatively new and paid for by the Makah Reservation. They made a big investment with their limited funds to get this place looking pleasant so more people would come and spend their tourist dollars in their town. I hoped it paid off for them.

The trail itself was a planked boardwalk with railings on each side that led ever downward through the forest. At some points, there were even some steps. It was an easy walk that would bore serious hikers and thrill older folks or people with children. Every now and then there was a little outpost for people to stop and take pictures. Small signs offered suggestions like how to recognize old growth Western Hemlock trees or a good spot where you might spot a black tail deer or maybe a bald eagle if you looked up. Lots of signs for birders, I noticed. The hardest part about the walk would be going back to the car, because that would be all uphill. I was grateful it wasn't raining or snowing. I imagined the trek would be slick. The wood was damp, and it probably stayed that way year round.

It was unnecessary for my parents to wear their backpacks stuffed with gear, but they did anyway. They were seasoned outdoor people, and they never went anywhere unprepared. I buttoned up my coat, wrapped a scarf around my neck, and slipped on some mittens to beat the chilly February air. Otherwise, I walked unfettered.

The hike was only a mile or so long before we reached the end, an octagonal deck with views in all directions. There were lots of great photo opportunities at this location, to be sure. The fog was beginning to lift, and I could only imagine how amazing this spot would be if it was a clear, bright day. Even from this platform, we were still a good ways up from the rough water below that spilled around promontories and rocks. Some of the boulders out there were as big as trucks. The earth curved out in each direction around us, sheer cliffs at least thirty feet high blocking any peripheral view to the north, and a forest of trees atop the slightly shorter cliffs to the south blocking any real view in that direction. I had to lean way out over the railing to even catch a glimpse of the Fuca Pillar in the distance. We weren't close to it at all.

I saw a couple caves cut into the cliffs, but they didn't resemble the one from my vision. They were also too obvious. Anyone could see and reach them if they tried hard enough, which made them a ridiculous choice for the mermaids to use as a hiding place.

"We missed the cut off to the waterfall," I said. "This was such a short hike I hadn't even started looking for it yet."

Mom snapped some pictures on her phone. Dad brought out a camera that he kept stowed with his camping gear.

"This really is extraordinary," Dad said. "I don't know why we haven't come here until now."

"I'm just going to backtrack a bit," I said, not sure they were paying attention to me. It was beautiful there and all, but I was on a mission. Sight-seeing wasn't my plan.

A dog yapped in the distance, and a moment later a young couple and their Golden Retriever clopped onto the viewing deck. The guy carried nothing but the dog's leash, and his wife/girlfriend only wore a small purse strapped across her chest. They didn't even have water bottles because it was below forty degrees out, and they knew they weren't going to get hot and thirsty on this quick jaunt.

"Ooh. It's so pretty!" the woman said.

The guy rubbed his hands and blew hot air into them. He'd forgotten to wear gloves. I pegged him from a state that doesn't get cold. Arizona, maybe? Nah, their puffy jackets were Lands' End. They had to be from Los Angeles or maybe San Diego.

The dog barked, and the lady hushed her. "Shh, Daisy." She gave us all an apologetic look. "Y'all are so quiet," she said to us. "We didn't even know you were here."

Not L.A. She was from the south somewhere. Maybe Georgia? I wondered what appealed to this couple to come all the way up here in February for their winter vacation.

"Just enjoying the view," Dad responded.

I let the couple pass me so they could get to the rail. "Mom, Dad, are you coming?"

"Don't let us chase you off," the guy said.

"No, it's fine," I answered. "There's just something I want to see."

"Ooh, what? Is it a secret path you know about? Would you show us?"

I took that to mean that she thought my dad and I lived in the area and were experts. "Uh…"

"It's best you stay on the marked path," Dad said simply. "Especially since you have a pet with you."

"Oh, sure," she said, her voice dripping with disappointment.

"Look," I said, pointing off in the distance. "People have whale sightings all the time here, and sometimes there are puffins on the rocks." I'd read that on one of the little signs.

As soon as they pressed against the railing to have a look-see, I jogged away. Mom shook her head a little and smirked as she followed me back up the path. Dad snapped a couple more pictures, excused himself from the couple, and then caught up to us.

"This place is fantastic!"

"You're glad we did this after all?" Mom teased.

"Good," I said, all business. "What we're looking for is, well I guess it would be on our right now that we're going up instead of down, a mark on the railing. It's two lines like parallel s letters. It's supposed to be a symbol for a waterfall. Naomi said she had to make it small so she wouldn't get in trouble and other hikers wouldn't think it was okay to start marking stuff up. Anyway, that's where we're supposed to duck under the railing and step off the path."

The three of us lined up side by side and made our way slowly along the railing, looking carefully at every little scratch and mark. There were quite a few, probably made from bird talons and falling branches. I found one heart with letters in it. *Jerks*, I thought quickly, and then let it pass.

"That looks fresh," Mom said, dragging her fingers across the heart. "You think that couple did it?"

"Probably," I said.

"At least it wasn't on a tree," Dad responded.

We kept looking. We were about a third of the way back to the start when I spotted it. The marks were very close to a post with one of those signs on it, so if it was late in the day, the shade from the sign would have hidden it completely. Luckily, it was still morning. I hadn't looked at a clock in a while, and the mountain hid the sun's progress in the sky. I thought it might be 9:00 or 9:30 at this point.

The railing was held up by posts, but there was plenty of space between them so that they didn't prevent any views of the fauna for the smaller people. We ducked under and climbed down a few rocks until our feet landed on some rich soil. There weren't any fresh footprints guiding us, but there was a bit of a dirt trench between the foliage that looked like it had been caused by some regular trekking back and forth along it.

We were all wearing hiking pants with thermals underneath and boots. More stuff Mom and Dad kept already stocked with their camping gear. Last minute nature trips were no new thing to them. I walked in front, but I let my parents give the directions because they knew the different kinds of trees and shrubs Naomi had told us to use as markers. A lot of the walk was uphill, and the ground was uneven. Twigs snagged and poked at my legs as I pushed through the overgrowth. It was an effort, and even with the weather being so frigid, I worked up a sweat and considered taking off my coat for a minute. I knew better, though, and kept it on. I did undo my scarf a bit.

We followed Naomi's final directions to walk through two matching hemlock trees, one with a bandana knotted around a low-hanging branch. There would be a bit of a drop-off before we got to the waterfall itself. She wasn't kidding about that. It was like someone took a bulldozer and carved a crevice out of the earth. I wasn't expecting the step to be as deep, and I turned my ankle. I lost my balance and stumbled forward. Luckily Dad was right behind me to catch my flailing hand, or I would have flown off the edge of a steep cliff into the rocky shore below. My dad pulled my trembling body into his and held me for a moment while my breathing calmed. Mom came up behind us and saw how perilously close we were to the edge. She sucked in a breath and then waved her hands at us, beckoning us to carefully come toward her. Dad guided me to sit down on the dirt a few feet back, and we all took a second to get our bearings.

"I didn't think we were still this high up," I said. "When she said small waterfall, I was picturing something only a few feet high."

"Me, too," Mom said.

Dad shook his head. "This area is all sheer cliffs. I have no idea how we're supposed to get down to the water if that's what you still want to do."

"It's what I want," I assured him.

"I don't see any waterfall. Not even a sign of one." He touched the soil and rubbed it between his fingers. "The soil is damp, but that's from the dew and mist, not from any stream or waterway."

I sighed. "Naomi said that it came right out of the rocks. There was no source, remember?"

My mom put her hands on both of our knees to still us. She cocked her head a bit to listen to the sounds of the forest around us. I closed my eyes and focused too. At first I heard only the birds and insects, a pinecone dropping from a branch, and something skittering in the brush. Mom wrapped her fingers around mine and squeezed.

"There. Hear it? The water?"

I focused my listening toward the ocean and not the forest. I heard the steady crash of the surf out at the breakers. Closer in, the water sizzled over the rocks at the base of the cliff each time a new wave thrust at them. Then I heard it, a steadier, more even sound than the surf, kind of like a bathtub faucet.

"It's this way." I pointed. We got up and carefully walked along the tree line, only a couple feet back from the cliff's edge. The sound got stronger as we got closer, and finally we were right on top of it.

It was the strangest thing because we could hear it but not see it at first. Like Naomi said, no stream led to the water fall. Where we stood was dry, hard rock. A few large stones and boulders rested on the edge of the cliff. They reminded me of gargoyles on a cathedral, somehow positioned like they were guarding the waterfall. I got down on my hands and knees and squeezed between them, sticking my head out over the edge of the cliff. A few inches below me, the waterfall broke loose from a crevice in the stone wall and cascaded ceaselessly down the thirty feet or so drop. The water down there was a deep bluish green and churned around the rocks and into a cave opening that was partially blocked by the waterfall. The cliff curved around both sides of the waterfall and cave, forming a narrow cove.

The waterfall was about the size of something you might see in a backyard swimming pool. It was about two or three feet wide, and while it didn't gush as a waterfall should a couple days after a giant rainstorm, it did have a steady flow to it. I could see the stone cliff through it, and a person would be able to stand underneath it like a shower without getting hurt or pummeled. As I leaned closer to it, a little mist from it caught in the wind and sprayed my face.

"Do *you* see its source?" I asked my parents.

Both of them shook their heads in dismay. Mom ran her hands along the ground as if maybe she could feel an invisible stream or something. Dad simply scratched his head.

"It's so bizarre," he said.

Mom rolled one of the smaller stones out of the way and got down next to me. She yanked off the glove on her right hand and reached into the water. It ran over her finger tips, and she squeaked at the icy temperature. Immediately, she brought her wet fingers to her mouth, tasted the water, and took them back out again, staring at them as if they were lying to her. "Naomi wasn't joking. It's saltwater." She got out of the way for him to see for himself.

"That's impossible." Dad knelt down and stuck his hand in and tasted the water. He also stared at his fingers after licking them. "*How* is it possible?"

Now it was my turn. I wanted to touch it, but I was afraid. I was afraid that the waterfall was just some anomaly that science would explain but had nothing to do with the legend or the mermaids or, ultimately, Carter. I didn't want to be let down. I didn't want to have to look at my parents and tell them I was wrong, that Dad was right, and we just should have gone home. I didn't want to attend Carter's funeral, or, worse, stand behind some tree to watch it because his parents wouldn't allow me to attend.

I took my mittens off slowly and stuffed them in my pockets. My parents watched me expectantly, both of them on their knees beside me. I was reminded of playing in a sandbox as a child, digging up toy dinosaur bones they'd hidden for me while they cheered me on with each find and promised how we'd assemble the skeleton puzzle when I found all of them.

"Here goes nothing," I said, shoving both hands down into the flow of water.

It was icy, and my palms and fingers went instantly numb. Other than that, nothing happened. I kept my hands in the water and looked at my parents. Could they read the disappointment on my face?

"Anything?" Mom asked quietly.

I couldn't answer her. I refused to let the word "no" out of my mouth. I also refused to take my hands out of the water even if I knew I'd suffer frostbite. The numbness shifted to a sharp pain, like shards of ice slicing at my hands. I got all the way down on my chest and pushed my arms down further, wetting them all the way to the wrists. I heard my mother call my name, and my dad grabbed my legs to steady me. He began pulling me backward, but I grabbed onto a root sticking out of the rocks and held on tight.

Concentrate on something but the pain, I thought, *something but the icy pain.*

I closed my eyes and put the vision of the sea cliffs there again. I focused on it as hard as I could, the picture becoming vivid in my brain, the colors brightening as if the clouds were parting on the scene and the sun came streaming in on it. The vision became panoramic, allowing me to see more than I could before. In this new wider angle, I could see that the cliffs from my vision included this cave and the waterfall to the side of it.

I was about to open my eyes and tell my parents we were in the right spot when the whole vision aborted. Everything went black for a moment. All I could hear was my breathing. It was hard and fast, drowning out the sound of the water. Come to think of it, I couldn't hear the waterfall at all, and the breathing was much too fast to be my own. It was panting.

A new vision opened up in my mind. I was in the forest in the darkness before dawn. The forest was rushing past me, and it took me a moment to realize I was running through it. The breathing was from me as I ran, and someone was beside me breathing hard, too. I looked to the right to find a handsome young American Indian warrior running beside me. His expression was serious, maybe even afraid.

Then something pounced at him from above. I thought it was a mountain lion at first, but it was a man. He threw my running mate to the ground, and they rolled in the dirt. Knives glinted against the rays of rising sun. I couldn't tell in the jumble of shrubs, rocks, roots and shadows which one of them was prevailing, and then they rolled off the cliff, locked in battle, screaming on the way down.

Whoever's memory I shared ran to the edge and watched them plummet to the shallow ocean full of rocks that would break them both. Neither man could survive the fall. In grief and desperation, I leapt.

"June!" My mother was screaming, and my dad shouting.

Reality came back to me in a rush only to discover the top half of my body dangling over the cliff. The icy water of the waterfall pouring against me from hips to my face. I gurgled and struggled to pull my face away from the water so I could breathe. My father had his arms around my hips and his whole body weight on my legs, preventing me from falling any further.

"June! June! Are you okay?"

"Yes!" I sputtered. "I'm okay."

I used my hands to press against the rocky cliff and inch my body away from the waterfall. When I got to dry rock, I was able to push hard enough to give my dad some leverage to pull me back up. Safe at the top, I rolled to my back and exhaled deeply. Mom was immediately on me, checking my pulse and inspecting me for injuries. She took my soaked scarf off and then grabbed the towel my father got out of his backpack and dried my face and neck as best she could.

The shivering began in earnest as soon as the shock wore away.

"We need to get back to the car and warm her up," Mom said. "Now. She'll get hypothermia."

"I'm okay," I said through my chattering teeth. "I've been through worse than this."

"And wound up in the hospital," Mom reminded me.

"Do you have anything in your pack like a sweatshirt or something?" Dad asked my mom. She took her backpack off and rummaged through it. After a moment, she pulled out a fleece sweatshirt. They helped me out of my once-again water soaked coat and put the dry shirt on me. It wasn't warm enough for the weather, but it was dry. She loaned me her gloves to warm up my hands. Thankfully, my hair was pulled back, so it didn't get too wet. I patted the poor wool pea coat my boyfriend had given me just a few days ago. It had already been through so much.

"Are you okay to walk?" Mom asked.

"Yes." I got up and brushed myself off. I started away from them.

"Where do you think you're going, young lady?" This was from Dad, but Mom was right behind him with her arms crossed, nodding severely.

"To find a way to that cave. It's right below us."

They both took a step toward me. "You saw something?" Dad asked.

"Yes." I put my hand out for him to take and told him as seriously as I could, "That waterfall story Naomi told us about is real. It happened right here. It's somehow connected to everything that's been going on."

Mom started, "Is that why you…?"

"Jumped off the cliff?" I finished for her when she couldn't get the words out. "I think so. I didn't know I was doing it. I was dreaming I was doing it."

"These visions are too dangerous," Dad said. "True or not, we can't risk your life over them. We need to head home. This is too much."

"We can't," I said. "Not now. We're so close."

In her continued mission to amaze me, my mom said to Dad, "No, honey, June's right. We have to finish this. The visions mean something, and you know it as well as I do. We've got to get to the bottom of it. Let's go."

Mom zipped up her backpack, stuck her arms through the straps and took the lead. She hiked past the cave and kept an eye out for a way down to the shore. Still holding my hand, Dad walked with me a few paces behind her. Not far from the cave, a piece of the cliff jutted out into the water, that far part of the cove I'd seen. It was too steep and narrow for us to traverse. We stumbled a little way further, noticing the cove beneath us now was a bit wider and had some beach to it. On the far side a series of mossy-topped boulders, formed from a long-ago avalanche, gave us a way to descend to the shoreline.

"It won't be easy," Dad said. "Want to keep looking for another way?"

I shook my head. Trying to find any other path would keep taking us farther and farther away from where we needed to be. We were just about to start navigating the slippery stones when we heard that dog Daisy barking in the distance. I figured the tourist couple had headed back to their car until I heard their voices clearly calling to us.

"Hey! Hey, there you are!"

"Wait for us!"

They'd followed us. My Dad and I looked expectantly at Mom. She was the one with the talent for coercive speech. She could get them to go away.

The woman stepped into sight first. "Whew! You picked a hard hike. I am all scratched up."

The guy nodded at my dad, breathing hard. "Had a feeling you'd know some secret things to look at. What are we aiming for?" He stuck out a hand. "Name's Sean, by the way. And this is Casey."

Casey wiggled her fingers in a way that was too young and cute for her. Dad shook Sean's hand.

"We're not tour guides if that's what you're thinking," I said as bluntly as possible. "We're here for the first time, just like you."

Casey put a hand to her chest like she was embarrassed, and Sean chuckled a little. "Oh, sorry about that," she said. "Ya'll just look so *prepared*." She noted my parents' backpacks.

"Where's your dog, by the way?" I asked.

"We tied her up to the post on the walk. She'll be all right."

"This is a forest," I reminded her. "There are wild animals, you know."

A flicker of nervousness crossed her face, but Sean shook his head. "Daisy will be fine for a few minutes. Are you aiming for something specific, or did you just feel like veering off the path?"

Mom stepped forward then, stopping me from saying anything else. "We just wanted a closer view of Fuca Pillar. That's all. We're seeing what we can find."

Casey put on this sheepish expression, like all of a sudden she realized she should've asked before following us, "Do you mind if we tag along and see it with you?"

"I don't know how long we'll be, and you have your dog to think about," Mom said.

"If it seems too long, we'll turn back."

My parents and I shared an unspoken frustration, and finally Mom said, "Fine."

Without another word, we crawled down the boulders. Casey chattered the whole time about how tricky it was to get over these things and how she sure chose to wear the wrong shoes. Sean told her to be quiet about ten times, but it didn't seem to make any difference.

At last the ground sloped down again and got us to a point where we could lower ourselves over the edge of the cliff and land easily on our feet. Casey was dramatically shorter than the rest of us, so she came down last and needed Sean and my dad to help her. It was a beautiful, peaceful cove. The water was an astounding sapphire blue except for where it washed over the pebbled beach. There, it was clear as a stream, and I could easily see a foot deep into it. The sea stacks were massive now that we were closer to them. They stood in a line like soldiers on parade. Biggest of them all and leading the march was the Fuca Pillar. It appeared to be the size of a ten-story tall tower. From where we stood, it blocked most of our view of the horizon. Cameras clicked as Casey, Sean, and my dad snapped pictures of it.

"It's amazing!" all of them were saying in turn.

Sean had his arm across her shoulders like they were posing for some romantic postcard. Casey snapped a selfie and then said to me, I guess because I was the teenager and therefore good at cell phone stuff, "Could you take a picture of us?"

I took her phone and snapped a couple shots of them and handed it back. I made sure at least one of them was out of focus.

"I can't tell you how grateful we are that you let us follow you down here. This is terrific."

"No prob," I said. "Maybe you should get back to your dog now."

They ignored that comment and went back to gawking and picture taking and talking about how lucky they were. I was pretty sure Daisy didn't feel lucky.

I tore my attention away from the giant stone and looked back in the direction of the waterfall and cave. It was impossible to see them now, because of the way the cliff curved out into the ocean. I had no idea how we were going to get to it with this wall blocking the way. While the adults talked about the view, I walked along the base of the cliff, running my fingers against its rough surface.

In the back corner of this small beach, in the darkest part of the shade, I noticed some rocks and driftwood. The pile was nearly as tall as me, and I figured the tide had pushed and prodded it all into that place over time. I continued along the cliff until I came up to it and discovered, wedged between the rocks and the wall, a beat-up blue kayak.

"Dad! Mom! Come here!" I shouted. Dad dashed right over. Mom took a second to suggest Casey and Sean wait where they were before joining us.

"Do you think it's the one Juarez was using?" I asked quietly after I showed them the kayak.

"That's my best guess," Dad said, his voice somber. "I feel like if he crashed here, he should have easily found his way back to town."

"He might have been too hurt," I offered.

"Or he drowned out at sea, and the kayak was pushed to shore by the tide," Mom concluded logically.

There really was no alternative answer. If he'd survived somehow, he would have been found or rescued. If he had made it to shore but died of wounds or hypothermia or something, there would be a body, unless some animal had dragged it off. All the thoughts were dismal. I shuddered.

Dad tugged at the kayak and managed to loosen it from where it was wedged. It was pretty dinged up, but the blue polyethylene hull was intact as far as I could tell. I didn't see any gaping holes in it. We rolled it over and dumped out the water that had gathered inside.

"Do you see an oar?" I asked.

Mom put her hands on her hips and scanned the area. Dad didn't bother.

"Come on, June. Those are at the bottom of the ocean somewhere."

"They're plastic, and probably floating somewhere," I snapped back.

He huffed. "Okay, then they have floated off to Alaska. How about that?"

Dad's attitude was raging. He was cold and tired of all of this, I could tell. I wished I could tell him I was done, that I'd found what I was looking for so he could get back to town, slug down some hot coffee, change his clothes, and point the car back to Olympia. Only, every new clue I got increased my desire to search for more.

What had Juarez been looking for out here in the freezing January weather? Was it a storm that ended his life, or was it something to do with that giant stone sticking out of the water? If it held a spirit in it like the tree, it could have hurt Juarez just like the tree had hurt Ronnie.

I fought off the memory of Ronnie stabbed by the tree's thorns and then smacked by the tree's limb until he fell forty feet to the ground.

Could something like that have happened to Juarez if he'd tried to climb the Fuca Pillar? What would happen if I tried it?

I began dragging the kayak to the water.

"What are you doing?" Dad asked,

"I've got to get to the Fuca Pillar," I explained. "I have to touch it."

"You can't paddle the boat," he said. He looked back at Mom, who to my surprise was digging through the driftwood. "Are you going to do anything about this?"

"Yes." She stood up and walked over to me with a five-foot long piece of driftwood. She handed it to me. "This should work. Just keep my gloves on to protect your hands from splinters."

My dad bunched his fists in his hair as he gawked at his wife. "Are you out of your mind, Natalie?"

She pinched her lips tight and spoke as calmly as she could. "I promised her I would be here with her for this journey, and that's what I'm doing. Frankly, I'm a little tired of your doubt and whining. If anyone should be gung-ho about all of this, it's you."

"Me?"

"Yeah, you," she said, crossing her arms. "I've traveled all over this country with you to protect everything from eagles to muskrats to butterflies. I've been to Pow-Wows in seven different states and listened to you tell stories and patiently waited while you learned new ones you hadn't heard before. Now, when your own daughter is telling you a person she loves is missing and could still be alive because the creatures from your mythology have turned out to be real, you're suddenly not interested? You're not concerned? Does Carter's life mean less to you than a freaking butterfly?"

Mom's lawyer tones vanished. She flat out yelled at him. "She has rescued mermaids. She has survived the clutches of a manic tree spirit. She almost drowned in a waterfall while receiving psychic images a few *minutes* ago." She put up a finger. "But she didn't. You know why? She's special. She's some kind of messenger between that world and this one. If she says there's something to be learned from that giant rock out there, then I believe her, and I think it's high time you did, too."

All the yelling caught the attention of Sean and Casey, and they wandered over to us.

"Everything okay?" Sean asked cautiously.

"It's fine," Dad grumbled.

"Did you say something about mermaids?" Casey asked. She did a side glance at Sean and the corner of her glossy lips rose. "There were all those news reports about mermaids in this area."

Sean patted her on the head like she was a child. "It was all bunk, remember. That video was proved to be a fake."

I lowered my head, but it was too late. Casey figured it out. "You're her! Oh, my goodness! You're the girl from the mermaid video! I totally recognize you now. I must have watched that thing a hundred times."

"No joke," Sean said, putting up a hand like he was taking some oath.

Casey leaned toward me and asked, "Are you still looking for them? I secretly always believed the story was true. It's one of the reasons I pressed for this vacation. Just in case, you know?"

Sean threw his head back in exasperation. "*That's* why we're here? I wanted to go to Florida. It was closer, cheaper, and warmer."

The three of us stared at them, not knowing what to say. Did we fill them in on what was happening? Did we try to get them to leave? *Could* we get them to leave?

After a moment of awkward silence, Sean cleared his throat. "What's the kayak for? It looks in bad shape."

"We found it here," Dad told him. "Probably abandoned by some tourist, or maybe it got pulled away from the docks at Neah Bay during a storm and wound up here. Would you mind helping me carry it to the water? I want to see if it still floats."

The men lifted it up on their shoulders like it was made of feathers and then lowered it onto the water. The tide tugged at it, but Dad kept his hand on it while he watched to see if it filled up with water.

"Looks okay to me," Sean said.

Without hesitation, I took the board from Mom and made my way to the kayak. Dad held it steady while I got in. My experience with the tree boat a month earlier prepared me for the unsteady feeling of being in the craft, and I found my balance quickly.

Sean and Casey gaped at what we were doing while Mom sidled past them and approached ankle deep into the water.

"Be careful. It's further out than it looks. Stay on this side of the stone where we can see you. The ocean current will be too rough if you try to go around, and that board isn't going to help you much."

My mother of the business suits and briefcase was really an outdoor adventurer at heart. That's what she and Dad had in common back in their younger days, wasn't it? Not being at all experienced with kayaking, I took her advice to heart.

Dad waded out to his thighs, still steadying me in the kayak and making sure I was comfortable. "For the record," he said just loud enough for Mom and me but not the other two back on the shore to hear, "I believe you about the mermaids and the stone. I saw you morph into my dead sister, for Heaven's sake. I'm just terrified that nothing good is going to come of this. You can understand that, can't you? My sister disappeared into a tree. You were almost killed by that tree and then almost drowned by a mermaid a week later." He shook the thought away. "I don't trust any of this. That's why I wanted to leave. Do you understand?"

Mom came out further into the water and slipped her arm around his waist, resting her head against his arm. I simply nodded. I had nothing encouraging to say to him. He might be right. If the story Naomi told us was remotely true, the spirit trapped in that big stone was a murderer. The vibe I might get from touching the rock was not bound to be a good one. Still, I had to know.

"Just be cautious," Dad said.

"I will," I croaked.

He gave the kayak a push, and then I paddled away from them. My parents stood in the water, watching me go.

Chapter Thirteen

The current pulled the kayak outward, so I got distance from the shore pretty quickly and was soon out far enough to see a more panoramic view of the shoreline. I should have brought Dad's camera. It was stunning, and he'd have loved to see it for himself. I could see clearly now how the cliffs were scalloped into coves, one after the other. The observation deck at the bottom of the hiking trail was difficult to see because it was set in the middle of one of the deepest inlets. Once I found it, I realized how far we'd walked from there. It was further than I thought. The forest above the cliffs was lush, and the sun was now coming up over that tree line to brighten the hazy morning. That extra golden light filtered down like a spotlight on the cave and salty waterfall, and I felt my chest tighten. This was the exact scene from that mermaid's vision. She had been in this spot, looking back at the shoreline. This is the place she wanted me to find.

As much as I wanted to enjoy the view, I needed to focus on what was further out to sea. The sea stacks towered over me and became more daunting the closer I got to them. They were so tall, it felt like when we drove downtown and I couldn't see sky for the buildings. The Fuca Pillar was simply massive up close, making me feel like nothing more than a mackerel beside it. I wondered what the sea stacks looked like under the water, how deep they went. It was probably too dark and murky for anyone to ever snorkel here, and no one ever mentioned this place when they talked about great scuba diving spots. I wondered if the mermaids liked living here because of all the places to duck around and hide.

There was a bit of a vacuum as I drew close to the Fuca Pillar. The current was doing its best to spin my kayak and drag it by the tail out into the open sea. I had to paddle hard against it and get myself squared behind the stone. The wind came around the stone like freezing whips, and the sweatshirt and still damp thermal under it weren't enough to keep me from shivering.

It took considerable effort to get the kayak close enough to the base for me to touch it. Holding the wood I was using as an oar in the crook of my left arm, I reached out with my right fingers splayed. The rock was moist and mossy. My instinct was to retract my fingers, and I forced myself to ignore my squeamishness and press hard onto the rock.

I wanted to close my eyes to concentrate, but I was afraid of not being able to see any dangerous waves or, I don't know, mermaids that might sneak up on me. I breathed slowly through my nose to calm myself and thought only of my connection to the stone.

Nothing.

Okay. There was nothing at first with the waterfall. I had to be patient. I concentrated again, harder, if possible.

Still nothing.

I heard the ocean waves crashing on the far side of the sea stack. The wind whistled. Gulls cried. I saw the sky change colors three times as the varying thickness of gray clouds blew past, but I got nothing from the rock.

My jaw ached from my teeth rattling. I took in a deep breath and then resigned myself to having to close my eyes. I leaned over as far as I dared so that the top of my head touched the stone and shut my eyes tight against the wind.

"Come on," I moaned before willing my thoughts to be still, silent, and open. I waited for what seemed like minutes but was probably not that long. Still, all the other visions had come to me relatively quickly. Why was this taking so long? Was it harder for the spirit to communicate through stone? Stone wasn't alive like a tree or a mermaid, so maybe it wasn't as easy to break through.

I was nervous about keeping my eyes closed and my body unbalanced this long. The swells beneath the kayak had increased, and seawater splashed harder on the hull and the rock beside me. I bobbed up and down, and the kayak began to drift away from the Fuca Pillar. I had nothing to grab onto. My head broke contact and in a heartbeat, all that connected me to the stone were my fingertips. Then a wave sliced between the kayak and the stone and thrust me forward, nearly causing me to fall out.

My eyes were fully open now, struggling to focus and get my bearings. I heard a loud noise, similar to the sound of a city bus belching exhaust. I'd been on enough whale spotting trips with my parents to know the source of that noise, being that there weren't any busses around. I craned my neck to see where the whale could be. In all reality, no whale should be on this side of the sea stack. It was too shallow and full of stones for a creature that large. Maybe it was a walrus or even a seal. It just seemed too loud for that.

Another wave came at me, and as soon as I got myself straightened out I saw it – the sleek black back of a killer whale. Air blasted out of its blowhole, and then it dove again. Not deep though. The dorsal fin stayed above water as it came around the Fuca Pillar and right toward me. It pushed the ocean water in front of it like it was a bulldozer cutting through mud. My kayak tipped forty-five degrees, making me use every bit of strength in my legs and torso to keep taut and stay in the craft. The stupid piece of driftwood I was using for an oar did nothing to keep me steady in the water. I tried rowing with it, but it couldn't give me any speed.

This killer whale was going to dump me into the water the same way it happened three days ago. Was it possible this was the same whale?

Everything was loud, the crashing of the waves, the screech of the wind, and the snorts of the orca. Somehow, seemingly too far away, I could hear my parents screaming my name. I prayed my father wouldn't do something stupid like dive into the water and try to swim for me. It was too far, too deep, too cold, and there was a killer whale circling me.

At least it seemed like it was circling me at first. It took a minute to realize that each wave he thrust at me pushed me a little closer to shore. The creature was herding me, purposefully forcing me away from the Fuca Pillar and back toward land. Was it some kind of protector of the stone spirit? Did the ancient spirit in that stone have some sort of hold on the creature?

I began to relax, accepting that the orca wasn't trying to kill me after all. I loosened my body and allowed it to roll with the waves instead of fighting against them. I took the oar out of the water, trusting the whale to push me. My parents screamed, "No!" I felt confident Sean and Casey were screaming, too. There was a high-pitched sound that I couldn't imagine my mother making.

"It's okay!" I shouted.

I was more than half-way back to the beach, where the water was increasingly filled with rocks and stones jutting out in every direction, some causing whirlpools that threatened to tip my kayak. The orca couldn't swim in this place and gave one final shove against the kayak. It failed to propel me in the right direction. The front of the kayak jammed into the crevice where two rocks met and wouldn't budge any further. I climbed out of the kayak, onto the rocks, the frigid water coming up to my waist, and tried without success to loosen the kayak.

"Oh crap!" I shouted at the shock of the water. "Bad idea. Bad idea."

I spun around to search for the whale, hoping it noticed that I was far enough away from its precious stone and wouldn't try to follow me any further. I spotted it right away. It was too late. The whale had swum too far into the lagoon, and now it twisted back and forth in the water, appearing to be trapped between stone barriers. Some of the stones I could see, but others had to be under the water line. It couldn't figure out how to get free and back to the open water.

I didn't know how to help the poor creature. All I could do was gesture wildly with my arms and holler, but I knew it couldn't understand me. I think all my noise agitated it, for it became panicky and began flipping from side to side. Frantic, I turned to my parents.

"What do I do?" I shouted at my dad. "It's trapped!"

Dad shouted something, but I couldn't hear it because the whale began keening. The sound broke my soul. The last time I heard that noise was when Dr. Schneider played it on the speaker and caused all the trapped mermaids at the Affron facility to slam themselves against the aquarium glass in panicked agitation. Tears lurched to my eyes, saltier than the ocean water spraying on me, as I remember the mermaids that had been crushed and didn't get to escape with the others. I knew the sound meant the killer whale was in agony, and I had to do something to help it.

I lowered myself down into the water, feeling a little like one of those trainers at Sea World. Only, this killer whale wasn't trained to do tricks and could possibly bite me in half as if I were a seal. I held onto the rocks with one arm and used the other to help me fight against the whirling current the whale had created.

What did I think I was going to do? Lead it to the opening it couldn't find on its own? And even if I could do that without getting killed, how would I get back?

"This is stupid," I said, rubbing my sopping sweatshirt sleeve across my face to wipe off dripping snot and ocean water like I thought that would work. I rotated my body to climb back up the rocks. Only, the cold water and my nerves had zapped my energy. I couldn't bring myself to lift up my legs high enough, and my arms were weak. I couldn't get back up, and I didn't know how much longer I could hold on. I dared to look behind me and saw the whale coming toward me, its jaws open. I shut my eyes, praying it wouldn't hurt.

The bite didn't come. Instead I felt pressure underneath my legs. The whale had gone under the water and was nudging me up on top of its head. Now, I really felt like one of those trainers. Would it throw me into the air? Those Sea World trainers knew how to do that trick in their very deep aqua-blue pools. I was pretty sure I'd wind up smashed on some rocks with a broken spine. But the killer whale was gentle. It lifted me up so that I could crawl off it and get more securely onto the rocks. Then it lingered. My parents screamed my name from the shore. They couldn't see the close proximity of the whale to me. They, also, couldn't see it swimming away from me. I put up a hand to them to signal I was all right without taking my eyes off the whale. Ocean water beat at the side of the creature, bumping it against the sharp rocks over and over again.

"Swim away," I told it. "Why are you staying here like this?"

It raised its head enough so that I could see one of its eyes. The small orb expressed so much exhaustion and sadness, in stark contrast to the dash of white right behind it.

"Don't give up," I told it. "You can get away."

The eye focused on my face, and the killer whale spouted weakly. It opened its mouth, top jaw rising above the water, revealing a giant pink tongue and all those massive sharp teeth. I was out of its reach for biting, but it could easily swim around in a circle fast enough to gain enough momentum to leap for me. For some reason, it didn't. The poor, tired creature tilted against the rock as if using it for support.

I dared to reach a hand toward its shiny black head. It flinched, but then the whale relaxed as I pressed my hand flat on it. I tuned out the sound of my parents shouting for me to come back to them and questioning what I was waiting for. I petted the killer whale, thinking how thrilled Carter would've been to have an experience like this.

Its sad eye looked up at me, my face much closer now that I was leaning over. Only now did I observe the eye was brown. The eyes of orcas are usually gray with very large black pupils. This iris was most definitely brown with a much smaller pupil like a human's eye.

"What is this?"

In answer, the whale blinked, and then a rush of emotion went from my fingertips to my heart, causing me to gasp. I almost lost my balance, but I gripped the rocks with my legs. The whale lifted up its body as high as it could manage, and I wrapped my arms around its head for support, my face against its slick black flesh. The creature sighed deeply, hot, fishy air billowing around me.

It was a mixture of fear and sadness that eclipsed anything I'd felt before, including the sight of the mermaids crammed in that tank, the belief I'd been swallowed by a tree, and the disappearance of the boy I loved. My chest ached so deeply I felt the pain of it rush through my veins to my toes and fingertips like poison. Keeping one arm wrapped over the whale's head, I traced around the strangely human eye with my fingers.

"What are you trying to tell me?"

The brown eye closed, and I took that as a signal to close my eyes as well. I had my arms around a killer whale, sitting precariously on a rock in a deep lagoon, and I had my eyes closed. Everything about this choice was stupidly perilous. I did my best to shake away my own doubts and fears and tune into what the whale was trying to share with me.

As soon as I got my head clear, the images came to me. It was a cold, cloudy day on the ocean. I saw the Fuca Pillar in the distance. Deep water, bubbles, and blackness. A narrow cave with a low ceiling and very little natural light. And mermaids. All of them silver and bald with strange ridges in their skulls and webbed fingers reaching.

The vision faded away until all I could see was empty ocean, like the view from a shipwrecked sailor. Nothing in any direction but dark water.

I opened my eyes, and that mysterious brown eye was staring at me, boring into me, pleading with me. A voice seeped into my mind, both far away and very close at the same time.

Juniper.

I stiffened as if shocked by electricity.

Can you hear me?

The whale moaned and clicked.

"Yes," I said. "I can hear you."

I'm... changed.

It was as if the killer whale had to struggle for the right word, and yet it shouldn't know words at all. What was happening?

"How are you—?"

I wanted to see mermaids.

I gasped. "Juarez? Juarez, is that you?"

Yes.

"But how? How could this happen?" I ran my hands over that black head as if my hands would help me understand the unbelievable.

Too weak. I'm too weak. Not strong enough.

"What can I do? How can I help you? Is there a way to turn you back?"

Part of me wanted to resist the thought that a man could be changed into a killer whale. That was ridiculous and impossible in every way. Yet I knew a man had been turned into a tree. My aunt's spirit lived in that tree. A woman dove over a cliff and became a waterfall of her own tears. I lived in a world where things like that happened. Even so, how did a TV news reporter end up this way? He got fired from his job because of me. He had been out here on a kayak looking for a giant rock in the bitter cold of January because of me.

"I did this to you."

No. The mermaids. And the creature. I wanted to see the mermaids. I've seen them now.

The mermaids? A creature? It was almost a month ago when that mermaid pulled me out to sea and gave me the vision of these cliffs and the cave. I told Juarez, and he went to investigate. I never thought to follow up. I figured he'd contact me when he knew something. I didn't know he'd gone missing. If I had gotten here sooner, could I have prevented this horrible magic from happening? And I couldn't help but wonder... "Carter? Is Carter with the mermaids and this creature? Is he going to be...?" I couldn't finish the thought.

The heavy whale sank deeper into the water. I had to let go so I wouldn't be pulled off the rocks. It rolled to its side and floated away from me, its brown eye staring up blindly at the cloudy sky.

"Juarez!" I shouted. "Come back!"

The killer whale didn't respond. It looked very ill, and it didn't even try to swim anymore. I stood up and faced my parents. I waved at them that I was all right. My mom clutched at her chest. Casey covered her mouth with her hands. My dad beckoned for me to come to them. Sean stood there with one hand on his forehead and the other on his hip, slowly shaking his head back and forth.

I swam back to shore. It wasn't too far, and the water never was deep enough to go over my head. I was able to put my feet down a couple times to rest, breathe, and make sure I was going the right way. I crawled onto the pebbled shore to my parents' feet.

"Oh God, she's blue!" Mom shouted, crouching next to me and taking my pulse.

Dad crouched down on the other side and inspected me for bites or wounds. "Did it hurt you? We couldn't see you very well."

My shaky voice sneaked out between teeth that chattered uncontrollably. "I'm okay. The whale... He's not okay. I think he's... dying." I decided that was the more urgent news, and we'd get to the magical metamorphosis of our friend later.

"We need to get her back to the car," Mom said. "Now."

"Okay," Dad said. "Do any of your phones work?" Mom, Sean and Casey all checked, but none of them had any service. "That doesn't surprise me." He rubbed his jaw and then tugged absent-mindedly at his braid. "This is what we're going to do. Natalie, you and *Sean*?" Sean nodded that it was his name. "Need to take June back to the car. Do you mind carrying her?" Sean nodded again. "Drive toward town. As soon as you get to where the phones start working, call the Coast Guard and let them know about this killer whale. Maybe there's still time to get help for it."

"Can I go with them?" Casey asked. "I need to check on Daisy anyway, and frankly I'm a little freaked out by what's happening here."

"That's fine," Dad said. "I don't care." To my mom and me, he said, "I'll stay here and keep an eye on the whale until the Coast Guard gets here. Maybe I can do something to help it."

"Dad." I gestured for him to come close to me. I croaked out, "Don't go out there. Please."

"She's right," Mom said sternly. "I don't need both of you with hypothermia in the hospital. And besides, if you get caught out there, who's going to rescue you if we're all gone?"

"I'll be fine," he said. "I've done this kind of thing before."

I shook my head wildly. "Not *this*. The mermaids…"

He whispered. "You saw the mermaids? Are they out there? Is that what took you so long?"

"The mermaids did something to Juarez."

"Juarez Peña?" Dad frowned. "He's gone, Junie."

"He's not gone." I pointed at the killer whale floating weakly in the distance. "He's right there."

My parents gaped at me, but neither of them said I was crazy. We were all beyond that now. No one asked for details, though. We'd discuss all of that in time.

"Sean, help."

The tall southern man tore himself away from his wife who was gesticulating wildly and whispering something apparently very urgent to him. He rolled his eyes when she couldn't see his face anymore. Before he knelt down to pick me up he said quietly, "She thinks she heard you say you saw mermaids. She said she wants me to check on the dog, and she's going to stay here with you if that's okay."

She must've been closer to us than I thought.

"She heard wrong," Dad said firmly.

"That's what I told her. Ridiculous, right?"

From behind him, Casey said, "Don't you poo-poo me, Sean. Besides, she just said she wanted someone to stay with her husband to keep him from killing himself. I can do that all right."

If I could have, I'd have laughed at that. My dad and I shared the same blood and brain patterns, and if something got him motivated enough, he'd chase after it. Nothing tiny Casey could do or say would stop him.

Sean lifted me up in his arms. "Whew. You're an ice cube."

"You got her?" Dad asked, and Sean nodded one more time, even though I didn't think he had me that well as he struggled under my weight. I wasn't a slight thing like his wife.

My body was super stiff from the cold, and that might have been a help to him. I think people are heavier when they are relaxed. I was getting to a point where I couldn't have moved if I wanted to. I think my blood was freezing, and the pain shooting through my limbs was intense. My neck was so rigid I felt like it was about to crack. A headache began, and my nose ran like a faucet.

Casey tried handing me a bunch of tissues from her purse, but I couldn't close my fingers on them let alone bring them to my face. She handed them to my mom who cleaned me up a little.

"Let's go. We don't have a lot of time. Hold her as tight as you can to you," Mom directed.

Sean rolled me up a little more in his arms so that the whole front of my body was pressed against his torso and my forehead could rest on his shoulder.

Mom gave Dad a quick kiss on the check and pointed her finger at him in a silent warning. Dad squeezed my hand for a second before we left him there.

Chapter Fourteen

We went as fast as possible through the woods back to the trail, but it was hard going. Sean had to put me down a number of times to catch his breath. Finally, we made it back to the boardwalk where Daisy greeted us enthusiastically. Mom grabbed the dog's leash and took the barking dog with us. It was all uphill, but it was a wooden walkway without any tree roots, rocks, or spiky bushes. By the time we got to the car, Sean's warm, sweaty body had helped my temperature rise a little bit. Mom slid me into the back seat of the car, propping me up against all the camping gear with my legs dangling out the door, and shooed Sean away.

He took Daisy to his own car where I figured he'd give the dog a treat and change his own shirt. Mom started the car and turned the heater on full blast. She then rummaged through our bags in the trunk as fast as she possibly could. I heard things plopping and banging on the asphalt as she threw them out of her way to get what she needed. She came back around to me and with great efficiency peeled all my wet clothes off, underwear and all. I was reminded of this happening not that long ago on the Coast Guard ship. She tossed two blankets over me and shoved my legs into the car. With a cruel yank, she took the elastic band out of my hair and then dried my hair roughly with a towel before knotting it all up inside it like I'd just gotten out of the shower. After all that, she squeezed herself in beside me and held me tightly to her while the car filled up with heat.

Finally, my jaw and neck loosened. My shoulders began to drop. I felt so weary and drowsy I could barely keep my eyes open.

"Stay awake, honey," she said to me. "I need you to stay awake. We're going to get you warmed up, and then I'll give you some clothes

154

to get dressed in while I drive. Okay?"

Mom kept checking the time, both on her phone and on the dashboard. It was 12:35 in the afternoon already. Clearly, it was taking longer for me to thaw than she wanted. Dad was still down at the water, and he'd need to get out of there before the tide rolled in. That would only be a few hours from now.

There was a tap at the window. Sean was outside, uncomfortably looking away from us so that we only saw him from waist to shoulder. He wore a zipped-up olive green hoodie now. Mom rolled down the window an inch. At the sound of it, he leaned over to tell us, "Hey, so I'm going to go on and see if I can find a place where the phone works. Okay?"

"Yes. Thank you."

"Cool. Is your daughter okay now?"

"I think so," Mom answered.

He put his hands on his hips and looked toward the forest trail. "You think Casey's gonna be safe down there? I mean, I don't really know your husband."

"She'll be fine."

"She's pretty keyed up about mermaids, and I don't want her to do anything stupid."

"Look," Mom said patiently. "Why don't you go on back down there? We're going to head out now that June's warmed up. I can make all the calls. You go back to your wife, all right?"

He nodded. "Yeah, I think that would make me feel better."

We took the dog into the front passenger seat, so Sean could hike back without Daisy hindering him. As soon as Sean was out of sight, Mom backed the car out of the parking spot and headed down the road to town. She handed the phone back to me and told me to keep checking until we got in range of service. The mountains and trees were no help at all, blocking any kind of cell tower signal. The first few buildings of town were in sight before bars appeared.

"I think it's working," I told her.

Mom cursed quietly before saying, "It's about time. We're practically back to the museum." She went ahead and drove into the museum's parking lot. There were a few cars, and I was still naked under some blankets and didn't feel like changing out in the open. I wrapped myself up as tightly as possible while Mom took Daisy out of the car and tied her leash to a bike rack near the front doors. I gathered my clothes and clumsily followed her inside, heading straight to the bathroom to change. She tossed an extra-large sweatshirt from the gift shop at me before I went through the door. There was an air dryer in there, and I crouched awkwardly below it to get my hair as dry as possible and then I held my hands under it until they stopped tingling.

By the time I came back out, Mom was behind the counter, well into a conversation on the museum's phone with the Coast Guard, giving them precise information about where Dad and the killer whale were located.

Greig's pleasant optimism had been replaced with all kinds of worry, and he was on his own cell phone telling someone, I assumed it was Naomi, about what happened to my father.

"No. I don't know if it was near the waterfall." He covered the mouthpiece and asked me as I approached him. "Was it near the waterfall?"

"We passed it, yes," I said.

Mom turned her back to us, tying herself up in the phone's cord.

Greig pointed at her with his thumb. "I told her the Coast Guard base is, like, right across the street, practically. Right before you enter Makah land. They can get to your dad quick."

Well, that was good to know. I was surprised we hadn't noticed the facility when we arrived yesterday. Then again, it had been getting dark, and we weren't looking for it.

"It might not be quick enough," I said. "I don't think that killer whale is just trapped. I think it's dying. Something's wrong with it."

Mom hung up the phone and immediately picked it back up off the receiver. She shot Greig a quick look requesting permission. He nodded once, and she punched in a number.

Greig mumbled something to his wife and ended his call. "You all right?" he whispered to me, so he wouldn't bother my mom. "You need some coffee or hot tea?"

"Tea would be great, actually," I said.

He went into the office to fetch it. Mom's cell phone was on the counter, and I pointed at it. She nodded that I could use it while she said, "Hey, Randy…"

I walked into the gift shop and texted Haley. I knew she'd be in school, but if she saw a text from this number she'd try to figure out a way to get out of class. I just hoped like heck she hadn't put her phone in one of those Cell Motels she told me about.

Greig came over and handed me a mug of hot water and a tea bag pouch already oozing brown into it. I didn't ask what flavor tea it was. I just thanked him and took a sip. It was too hot and burned my tongue. I saw that he'd brought my mom some coffee, and she had the same reaction to her first sip.

"If there's anything…" Greig put his hands out in some feeble gesture and then headed back to the cash register.

Some tourists came out of the exhibit, an eager dad with two bored kids and their mom who headed straight for the clothing racks in the gift shop. I turned my back to them and stared at the cover of a book. It had an image of a killer whale on it done in the chunky black and white artistic style of the Makah people. In fact, now that I was paying attention, I noticed the whole gift shop was full of this image and ones of the Thunderbird. I marveled at how the mythology of this region included a killer whale beastly enough to cause a tidal wave when less than two hours ago I was holding one in my arms.

The phone chimed with a message.

Give me a sec.

It was Haley. I wandered back toward the front door of the museum and knelt down so that Daisy could see me through the glass. She barked and wagged her tail at me. Poor thing. Sean and Casey should have left her in Georgia, or wherever, with a pet sitter if they were going to go on all these hikes and excursions with her tied to a rail in the freezing cold. I was about to ask Greig if I could bring her inside when my phone rang. I wanted to go outside to talk to Haley in order to get some extra privacy, but I knew Mom would get pissed if I got myself chilled again. I'd only just warmed up.

"I only have a couple minutes," Haley whispered. "I'm probably going to be in trouble for this."

"Where are you? The bathroom?"

"Are you serious? The bathroom is the first place Mrs. Slater checks for people using phones. She and her minions are constantly roaming the hallways. Regina is one of them. She's become such a suck-up to Slater-the-Hater she's hardly ever in class anymore. I'm in the janitor's closet."

"Oh, I see."

"No, you don't really. It's really bad here right now. I told all my teachers, well, all but Mr. Wadsworth, who is totally on Mrs. Slater's side because he's like ninety and hate cell phones, that you lost your phone in the same accident that killed Carter, and you were having an emergency and I needed to be able to answer the phone if someone from your family called. They all said I could keep it on me as long as I had it on silent. So, when I saw your mom's number—"

"Haley!" I interrupted. No choice. She didn't seem to be using periods. "I don't have a lot of time either. I *am* in an emergency, right now."

"You are? Oh, my God. Are you okay? Where even are you? You guys didn't come home last night, and there are reporters camped out on your yard—"

Apparently, I was going to have to fight for each word. "We're way up in the northwest corner of the state, on a reservation."

"Why?"

"I think this is where the mermaids were telling me to go to find Carter, and guess what?"

Haley squealed as quietly as she was capable, sounding like a mouse. I hoped for her sake no one was walking by the door of that closet right then. "I can't believe it! Did you find him? Is he really still alive?"

"I haven't found him – yet."

"Oh."

"But I found this killer whale, and I think…" It was going to sound crazy to her, so I amended what I was going to say. "I think it's the same one from the other day, and it's trying to show me where to go. I think we're really close."

"That's great, June." No squealing now. Her voice was as opposite of enthusiastic as a voice could get. Haley was convinced that Carter was dead.

Awkwardly, I continued. "Anyway, the killer whale is trapped, and I think it might be hurt or sick or something. So we've got the Coast Guard helping to rescue it, and we have to get back there. I just wanted to check in while I could."

"Are you coming back soon?"

"I still have some things to investigate, so we'll be here a while longer. I can't say exactly."

Haley didn't respond right away. "Is it true that Carter's dad is trying to blame you guys for Carter's... *disappearance*?"

"Yeah."

"Everyone's talking about it. Can you or your parents go to jail for that? Nick wrote a column for the school paper that you were going to jail."

"Nick's an idiot. It was an accident. Mr. Crowe is going to try to sue my parents for negligence."

"I get that he wants to hold you responsible, I guess, but aren't the Crowes pretty wealthy? What does he expect to get from your family?"

I really didn't want to talk about this. I wanted to find Carter and bring him home so all the charges would be dropped.

"The news is also saying that you and your parents aren't credible witnesses for Mr. Mains anymore, and all your testimony will be disregarded."

"What?"

"A bunch of us are planning a walk out this afternoon in protest. Halfway through sixth period we're all getting up from our seats and heading out the doors."

"How is that going to help anything?" I asked.

"It's going to prove that Mrs. Slater has no control over us."

"Whose big idea was this?"

"Mine." The squeal was back in her voice. "Aren't you proud of me? I'm a protester just like you."

"I don't know if that sounds like a good idea, Haley."

Mom rushed over to me, pointing at the phone. "Is that Haley?" I looked past her to see that she'd left the museum's phone receiver on the counter. She yanked the phone out of my hand before I answered. "Haley? Is that you?" After a beat, Mom continued. "I just heard about this protest you're staging today—"

I heard Haley's voice whining, but not the actual words.

"—it doesn't matter who told on you, just that someone did. My legal aide said it's been leaked to the news, so my best guess is that redheaded twerp that goes to your school spilled the beans to his sister. The press is gathering outside the school, and I'm sure Mrs. Slater will be prepared with the police to stop all of you. This is not going to be helpful to Mr. Mains. You want to be of value to him? Be respectful students like he would expect you to be. Do you understand? You need to call the whole thing off. Now."

Mom handed the phone back to me and said, "Knock some sense into her, June. I don't have time for this." She rushed back to the cashier desk. Watching her go, I saw that her boots and pants were still covered with mud. Her hair was a tangled mess. Mom hadn't taken a moment to clean up at all, and that wasn't like her.

The tourist family was standing together like they were posing for a picture, kids in front of their parents, all four of them watching us like we were some kind of entertainment.

I lifted the cell phone to my ear and heard Haley saying, "Mrs. Sawfeather? Are you there?"

"It's me."

"Geez, June. Your mom scared the pants off me. Do you think we'll get cited or arrested or something?"

I sighed. "I'm not sure, but my mom *is* a lawyer and an activist, so if she says don't do it, you should listen to her."

"This is going to be hard to call off this late."

"I don't mean to be dismissive or anything, but did you really have that many people planning to do it? The Recycling Club is pretty small." I couldn't imagine Haley having enough sway over people to make an event of any impact.

"You'd be surprised, June. I'm a lot more popular now than you know. I organized the whole thing, and there are lots of people planning to do this today. I mean, lots, like maybe a hundred or more people." The defensive tone in her voice was hard to miss.

"Sorry," I replied. "I'm not there anymore, remember?"

"Well, it looks like we have a… What's it called when someone spies on you?"

"A mole?"

"Yeah, one of those."

"I bet it's Marlee or Ted or Gary," I said.

There was a moment before she said, "Nah. I don't think so. Someone else had to have told Regina or Nick. I'll find out." Once again Haley had her blindfolds on about those three. Mom was off the phone again and dashing toward me. I didn't want her to talk to Haley again, so I said in a rush, "Okay. Well, I leave you to that. I really have to go."

"Oh. Okay. Bye. Be caref—"

I think I hung up before saying bye back. I handed the hot phone to my mother. Then I put up a hand to the tourists and said, "Show's over."

Embarrassed, the parents bustled their children back to the toys where they would surely pick out some tom toms and tambourines to purchase. Greig came over to us and took my now empty mug from me. "I'm sure the Coast Guard and the Emergency Wildlife Team will be able to help Mr. Sawfeather and the orca without you. Naomi said you could clean up at the house if you want."

"We're fine," Mom said. "I need to get back to Peter and make sure he's okay. If you want to help, can you watch this dog?" She gestured toward the window. "Her name is Daisy, and she belongs to the couple that were hiking. They stayed behind with Peter."

"Of course." Greig opened the door and untied the dog from the bike racks. He led the cold dog inside and gave her a rough massage to get her blood flowing. In a babying voice, he said, "Poor, Daisy, out in the freezing cold."

We thanked him and left him like that. The children from the tourist family headed over to pet the dog, too, as we walked out the door. Moments later we were driving back up to the hiking trail with the heater still set to high. I think the intention was to try to suck in as much heat as possible before going out into the cold again, if that was at all possible.

Mom told me, "When we get there you can stay in the car while I go down there. Stay warm."

"I'm fine now," I assured her. "I need to go back down there and see what's happening."

Mom only nodded. She knew she wouldn't be able to stop me at this point. "Did you talk some sense into your friend?"

"Not sure. She's enjoying the popularity that comes with staging protests against monster vice principals."

"It's intoxicating, I'm sure." Mom said with a smirk and a pat on my knee.

She sped up the mountain and we were back at the trailhead in minutes. It seemed like it took a lot less time to get back up to the trailhead than it did that morning. I was glad to see Sean and Casey's car was still there and that they hadn't abandoned my father. Back at the museum I had changed into new dry clothes, and I triple layered my shirts because I didn't have another coat with me, that oversized sweatshirt over all of it and hanging down past my butt. The pea coat was still super damp. With my arms wrapped around me for warmth, I followed my mom down the trail to the spot where we needed to cut off. There were a few stones next to the tiny waterfall etching. I assumed Sean put those there for himself, something a little more obvious and easy to spot. The only part of our trek back that wasn't easier was hiking through the forest. If possible, the foliage seemed even denser than earlier, and I tripped on every hole and rock, falling all the way to my knee at one point and swearing.

"Come on," Mom said instead of checking to see if I was all right.

"Mom, he's okay," I grunted at her.

"I know. I'm not worried about him."

"Then slow down a bit, okay?"

"I'm trying to get there before the Coast Guard or whoever they send leaves."

"Why?"

"Randy said all the water tests came out positive for dangerous toxin levels. You said the orca seemed sick, so I want to make sure that they take blood samples from it before they let it swim away."

"Mom, it's not sick from toxins," I explained. "It's sick because it used to be a person. People are not meant to be changed into giant sea mammals."

Mom stopped in her tracks. She rolled her head, and her neck made a hundred crackling noises. She put her hands on her hips and without looking back at me said, "There are magical things and there are science things. Whether we accept both or not isn't relevant here. Mermaids, rock monsters, and mysterious shape shifters aside, I have a case to build against Oceanside Construction, and that whale's blood can help."

"Or it could turn out to be Juarez Peña's DNA, and how will that help?"

Mom chewed on her lips for a second and then kept walking. "We'll just have to see what we get, won't we?"

There it was. Mom was still on the fence about it all. She was supporting me, because she was doing her best to be a good mother. Ultimately, though, she was going to need proof. She needed to see the magic happen and not just take my word for it. Anger built up in me, and I did my best to dampen it. Why should I be angry that my mom was being reasonable? That she was being intelligent and realistic? And worst of all, practical. Yes, I wanted her to accept what I was saying without question, but support was all I could really expect. I had to be thankful for that. What would I have done if she and my father hadn't come with me on this journey? I might not have made it this far. I might not have found Juarez. Or worse, I might have found him and drowned or died of hypothermia.

"I think we're close now," she said. "I remember this tree."

I didn't, but I took her word for it. She was right. A few feet further and we came to the ledge of the cliff where the giant avalanche of boulders made it possible for us to get down to the beach.

I saw the Coast Guard ship anchored out past the Fuca Pillar first and then the raft with two men and a woman riding in it toward us. I didn't see the killer whale.

"Hey!" came a cheery Southern voice as Casey darted over to us. "You're back. Are you feelin' better, honey?"

Sean moseyed over to us as well. "Where'd you put Daisy? Is she tied up at the rail again?"

"We left her at the museum in town," Mom said. "She'll be in good hands there."

"And warm."

Relief flooded Casey's eyes, and Sean grimaced guiltily. I was sure they never meant to be outside this long. The hike should have only been about an hour, not three or more. I wasn't even sure what time it was. I forgot to look while we were in the car.

"Where's Peter?" Mom asked.

"Where's the killer whale?" I asked.

Casey pointed in the direction of the waterfall, and Sean pointed toward my abandoned kayak. They began speaking at the same time, but my mom put up a hand and stopped them. She gestured for Sean to speak first.

"The whale is still stuck where you were earlier," he said. "It's floating on its side, so I think it's hurt or sick or something."

Mom said nothing to that and gestured to Casey.

She perked up and said, "Oh, well, your husband was with us the whole time, and then he said he thought he saw something over in that direction and wanted to check it out. He told us to wait here and he'd be right back, but that was a bit ago now."

Again, Mom offered no response, simply walking away from them toward the cliff that separated this cove from the one with the cave and waterfall. I expressed my apologies for my mother's curtness and followed her. Mom deftly climbed the rocks, and I matched where she put her hands and feet to follow her around the steep promontory that went out into the water. I wasn't keen on getting all wet again. I didn't have any more dry clothes in the car.

Above us the sun broke through the clouds, and judging by its position in the sky, I guessed it was somewhere between one and two o'clock. As we came around the corner over the deepest part of the water, Mom found a thin ledge for our feet that would take us all the way to the cave. It made it a little easier to scoot along the wall, but not much. Our fingers were still grasping at whatever we could find big enough to hold onto, making our progress slow. Now that I was near the bottom of the waterfall instead of above it I saw that about half of the "tears" poured across one side of the cave opening while the rest trickled down the cliff wall directly into the sea.

What I didn't see was my father.

"Do you think he went into the cave?"

Mom huffed. "Why can't he ever do what I ask?"

"He's an explorer, Mom," I reminded her. "Would you have just sat on the shore and waited?"

"That's neither here nor there," Mom evaded. "He was supposed to be waiting for the Coast Guard."

"I guess he figured he had a minute or two."

Mom kept going around the point of the cliff and settled her feet on that ridge. It was wet and slippery, but wide enough for her dainty feet. My feet were bigger than hers, so my heels stuck over the edge, and I kept all my weight on the balls of my feet. It was slow going, and we were about halfway to the cave opening when I heard my dad shout at us.

"What are you two doing?"

"Coming to find you, you idiot!" Mom shouted back.

"Well, go back. I'm fine."

If I wasn't holding on to this steep rock wall with the tips of all my fingers, I'd have flipped him off right then. "Look, we're halfway there," I said. "I'm going into the cave and see what's there."

"There's nothing to see," Dad responded. I dared to pull my head away from the rocks enough to look at him. He was standing with both feet on a boulder, one hand balancing himself against the rock wall and the other hand out, palm up as if to present his empty find. "It's a shallow cave. The roof is low enough that I couldn't stand straight, and it comes to a dead-end only a few feet in. If the tide were any higher, the whole thing would fill up with water."

How could that be? A shallow cave? I was so certain it was an opening to some secret labyrinth of tunnels that led deep into the mountain. The magic waterfall was at its opening, and that had to mean something. Was it all just a stupid story by Naomi DeSilba, and I was gullible enough to buy into it? I mean, what did I know about waterfalls anyway? Maybe there were saltwater waterfalls everywhere. I probably shouldn't take my scientific facts from a romance writer who gets all her information from random internet sites.

"What are you doing here?" Mom asked, disdain filling her tone.

"I thought I saw something," Dad answered, beginning his climb toward us. Mom nudged me, and I reluctantly began scooting back the way we came. "At first I thought I saw the head of an animal or person peek over the top of this cliff, but when I approached, it vanished. I thought it might have been someone watching us, so I decided to climb around and take a look to see if anyone was there. Then I saw these roundish stones in the water that didn't quite match the other rocks. When I got closer, they were gone. I got almost to the tip, over the water, and I swear I felt something staring at me from behind. I turned around and something flashed out of view. It seemed way too high up to be a seal or otter or something, but what I thought I saw seemed too big to have been a bird. At any rate, by the time I climbed around the edge of this thing and got to about where we are now, there was obviously nothing here. If there had been anything, it was long gone. Swam off or flew away."

"It was a stupid, dangerous thing to do by yourself," Mom said.

"Sean and Casey were here, and the Coast Guard was coming. I was fine."

Mom huffed again. We rounded the cliff and as soon as I could, I jumped off the cliff onto the rocky beach. My fingers were killing me.

The team in the raft was inside the lagoon area now. They had sidled up next to the killer whale. One of the men was inspecting the animal while another kept the raft steady. The woman put a small megaphone to her mouth and addressed us. "Are you the Sawfeather family?"

Mom and Dad took a step toward the ocean. Mom answered, "Yes. I'm Natalie Sawfeather. This is my husband, Peter." I didn't warrant an introduction, I guessed. I was only the person who found the killer whale and communicated with it.

The officer conferred with the others on the raft who were now wrapping a net around the whale's body. "It looks like the orca is deceased. We're going to take the body back with us. Thank you for reporting this."

"We'd like to go with you, if possible," Dad said, "so we can be part of the autopsy and use the findings for our research."

There was more discussion amongst the officers, and the female officer responded. "You can meet us at our facility near Neah Bay. We'll discuss it there."

Mom and Dad seemed pleased with that response. They knew they could use their influence and credits once they got to the facility. I stepped forward and shouted, "Hey! Do you think you can dislodge the kayak while you're out there and float it toward us?"

One of the guys put up a hand to acknowledge me. After they got the killer whale's body strapped up enough to be dragged by the boat, they motored over to the kayak and tugged it free of the rocks. As a team, they lifted it over their heads and passed it until they got it over the larger rocks blocking it from shore. The current pushed it toward us, and when it got close enough I waded out to fetch it.

"You might want to check that over before you use it," the woman said through the megaphone. "It's pretty dinged up."

"Thanks!" I shouted.

They waved at us and pointed their craft back to the ship waiting for them. The whale weighed down their raft, and it struggled to make it through the pass to the open sea. I wished my parents and the animal rescue team didn't need to do research on the whale to find out why it died. I wished Juarez could just be allowed to sink to the bottom of the sea in peace.

After dragging the kayak back to shore, I tipped it over and gave it a careful inspection, looking for any holes or rips. Despite being lodged between those rocks, it looked like it was only scraped and dented. The hull was still sound.

Sean and Casey approached cautiously, and Sean touched my dad on the forearm. "Hey. Are you folks all set now? Casey's freezing, and we'd like to go find our dog and get some lunch if you don't need us anymore."

"It was all very exciting, though," Casey said. "I mean, I'll remember this for years. I took lots of pictures."

"Did you now?" my mom asked, overly friendly. I wondered what was up.

"I mean, a secret path, a hidden kayak, a girl hugging a killer whale. I didn't get very good pictures of that, unfortunately, because you were on the wrong side of that big rock. I don't think anyone will be able to tell what's going on. And *then*, the Coast Guard came. Goodness."

Sean made a sour face and shook his head. "She keeps a little blog about our travels and stuff like that. Nothing big. Read mostly by our family and friends."

167

"Hmmm," Mom said, her finger stroking her lips as she thought for a moment. "Casey, would you mind sharing your email and blog address with me? Maybe we can talk about a way to get you some more hits. Would you like that?"

"Oh, sure. I was kind of hoping that…well, y'all are a little famous, so…"

"Sure," Mom said. "I understand exactly. I'd do the same thing if I were in your shoes. We just have a little image problem right now, and some positive publicity wouldn't hurt a bit."

Sean raised an eyebrow. "So, you're basically asking Casey to write her blog to make you all look heroic or something?"

Mom waved that thought away. "Heroic is a broad term. I just want to make sure the spin is on the side of helping our environment and the creatures that inhabit it, and not about—"

I had to speak up. "Basically, Mom is trying to make sure you don't post something about how I was out in the ocean doing something stupid and dangerous while my parents watched. Again."

"That's kind of what happened, though," Sean said plainly. "Isn't it?"

Dad shook his head. "Nope. What I think happened was a brave girl took a kayak out to try to help a stranded sea animal."

Sean shook his head. "It wasn't there when she first went out. She went out there for another reason."

Casey whispered, "I think it was to find mermaids. Right?"

"No!" all three of us answered at once.

Casey recoiled, and Sean stepped in front of her protectively. "What happens if she writes whatever she wants? Are you going to sue her?"

"Of course not," Mom said. She smiled at Casey. "Because what any blogger wants are followers. A positive spin on what you saw will get them."

Casey nodded from behind Sean where he couldn't see her. She was all for Mom's help. "Hey, honey," she said to her husband. "I really need to go. I haven't been to the lady's in hours, and I'm worried about Daisy."

Sean took her hand and kissed it. "Sure." He gave one last look at all of us. "We waited here with you all this time, and I don't much appreciate being threatened."

"Nobody's threatening you," Dad said.

"Whatever." Sean tightened his grip on his wife's hand and led her away. She looked back at us one more time and winked. That situation was handled.

"Put that thing down," Mom said to me, tapping the kayak. "We've got to go."

I stuck it back where we'd originally found it that morning. It seemed to be pretty safe from the tide there.

"We really should bring that back with us," Dad said. "I hate leaving it there like litter."

Mom groaned. "I'm too tired right now to lug that thing through a rainforest. We'll make sure Eddie from the docks knows about it, and he can send his guys to come get it."

"We don't have to tell them right away, do we?" I asked. "I might want to come back—"

Dad put a hand on my shoulder and sighed deeply. "That's not going to happen, June. We're done with this search. That cave doesn't lead anywhere. It's not some secret mermaid home where they're keeping your boyfriend. That's a fantasy, and it's time you let it go."

"But what about Juarez? And the waterfall?"

"Stop it, June." Dad's voice was stern. Mom looked away, like she couldn't bear to see this happen. "We're going to deal with the killer whale because we need that evidence for our cause. Then we'll head home."

Mom put her hand between us, her body facing Dad's. "It might take hours with the animal rescue team. I suggest we stay tonight, because I don't want to be driving all night long."

Dad exhaled. "Fine. We'll set up camp one more night—"

"No," Mom interrupted again. "I want to rent a room. We can afford one night. June needs to be kept warm tonight so she doesn't get pneumonia or something, and I want a good night's sleep."

I'm not sure what my mom was after. Maybe she was just softening the blow a bit, but I appreciated her effort.

"Sure, we can do that," Dad agreed. He looked at me uncomfortably and added so he was perfectly clear about it, "But we're leaving early."

We gathered up their backpacks and started our trek back to the car. When we got to the top of the ridge I looked back out toward the Fuca Pillar and stared at that massive stone that was nothing but a massive stone. We walked over the top of the cave that was nothing but a shallow cave. If these places didn't hold magic, then why did I feel so strongly that the mermaid's vision had led me here? What was I missing? What had Juarez been trying to tell me about the mermaids? There was still a mystery about this place that I had to solve. I wasn't giving up yet.

Chapter Fifteen

I sat in a waiting room just inside the front door of the Coast Guard facility. The walls and floor were stark white but smudged everywhere from dirty hands or feet, chairs being moved and scuffing everything they touched, and whatever else bustled through this place. It wasn't a big room, not a whole lot larger than that tiny room at the place where we got the oil changes done on our cars. Only five chrome chairs with black vinyl seats and backs lined the walls, with a dirty table in the corner covered with some old magazines and a used Styrofoam cup. My blood boiled a little at the sight of the cup, less because someone left it behind and more because a place dedicated to taking care of the ocean served their coffee in non-biodegradable containers. Why couldn't they use paper? Or even better, real mugs? Some things my parents taught me were deeply ingrained.

Across from me was a door, also white and smudgy, leading to the rest of whatever secrets were back there that I, apparently, was not allowed to see and an open window with a bored uniformed office attendant. That woman never looked up from her desk, and I was pretty sure she was playing a game on a tablet or phone because I heard the faintest of beeping and whirring.

I tried thumbing through the magazines and the Coast Guard pamphlets that were in a slot on the wall by the front door. I braided my hair again because it felt sticky and gross around my face. I felt time slowly eating me alive. My muscles ached from the hiking and climbing, not to mention from how tense I had been during my bout of nearly freezing to death. Still, I didn't care. All I wanted to do was thrust open the entrance door and bolt out of this place. I would have run all the way back up the mountain if I could have. I would have been long gone except every ten minutes or so – I'm only guessing because I had no watch, no cell phone, and there was no clock in the room – the phone at the front desk would buzz. The office attendant would pick it up and glance at me. Why? I don't know. Double checking that I hadn't moved? Then she'd say, "Yes, ma'am," before hanging up again. It had to be Mom. She didn't trust me to stay put. She was wise that way.

I stood up and opened the door. The office attendant cleared her throat, and I looked back to see her hand hovering over the phone.

"I'm just looking," I said. The sky was very yellow. The sun was careening toward the horizon. It had to be close to four, I assumed. There wasn't much daylight left. I closed the door and approached the window. "Could you ring up my mom or whoever is with her?"

She did and handed me the receiver. I asked Mom if I could borrow her cell phone. A couple minutes later Mom appeared at the interior door, which she had to unlock to come through.

"Mom, this is torture. Why are you making me sit here?"

"Where else can you go?"

"If I can't be back there with you guys learning something useful, then maybe I could go back to the museum or sit at the diner. Maybe one of you could take a minute and check me into the motel we're going to stay at tonight so I can take a shower or something. Do I have to just sit here? I'm climbing the walls."

Mom handed me the cell phone. "It's almost dead. If you're calling Haley, it'll be a short talk."

"Then can I have your car keys and charge it in the car?" I asked. I flicked my gaze over to the office attendant and back to her. "A little privacy would be nice." Mom reached into her pocket and put her hand around the car keys. A glimmer of hope rushed through me. I could take the car back up to the trail and…

Mom brought her hand back out empty. She'd read my mind.

"I think you can sit tight in here a little longer. Your dad's making sure we get the blood and tissue samples we need."

"Are they running a DNA test?" I asked.

"There's no reason for that," Mom said, almost a whisper.

"I think there's a reason."

"Not right now, June."

172

Her expression was harsh enough that I had to look away. I punched the on button on her phone. The battery was in the red.

"I still need a charger. Is it in the car or your purse?"

Mom walked me to the car, not even trusting me to go out and get the charger myself and return her keys to her. While we were out there, I pointed at the totem poles in front of the museum across the road. "Come on, let me hang out over there with Greig. I can visit the exhibit before they close. You know Dad would approve of that."

Mom licked her lips, which I noticed were red from being chapped and not from lipstick. When was the last time she'd touched up her makeup? Her face was unusually plain. Finally, she nodded. "Sure. That's fine. Stay there, though, until we come get you."

"Okay."

"You know this is important, June," she told me as if she had to explain herself. "Getting some solid data on the level of toxins in the creature's blood and blubber will be a major boon for our case. Also, it will validate our time spent here for our businesses. You understand why it's our priority right now, don't you?"

I lifted one shoulder and dropped it again in response, allowing my gaze to drift off toward the ocean. "I think there's a different priority, but whatever."

"June."

"Just leave me alone. I'm kind of tired of your *parenting* me all of a sudden, especially when it isn't even real. When the second something related to your causes happens, my needs and concerns are pushed to the side again. You guys don't believe me about the mermaids at all, do you?"

"Your father is convinced that Carter is gone. I can't say I totally disagree, although I'd like to have hope like you. I *do* feel like that woman, Naomi, planted some suggestions in your mind this morning with her big story, and when you were shocked by the frigid water of that waterfall you might have had some kind of a hallucination—"

"It was a vision, Mom. Just like the ones I got from the tree and the one I got from the mermaid. At this point I find it incredible that you guys don't believe me about this."

"You *want* to believe it," she said. "Sometimes when we want something so bad, our mind helps us see it. You're gullible."

I snorted in response.

"You are. I've been like that, too. When you follow issues and causes like I have for the past twenty-five years, occasionally stories come up that are sensational. I've latched onto more false leads over my career than you can imagine. This one time I was full-boar ready to prosecute a hotel company in Oregon for destroying Northern Spotted Owl nests near their property because the owls were defecating on their balconies. Turns out the so-called poop was just dried toothpaste, and the people making up the story were birders who were angry that the place didn't provide them with enough view. There weren't even any Northern Spotted Owls in the vicinity." She saw me cross my arms and said softly, "The thing is, they knew I was going to stand up for the owls because they're endangered, and they were hoping they'd wind up with a pot of money."

I jerked my head back. "Money? How was that going to happen?"

"Well, clearly they didn't understand how environmental law works. It's not a profitable gig."

"You could say that again."

"Anyway, when they found out they wouldn't get anything from the trial, they backed off and told the truth."

I took a deep breath and said, "Mom, that's an interesting story, and a rare one that I haven't heard. I don't think it applies to this situation, though. Naomi DeSilba's romance novel plot didn't factor into my vision. I swear it. I rather feel like somehow, she's tapped into the real story of the three warriors. I don't know how. Maybe she's sensitive to the magical world like I am. I can't be the only one, right?"

Mom pressed her lips together, probably to prevent herself from saying something hateful or casting more doubt on me. I wondered if it hurt, her lips being so chapped and all. She reached out a hand and pulled my long, dirty braid over my shoulder before saying, "I've got to get back. We're mostly just watching, and your dad knows more about what we need than I do. Still, I want to be there in case there are any technical terms that need clarification or forms that need signing."

She walked away from me and went back into the facility. I yanked the elastic band off the end of my braid and ran my fingers through my thick, dirty hair and shook it out so it fell behind me. The wind off the bay was sharp and cold, so I ran across the highway to the museum. As expected, the place wasn't exactly bustling. Greig was at his usual place at the counter and asked after my parents. I told him I was killing time while they did the autopsy, and he sweetly gave me a free pass to view the exhibit.

It was an exceptional museum, well laid out and cared for. It had all the warmth and color that the Coast Guard office lacked, and I soaked it in. Authentic tribal music played softly through the speakers. The lights were dim and amber tinted, creating a soothing ambiance, and wood panels lined the walls. The whole place smelled of dust and old paper. I read every sign and studied every artifact. I was particularly interested in the whale skeleton suspended from the ceiling, and the exhibit about fishing and hunting tools. Around one bend, I found myself staring at a diorama with stuffed, mounted animals that are often seen around the area. Among them were puffins, an eagle on a low tree branch, a boar in the dirt, and a sea otter and a seal sticking their heads out of the plastered and painted water.

The seal. Seals were common in this area. Of course they were.

I pulled Mom's cell phone out of my pocket and stared at my reflection in the dark screen for a moment. My thumb moved on its own and clicked on the screen. I went to the contacts and scrolled through the names. I didn't know the last name I was looking for, but thankfully Mom lists her close friends by their first names only. It was pretty easy to find.

The battery on the phone was low. I'd forgotten to charge it like Mom asked. I didn't know how much time I'd have on this conversation, so I'd have to be brief. I punched the number. A moment later I heard Vanessa's lovely French Canadian accent.

"Natalie? Oh, I've been worried. Where are you?"

"It's me, Vanessa," I said. I felt a little awkward calling her by her first name, but she hadn't been introduced to me any other way. Plus, I figured after hanging out with her at her secret cove, we were past the formal stage. "It's Juniper."

Her voice was light as she responded, "Oh, Juniper. Good to hear from you. Have you found what you were looking for?"

"No, actually. I haven't. We found what I thought was the right place. I swear it's the right place, but the cave there is too shallow. I thought Carter would be kept inside the cave somehow, and now my parents say our search is over and we can't go back. We're leaving in the morning. I don't know what to do." I sat down on the edge of the diorama, the moss and fake bushes behind me. I crumpled over and put my forehead in my free hand.

"Okay. Okay, sweetheart. Don't worry. How can I help you? You want me to talk to your mother? Tell her you need to go back again?"

"It's not even her. It's Dad mostly, but it won't work for you to talk to them. You can't convince them. They're certain Carter's dead, even though…" I let the rest of that thought go. It was too complicated to tell her about Juarez and the killer whale just then.

"…even though you're sure he's with the mermaids," she finished in her own way.

"Yeah." I sniffed. "So, is there... anything… you can do?"

"Ah, I see. That's a long way from here. Hours."

"I know. Is it even possible?"

There was silence on the other end as Vanessa mulled it over. Or maybe she was just sipping some of her nasty tea. "Let me see what I can do."

"We're staying here tonight. I'm not sure which motel, but I'll text you when I know."

"I won't have my phone with me," Vanessa said.

Of course she wouldn't. I laughed quietly through my slow tears.

"I will leave you some kind of message at the beach at Neah Bay. You look for it in the morning. Early though. Before sun-up. Low tide this time of year is around eight am. If there's something to be seen in those caves, you'll need to be there when you can get in."

I agreed and hung up. Mom would wonder why I called Vanessa when she looked at the phone later. I'd figure out some lie then. I was too tired to think of one now.

I shuffled to the exit and asked Greig if I could charge my phone somewhere. He pointed to a plug by the drinking fountain. Only then did I notice Naomi was sitting in a chair beside him. Her kids were playing with toys in the gift shop. I glanced at the time on Mom's phone before I plugged it in and saw that it was well past the time the museum closed. Had Greig called his family to come over while he kept the place open for me? I didn't know how to express my gratitude for that, so I said nothing. I just smiled uncomfortably.

Naomi had lost a little of her polish over her day with the children. Strands had loosened themselves from her hairdo and gently framed her face where her makeup had faded into her skin. Her lipstick had long ago been licked away. She was still stunning, and I figured Greig was proud to have one of the prettiest ladies on the reservation as his wife. The three children looked like they ranged from two to six, and, by the way they banged on the drums and shook the maracas over there in the shop, I could tell they were a bit of a handful. By the way Naomi and Greig did nothing to stop them, I could tell they were worn out.

Naomi stood as I came closer and surprised me by pulling me in for a hug. "We found your waterfall," I told her when she let me go again.

She straightened her green sweater and swiped at her hair strands, beaming the whole time. "You did? That's great. What did you think of it?"

"I have to agree with you. It is very mysterious, coming out of nowhere like that." I was tempted to tell her about the vision I got from the water. The words were right on the tip of my tongue, and I was eager to see if she would squeal with envy at what I'd experienced. I held back, because, even though she was a creative person with a very vivid and strangely accurate imagination, I wasn't sure she was ready for her fantasy world to be true. "Do you know anything about the cave beneath it?"

"No, not really," she said. "Why?"

"Dad went inside and said it was really shallow, and I guess I thought it would be deeper than that."

"Makes sense it would be shallow, or how else would the paintings be on the roof of it?"

I'd forgotten about the paintings in the cave. Dad didn't mention seeing them, and that wasn't a thing he would leave out. In fact, given how he felt about American Indian history and heritage, he would have taken pictures of them. If he didn't see the paintings, where were they?

"Are you sure the paintings are in that cave?"

Greig and Naomi looked at each other as if conferring silently over the facts. After a moment, Greig said, "There are a number of caves along the cliffs. It could be a different one."

"But I like it being that cave, because it goes with my story."

I nodded and gave her a half smile. "It kind of goes with my story, too."

"What?" she asked.

"Nothing." I waved it away. "Maybe all of it is in another cave like Greig said. I'd just like to see for myself."

Naomi pointed back toward the office and said, "I could pull up some of my research if you'd like."

"Research on what?" My dad stepped up behind me. I hadn't even noticed my parents coming in, which was kind of amazing because their fish odor was foul.

The smiles on Greig and Naomi widened despite the horrible stench. Greig greeted them, "Mr. and Mrs. Sawfeather. Good to see you. We're just about to close up. We stayed open a little late for Juniper, and we were hoping to invite you to dinner when you came for her."

Mom put her hands to her face. "Oh, that's so kind of you. We're just so exhausted and filthy. All I want is a shower and a bed."

"You have to eat," Greig said.

"I just don't think we'd be good company," Mom said as apologetically as possible.

That I didn't doubt.

Naomi put up her hands like a magician showing his clear cuffs, "I was just about to show June some of my research on the waterfall and cave that you visited. She said you didn't see the handprint paintings."

"Oh, I saw them," Dad said. He put up a finger and dashed outside. We all shrugged at each other and waited until he ran back in with his camera. He turned it on and swiped through pictures as he walked toward us. He turned his back to all of us and held the camera up so we could all see the images he'd taken of the cave ceiling. Dozens of brown and black handprints covered the ceiling as though people had ridden in there on canoes and reached up.

Something was odd about the handprints. I grabbed the camera and zoomed in on one of the handprints as close as I could get. Yes. I was right. Those weren't normal handprints at all.

"Dad, do you see that?" I pointed at the picture.

He leaned in to get a better look. Everyone else was leaning in, but I lowered the camera to my chest where only my dad could see it.

I whispered. "Do those fingers look like they have webbing to you?"

Dad didn't need time to study the picture. He gave me a sharp nod, turned off the camera and dropped it to his side.

"What is it?" Mom asked. "Did you see something?"

I nodded. Dad said nothing.

"What?" Greig and Naomi asked.

"Mermaids have been in that cave," I said. Dad started to shush me, and Mom glanced at the DeSilbas uncomfortably. "The handprints were made by mermaids. I'm sure of it. I think they live near here."

"Mermaids?" Greig laughed incredulously. The children in the gift shop heard him, and they perked up at the word. Repeating the word 'mermaids' crazily, they came running toward us.

Naomi wasn't laughing, though. Her face was as eager as that of her children. "I remember now. You're the people who found the mermaids. You're the girl from that video."

"That video was a fake," Greig said, coming around the counter to hush his children. More to them than to his wife, he said, "Mermaids aren't real."

I shook my head. "They are real. I was responsible for the release of maybe a hundred or so of them that were being held in captivity by Affron Oil right here in the San Juan Strait on Orcas Island. My friend Juarez Peña said there used to be events around this area where our people made shell jewelry and tossed it into the sea—"

"Oh, the Potlatch," Naomi inserted.

"Yes, and the mermaids collect and wear those necklaces. They live near here in these cold waters. I believe they are the ancestors of the man from the legend, the man that is the boyfriend or lover or whatever in your novel."

"Torren."

"What's that?" Mom asked.

Naomi blushed. "Oh, that's the name I've given him. Torren. Do you like it?"

Dad scratched his head. "It's not very authentic, is it?"

Greig made a face behind his wife to show he didn't care for it, either.

Naomi ignored my father and said to me, "The mermaids are real? What about all the press after that video came out declaring the whole thing was a hoax?"

Mom answered. "We told her to say to that. We had to fight a court case against Affron, and the mermaid story was distracting and diminishing our credibility."

"And the tree sitting thing? Was the tree enchanted like I've heard from the rumors? They say Nathan Clark claimed the tree was alive and almost killed him."

I nodded. "That's true too."

Dad groaned. "Why are we sharing all of this right now, June?"

I turned on him. "Because I need someone to listen to me. You know all of this to be true, but you won't listen to me. I need an ally. I need someone who understands." I swung back to Naomi. "Plus, I need to know how you came up with the idea for your story, because it's... strangely accurate. What I mean is did you know the legend *before* you found the waterfall or the other way around?"

It took Naomi a moment to answer, like she was puzzling it out for herself. She even looked to her husband like he might remember for her, but he didn't give her an answer. "To be honest," Naomi finally spoke, "I'm not really sure how it happened. I've been to the waterfall at least a hundred times. I found it one day when I was exploring a few years ago. I remember putting my hand in it and discovering how salty it was. I remember going home that afternoon and trying to look up any information about it, to see if anyone had written anything to explain the kind of waterfall it was. I didn't find anything at all except the one legend of a heartbroken girl who dove over a cliff and turned into a waterfall. As sad as the story was, I fell in love with it and couldn't stop thinking about how wonderful or amazing it would be if that story were true somehow. Then I started having the dreams."

"Yes, the dreams," Greig said. The oldest daughter nodded just like her father as if she knew all about it, too. "She'd wake up in the middle of the night and go to her desk where she'd start clacking away at her keyboard."

"To get the ideas down before I forgot them. The dreams were so vivid and about my story. I saw everything that was happening to this girl and the men in her life. It was like a movie."

"Woke us all up," Greig said. "Our house isn't exactly big."

"I get my best writing done after the dreams. It doesn't hurt that the kids are asleep and don't need my attention, either. It's hard to find the time to write during the day."

Dreams. Another kind of vision. I had to ask. "Are the dreams frequent? Does something spark them?"

"I haven't had one in a while," Naomi said. "I have a lot more of them in the summer months when I'm guiding the hikes. I'm really blocked right now."

"Do you usually take people to the waterfall? Do you think the dreams could be connected to touching the water?"

Naomi took in a breath. "You know, you're right. It isn't every time, but all of my dreams about the story have been after visiting the waterfall. All of them."

I faced my parents. "Still think I'm hallucinating? That I'm susceptible to suggestion? Mermaid handprints on the cave ceiling. Naomi gets visions from the waterfall, too."

"Wait! You got a vision from the waterfall?"

I didn't answer her, and I saw Greig put a hand on his wife to keep her from interrupting my conversation with my parents.

Mom looked uncomfortably down at her hands. Dad rubbed his face and said, "We need to go, June. It's getting late. These people probably want to go home."

"No, it's fine," Naomi said. She shooed the children away, and they moved glumly back to the toys, looking over their shoulders like they were afraid they'd miss something. "We're happy to talk to you about this. I'd love to know more about, well, anything you've seen."

"Me too, actually," Greig said, not sounding sarcastic in the least.

"Maybe another time," Mom said. "Thank you for your help and the offer for dinner. I think the three of us have some *private* discussing to do this evening."

"Sure," Naomi said, looking identical to her dejected children. "We understand."

"If you change your mind," Greig said, handing Dad his business card, "just call."

Dad ushered Mom and I out of the museum. We drove in silence down the road to a small hotel on the beach. The rates were low, because it was off season, and my parents actually splurged and got me my own room. It was decorated like a cottage. The walls had white paneled wainscoting and the top half painted emerald green. All of the furniture was pristine white with green accents. Pretty little white shutters were on the window that overlooked the ocean. It was all very soothing. After I got out of the shower, I found some room service food on the stand next to my bed. A cheese and egg sandwich, fries, fruit cup, and a juice. I was dying for a soda and decided to scout out a machine later. I never did, though, because I put my head down on the pillow after I ate and knocked out.

Wham! A blow to the face. Fists flew, connecting with cheeks and jaws. The two men were at each other with a fury. I could see them from a distance, flailing and tearing, spinning around in a violent dance of hatred. I drew toward them cautiously. Their ferocity was out of control, and I didn't want to get slugged by accident. I couldn't imagine what had them so incensed, but I had to know who they were and find out why they were fighting here at the edge of the world.

I snuck up as close as I dared through the undergrowth of the forest and watched them whirl around each other. One was dark-skinned with thick brown hair. The other pale with a crown of white-gold ringlets. They matched each other in size and weight, but the darker man was older, his movements a little slower and more controlled. The blond man kicked sideways, but the other one grabbed his leg and flipped him over. He crashed to his back, and then I saw his face.

Carter. My Carter.

I screamed, and he saw me. A smile touched the corner of his mouth before he flipped himself back to his feet again to face his foe. Now I saw that man's face as well.

Juarez?

Juarez's expression was fierce. He rounded on Carter, fingers splayed, ready to tear Carter apart.

But why? These two were friends. Sort of. They'd only met briefly, but it was a good moment. It was when we'd saved the mermaids together. Juarez liked Carter. Carter had no problem with Juarez. Not that I knew of. Why were they fighting?

I ran toward them. "Stop! Both of you! You're friends! We're all friends!"

"He's no friend of mine!" Juarez snarled. "He's a thief!"

"You're a coward!" Carter shouted back.

They attacked each other again, hands at each other's throats. I came at them and tried to pry them apart. Juarez tossed me back, and I landed hard on my tailbone.

"How dare you hurt her?" Carter raged. He charged at Juarez like a bull. Juarez grabbed him around the waist, intending to fling Carter aside, but he lost his balance. They both toppled over the edge of the cliff.

"No!"

I dashed to the edge of the cliff, both not wanting to see but also needing to see them hit the water below. I needed to make sure they survived all the hidden rocks below the surface. They disappeared beneath the deep blue water and churning white foam. No blood darkened the water. I wanted to feel relief for that, but neither of the men surfaced. Could they have hit their heads and passed out. Were they drowning?

Then I saw movement. I crouched down and focused on the dark head coming out of the water. Was it Juarez? No, the head was too small. It was a seal, a seal with a blonde streak on the top of its head. It lifted its head to see me and began swimming toward the nearest rock. It didn't get there in time.

A killer whale, massive and shiny, erupted from the water, its jaws wide open. In a flash, it chomped down on the seal. Only as it lowered its head into the fresh pool of blood from the massacred seal, did I notice the killer whale's brown human eyes.

My own whimpering woke me up. It was as if I was too terrified in my dream to make my mouth and vocal cords work correctly. I sat up and tried to get my bearings in this unfamiliar hotel room, grateful my parents were on the other side of the wall and I hadn't woken them up.

The power of suggestion. That was my first coherent thought. We'd been talking about dreams last night, and I knew that Juarez had somehow been transformed into a killer whale. All of it mixed together in my mind to form this crazy dream.

But Carter as a seal? What was that about?

Then it came to me. Vanessa. She'd never outright said it, but I knew she was a selkie. She could turn into a seal, and she was supposed to be helping me.

I looked at the clock. It was nearing five in the morning. I slid out of bed and threw on my clothes. They were stiff and stinky from the saltwater, but they were dry. My coat was dry, too, finally. As quietly as I could, I snuck out of my room, past my parents' door, and down to the stairwell. We were only on the second floor. In moments, I was out on the dark beach. This part of the bay, being on the hotel property was much prettier and well-kept than the beach by the campgrounds. There was still quite a lot of debris, but I bet it was all cleared out by tourist season to make room for the beach towels and chairs.

Almost at the end of the property line was a wooden dock. Tied to one post out in the water was a rope of buoys that stretched across to a wooden spike sticking out of a pile of boulders. This marked off the safe swimming zone, I assumed. Also at the end of the dock was the lone figure of a person sitting, wrapped in a thick blanket, with her feet dangling over the edge. I approached cautiously in case it was a crazy person who liked to sit in the freezing cold and watch the sunrise as opposed to my mother's magical friend.

The sky got lighter as I approached, and I could see her outline better. Her long gray hair hung down her back. As I got nearer, I could see that it wasn't a blanket around her at all. It was her seal skin. Her shoulders were bare, and I suddenly understood that she was naked under that seal skin.

Vanessa twisted around when I got close to her. "Ah, there you are."

"Have you been here long?"

"Not terribly," she said. "It was a long swim, and it will be a long swim back. I'm already tired, and the water is so dirty. I haven't gone in it in a long time." She coughed. "I guarantee I won't go in for a long time again."

"I hope it didn't make you sick."

She gave me a wan smile. "Me, too, sweetie. A benefit I have over the other sea creatures is access to medicine and healing remedies." She patted the wood plank beside her, and I sat down. I averted my eyes from her bare legs sticking out from under the skins. I saw enough to learn she didn't shave.

"Did you find anything?"

"I did. The mermaids wouldn't let me get too close. They could tell I was not a real seal, and they were wary of me. Still, I could see that they were all gathered near the waterfall where the killer whale found you. It was hard to communicate with them, but they did seem distressed. It also seemed like they were protecting the area or guarding it somehow. I suspect that there is more to that particular cave than your father observed."

"I think so, too."

"Low tide is soon. If you can get there in time, maybe you'll see more. The mermaids will stay underwater. I don't think they'll try to harm you."

"I don't know anymore," I said. "I don't think the mermaids are very trusting of humans. Not even me."

"There is another presence there, too," Vanessa said. "I couldn't see it, but I felt it. Everywhere. It was almost in the earth itself. It's dark. It's angry."

"That has to be the spirit of the warrior that killed his friends. I'm not clear what kind of creature he is yet, only that it has something to do with rock or stone."

"Just be careful. Whatever the presence is, it's not welcoming." She winced at the sunlight beginning over the Eastern horizon. "I must go before anyone sees me."

I hugged her shoulders, the smooth hair of the seal skin gliding under my hands. "Thank you for this."

She kissed my forehead. "I hope you find Carter. I believe you that he was taken. I'm sorry to say that I'm not convinced that he's okay."

"Too many days have passed, I know."

"And there is evil there," she added. "Be aware. Be ready."

She launched herself off the platform into the water, and like my dream, moments later a small seal's head popped up out of the water. It barked at me and then swam away.

I heard a gasp behind me, and it jolted me to my feet. Three steps back from me stood my mother, her hands pressed to her mouth as her eyes stared dumbstruck at the seal swiftly moving away from us.

"Vanessa," she whispered in awe.

"Yes, Mom, it's her. Do you believe me now?"

"I saw her number on my phone, but I didn't think... And then I wasn't sleeping well and heard your door open, so I got up and followed you out here... How did you know about her?"

"She kind of told me."

"Why did she never tell me?"

"You wouldn't have believed her."

"I might have." I raised an eyebrow at her. "I would have if she'd shown me."

"Sometimes people just want to be believed on their word alone." I left it at that, and Mom didn't argue. "Did you hear what she said? Any of it?"

"Yes. I did. We need to go wake up your father. Right now."

Chapter Sixteen

Dad was already up, dressed, and drinking coffee in the continental breakfast set-up of the hotel lobby. He required no convincing. The look on Mom's face was enough. We swallowed down some stale pastries and packed the car as fast as possible. On the way back up to the hiking trail, Dad confessed that he hadn't slept a wink. Those mermaid handprints haunted him, and Naomi's confession of dreams and visions inspiring her work bothered him more. I don't think he was ready to admit that he had any hope that Carter was still alive, but his curiosity was definitely piqued.

We ran down the wooden walkway. My parents wore their over-packed backpacks, so they lagged behind me a bit, and I got a good lead on them when I slipped under the rail at the spot that led off the trail toward the waterfall. I heard them calling after me to slow down and wait, but I couldn't. It was low-tide, and I wanted to see if that cave had more to it than we thought. All the mist from yesterday morning was gone. Today was clear and golden. The water sparkled so bright on the horizon it hurt my eyes to look in that direction. The forest around me dripped with dew and smelled incredibly green and fresh. Maybe my hope colored everything with such beauty.

I got to the place where I could climb down to the beach and wasn't too terribly surprised to find two familiar faces waiting there. Naomi and Greig wore hiking gear and wading boots that went up to their knees. Naomi's hair was pulled back in a ponytail, and she didn't have a stitch of makeup on her face. A large duffel bag was unzipped on the ground between them, a wet suit spilling out of it.

"Are you going diving?" I asked.

"We normally advise against it in this area," Greig said. "The current is strong and there are whirlpools. There've been a number of drownings here. Plus, the water is so dark, being in this bowl between the mountain and sea stacks that block the sunlight, that it's hard to see anything."

"Normally I take tourists to snorkel over at Neah Bay, just past the buoy line," Naomi said. She lifted up the wet suit. "I brought two, in case maybe you wanted to take me with you to see the mermaids. If you think I could communicate with them like you do."

"I don't know if you can communicate with them," I said. "It's not easy, and I'm not sure it's safe. So far, I've only had a good interaction with one mermaid. It seems like the rest are hostile."

"I'd like to try," Naomi said.

Greig took her hand with both of his. "If Juniper says it's not safe, honey, we have to consider that. We have kids. What if—?"

"I'll be fine," she insisted.

My parents were climbing down now. Dad, who was holding a long tree branch in one hand, called over, "Curiosity got the best of you, huh?"

"Yeah," Greig said. "We had to see for ourselves."

Naomi's eyes implored mine.

"Tell you what," I said to her. "Let me go check it out first. If it seems safe enough, I'll come back and get you." I started for the kayak.

"Do you still want to wear the suit? Just in case?" She held it out for me. I stepped forward and took it graciously. Greig kept his back to me as I slipped out of my layers and pulled the wet suit on over my underwear. Meanwhile, my parents basically repeated the same conversation I'd just had with them about safety and such.

Mom nodded in approval at the wet suit while I reached over and retrieved the wreath made of Red Cedar tree twigs and remnants of Carter's clothing that I brought with me. I pulled the belt out of my jeans and latched it around my waist, placing the wreath in it like Xena's chakram. Meanwhile, Dad and Greig got the kayak back out of its holding spot and readied it in the water for me.

"I'm going to climb around like I did yesterday," Dad said.

"Me, too," Mom added.

He looked at Greig and Naomi. "You two are going to stay here and keep your ears sharp. If you hear any shouting or yelling, you'll need to run for help. Also, keep your eyes open for anything strange in the water. We've been told there is a whole…what would you call it? A *School*? Of mermaids out there. You shout to us if you see anything."

"Do *not* go in the water," Mom said. "Please."

Naomi and Greig nodded their heads like obedient children. I got in the kayak, and Dad ripped some leaves off the branch he had and handed it to me as a new oar. It was longer and smoother than the piece of driftwood I'd used last time. I dug it into the rocks under the water and got my craft moving forward. Dad raced to the cliff and began climbing, Mom right beside him. I saw her shake her hands a couple times. Her fingers probably still ached from doing this yesterday. I know mine did.

I couldn't keep watching them. This inlet was full of jagged rocks, some I could see and some hidden by the water, and I had to pay attention to where I was going. Bumping and scratching, testing the way in front of me with the reach of my pole, I slowly maneuvered out to where the water was deeper and around the corner of that steep cliff wall. The cave and the waterfall beside it came into view.

I rowed toward it. The branch had no flat end for a paddle, and I was fighting the current that pulled out to the sea, so it was no easy task to keep the nose of the kayak pointed toward the cave. The water here was pitch black, and I shivered wondering how many silver mermaids were underneath me at that moment, watching me pass over their heads. Would they allow me to get closer? Was my progress extra slow because they were somehow pushing against me?

My parents were coming around the point of the cliff. I heard Mom cry out. I looked to see that she had slipped a little, and her left foot dangled in the water. My breath caught in my throat as I saw a webbed hand reach for her foot and miss just as Dad pulled her back up.

"Mom! Dad! Be careful! They're swimming right beneath you!"

Mom pressed up tight against the wall and stared down as if what was down there were sharks. Maybe the mermaids were as dangerous as that. I didn't have a feeling they were friendly. I shivered. How many of them had been swimming right below me yesterday when I was interacting with the Fuca Pillar and the killer whale, and I didn't know it?

A rustling caught my attention, and I shot my attention toward the noise, wondering what was coming next. Naomi emerged from the shrubs above the waterfall, followed by Greig who squeezed out behind her. She knelt down where the water began.

"I thought Dad told you to stay at the beach!" I shouted at them.

"We can see and hear better from here!" Naomi shouted back. "We're completely cut off over there!"

"Besides," Greig added, "we're just that much closer to the car if we need to run for help!"

"Fine!" I shouted. "Just stay up there!"

I rowed a little further toward the cave. The water line was much lower than yesterday afternoon, making the cave appear taller than I remembered. From the ridge we were on before, we could have easily touched the ceiling of the cave. Now my parents would be several feet below it. From what I could see, the ledge for their feet at this level was wider and would be easier to traverse. It was still not wide enough for them to simply walk along.

A hard bump rocked my kayak as I neared the cave's mouth. I straightened up and searched for what I'd hit, but I didn't see anything. Another bump came from the other side. Then one from behind which caused my kayak to spin. I hadn't hit rocks. Something, or *things* were hitting me. Carefully, for fear of falling out, I leaned over to peer into the water. Something round and smooth zipped by just under the water level. A second later there was a splash behind me. I caught just the tip of a silver tail before it disappeared.

Naomi screamed from above. "They're everywhere! Be careful, June!"

From the cliff, I heard my mother. "Oh, God! June!"

"Just stay in the boat! Whatever you do! Stay in the boat!" That was my dad, and it was scary funny to hear him shouting this advice when at the same time, I could see half a dozen hands swiping for their feet, ready to grab ankles and pull them under.

I gritted my teeth and tightened my grip on the branch. My instinct was to use the branch as a bat and swing it at the creatures, knocking them away from me. I willed myself not to. Even though I suspected they're inclination was to drown me without hesitation, I didn't want to hurt them. I wanted them to see I was an ally. Carefully, I stuck the pole into the water until it hit the ground underneath. It wasn't too deep here. I pushed myself forward and then again, keeping the kayak as smooth and centered as possible. The mermaids continued to try to tip me or turn me, but I worked against them with my weight, balance, and determination. I aimed for the side of the cave closer to my parents so I wouldn't go through the waterfall, but a giant rock under the water prevented me from moving in that direction.

The mermaids used the ding against the kayak to spiral me away. The waterway had narrowed at this point, and the kayak butted its nose up against the wall on the far side of the waterfall. I reached forward and pushed off with my hand, sending the kayak backward toward the cave, and then I used the branch to keep me going in that direction. I'd turn around when I could. I just had to keep going into the cave.

I heard the water splatter over the back end of the kayak, and I jerked around to see there was no way I would avoid getting wet. Two mermaid heads rose out of the water and placed their hands on the nose of the kayak. I thought they were going to push down hard and flip me out of the craft, but instead they shoved the kayak. Perhaps they figured if I was here, I might as well get the full treatment. The freezing water showered over my head like someone dumping an ice bucket over me.

And the world went black.

It's a coastal village. Plank houses constructed of cedar wood are pressed up against the forest that rises up like a giant beast behind them. Night has fallen, and the water is peaceful. I watch the waves from where I sit in the sand weaving a new fishing basket. It is late, and I should get back to my family. I'm enjoying the moment away from them and want it to last a bit longer. If the men were here, I'd have gone back by now. I wouldn't risk the rumors of me being out alone with Tuari before our wedding. He will be back soon from the hunt, and we will be married then. He promised, and my father, the tribe's shaman, approved. Even my elder brother, who watches over my sisters and I like we are fragile eggs, agrees that Tuari is his preferred match for me.

I dream of building our own home, of having our children. I am so lost in my thoughts I think his voice calling my name is inside my head.

It isn't until he is touching my shoulders, gently shaking me that I realize he is kneeling before me and my basket has been tossed aside.

His face is full of fear. I've never seen his eyes so wide that the whites glow in the dark. "Do you hear me? We have to go, now!"

"Go where?"

"Away. Anywhere. Far from here. He's coming."

"Who's coming?"

"Jolon. He killed your brother in the forest, and he's coming after us."

"My brother? He's dead?"

"We don't have time!" He grabs me by the elbow and helps me to my feet. I dust off the sand as we rush back to the village. We weave through the huts to my family's home and dash inside so I can gather a few things. He stays at the door, his arms raised against the doorframe. My sisters cower in the corner afraid of his energy. My father stands and walks toward him, ignoring my frantic grabbing at clothing and blankets. In a quick exchange with Tuari, my father learns the truth. Jolon is determined to kill Tuari and take me for his bride.

"I will not permit it," my father says firmly.

"It doesn't matter," Tuari says. "He will take her, and he will be here soon."

My sisters scream at the news and reach for me to come and hug them. I only touch their fingers before wadding up my belongings at my chest and heading for the doorway. My father stops me and puts up a finger for us to wait. He goes to his wooden chest of medicines and pulls out several gourds and sniffs them before putting them back. Tuari taps his foot impatiently and takes fleeting glances over his shoulders. Finally, my father finds what he wants. He sprinkles some powder into a bowl and then pours in water and mixes it with his finger. He brings it to us and holds it for us to each take a drink.

It is bitter and burns my throat as I swallow. I cough and wipe my mouth. Tuari puts up a hand and refuses to drink, urging me to take his portion for extra protection. Before either of us asks a question, my father closes his eyes and invokes a quiet chant, moving his hand over my head and then that of my intended. "May Hohoepbess, the twin brothers of the moon and sun, guide you and shield you from harm." He finishes and opens his eyes. "Go now. Be swift of foot. You are protected from his evil."

Tuari thanks my father, grabs my elbow again, and we run up into the forest. With only the light of the moon to guide us, we run forever, until I can't breathe, until I can't stand up straight. We tuck ourselves under a wide stone and sleep fitfully. As soon as we wake, we run again. The sun rises and sets several times, and still we run. Until we hit the end of the world and can go no further.

I see giant stones sticking out of the ocean, but they offer no safety for us. We are stuck with nothing to do but turn back.

And then he is there, coming at us with a knife in his hand. His face is monstrous with hatred. Tuari pushes me behind him and rushes into his enemy. The knife glints against the dawning light of day, and I see dried smears of blood on it. I hope that is the blood of what animal he ate for his last meal and not my brother's. I haven't been told how my brother was killed. Tuari refused to talk about it, claiming to be protecting me from it or preserving my memory of my brother. Now, as my love and his enemy tear at each other, I want nothing but to know the truth. How has this animal killed my brother? And why?

"Stop!" I cry. "Why are you doing this?"

The knife gets knocked to the ground, and the two warriors lock their bodies in a hold.

Jolon grunts, "She is mine! I will have no one else."

"I will not see her with a creature such as you!"

"No. You will not."

Jolon dives for the knife, but I am faster and kick it over the side of the cliff into the water below.

Tuari pounces on Jolon's back, but Jolon doesn't have his balance and the two men tumble over the edge, flipping over each other as they fall. The golden light from the rising sun makes them look like they are on fire.

"No!" I scream, rushing for the spot where they last touched land. Their bodies hit the water and sink. The blue water fills with blood. Then I jump. There is no thought. Only grief. Then there is nothing at all.

So much screaming from all directions. It worked its way into my brain and forced my eyes open. Screaming from Naomi and Greig above me, leaning as far over the cliff as they dared. Screaming from my mother clinging to the wall across from me. Screaming from the mermaids roiling around the kayak, or whatever one could call the high-pitched horrible noise they made. I think I might have been screaming too, for my throat ached. For a brief moment, I considered opening my mouth and taking in some of the water pouring down on me, but then I remembered it was saltwater. Oh, and it was magical too. If it could give the kind of vivid vision I just had just by touching my skin, it might just kill me if I ingested it.

I had collapsed backward in the kayak, my face up to the sky. My hands had mercifully stayed in the craft, because I think if they had fallen into the water, I wouldn't still be sitting where I was. I would have been pulled under by the mermaids. My branch oar was missing. I sat up and looked around and saw it floating away, far out of reach. Great. I had no idea how to paddle back to the beach without it.

I signaled to everyone that I was okay, and the screaming from the humans came to an end. Questions followed, but I didn't have the energy to answer them yet. When the mermaids saw me alert again, they hushed as well, waiting for their next turn to rally. Carefully, I walked my hands along the cave wall entrance, trying not to push too hard and float away from it. Painstakingly slow, I made my way deeper into the cave, Mom coming toward me from the other side. If I could get around to her ledge, I could climb out of the kayak and go back around with her and Dad. Only...

"Where's Dad?" I shouted.

"He's not in there?" Mom was still close to the cave's opening. The cave wasn't deep, but it was dark toward the back of it. I didn't see anyone moving along the rocks.

"No."

"He said he was going on ahead to make sure it was safe. Right before you passed out."

"Well, he's not here! I don't see him anywhere!"

"Oh, God! June! You don't think he..."

I looked down at the pitch-black water, knowing those mermaids were right underneath me. Did they pull my father down to the depths while he was distracted by my passing out under the waterfall? They'd drown him!

Mom had edged a little further into the cave. I gaped at her, unable to come up with any words of comfort. She had also been staring at the water. She lifted her gaze to mine, and then her head jerked back as if she'd been flashed in the eyes with a bright light.

"June! Your eyes!"

"What about them?"

"They're blue. Not just blue. Brilliant blue! Sparkling! Like jewels!"

The water *had* done something more to me than given me a vision. Now it was time to see what these new eyes could do. I pulled my legs out from the kayak and swiveled to get them over the edge. Mom wasn't shouting at me to stop. Her tone was low, almost moaning.

"No. No. No. You will not do this. I didn't bring you all the way out here to watch you kill yourself."

"I have to find him, Mom. I'm the only one who can."

Not listening to her protestations, I pulled the wreath free of my belt and jumped into the water.

Chapter Seventeen

The mermaid hands were on me immediately. I felt them pressing against the wet suit and tugging off my boots. As they dragged me downward, I held the wreath out like a talisman which they avoided. Watching them recoil away from the wreath like it was on fire forced me to process that I could see amazingly well. The salt should have been stinging my eyes. The dank water inside a cave that faced the opposite way of the morning sunlight should have been impossible for my vision to penetrate. Not to mention the icy temperature already numbing my face and all the thick silver tails blocking any view. I could see as clearly as if at the bottom of a chlorine swimming pool in the middle of a bright summer day.

This cave pool was deep. I noticed that first, as the mermaids pulled me further and further away from the surface. Then I saw a cave opening that went further into the mountain. An underwater cave! Of course! That's where the mermaids were living their secret lives. They dragged me through the opening, which led to a low-ceilinged room filled with water. We kept going. My lungs were beginning to burn, and the reality hit me that their cave home might be completely submerged. I might wind up a drowned corpse at the bottom of this place alongside the bodies of my father and boyfriend.

For the first time, I thought I should have listened to Dad and not gone on this stupid quest. I pushed up with all my strength to try to get above the water, but the mermaids held me down and pulled me through another tunnel. I didn't think I could last a moment longer, and the edges of my vision began to go silver. We burst through the opening, and the mermaids flung me forward so hard a wave of water built up behind me, crashing me up on a sandbar.

I choked for air as water cascaded off my body. Then I collapsed onto my back. The wreath slipped out of my hand into the water. I got to my knees and reached for it, but the wreath quickly floated away. The tops of the mermaids' heads stuck out of the water like strange stones and moved backwards, like the wreath was warding them off. I screamed at them, "Why are you trying to drown me? Don't you know I helped you? Don't you know what I've been through because of you?"

"June. Come on. Get away from the water, before they pull you back in."

Strong hands tugged at my shoulders and ankles. I panicked, not knowing who had me, twisting against them and almost toppling back into the water. The hands tightened their grip on me, and they dragged me across the sand and then onto a hard slab of stone. I relaxed my body when they let go and finally turned my head to my rescuers. Crouched beside me was my father.

And Carter!

I yelped and lunged for him, wanting desperately to throw my arms around him so tight that he melded with me and we could never be separated again. Dad held me back with one hand and put a finger to my mouth to stop my noise. Carter plopped down beside me and rested his arms on his knees, as though that small effort of dragging me had worn him out.

"Careful," was all Dad said. I understood what he meant as I propped myself up on my elbows to get a good look at Carter. He'd lost too much weight in the last few days. Sticking out of what little was left of his shredded clothing were bony legs and arms, every bit of his skin covered with scratches or gashes. His normally golden locks were matted to his head, deep bags were under his dull eyes, and his cheeks were sunken in and covered with stubble.

"Carter," I whispered. "You're alive."

"Barely," my father said.

"I shouldn't be," he responded, his voice rough with disuse. "They've tried to drown me several times. I don't know why. I don't know why they brought me all the way here to try to drown me under a waterfall. It's not even a strong waterfall."

"What happened to your eyes?" Dad asked after looking me over to make sure I wasn't hurt. I felt guilty. I should have done the same thing to him. My brain was still reeling from surviving the journey into this cave and then finding Carter at the end of it. I was right. I wanted to shout it and hear it echo throughout the cavern. By the look of the stalactites hanging from the ceiling, I thought that might be a bad idea.

"The waterfall," I answered in a hushed voice, both acknowledging to Carter that the waterfall was significant and reminding my dad that it was magical. "It changed me somehow. I can see under the water. I think I can see like the mermaids do."

"You can't breathe like them, though." Dad ran his fingers along my neck, looking for gills.

"No, that's clear. I wonder if I'd been under it longer—"

"You'd be dead," they both said.

I shook my head adamantly. "No, I think I might have turned into one of them. Maybe. Like the lover in the story, Dad. The water of tears might have changed me. Think about Juarez. He became a killer whale. Maybe it was the waterfall."

Carter put his hand on my shoulder. His fingernails were worn down to nubs and the skin on his hands was so dry it cracked. "Juarez? Juarez Peña? You've seen him?"

"Yeah," I said. "I know this will sound crazy to you, but he was turned into a killer whale somehow, and now he's dead."

"Normally I would say that's crazy, but…" He took a deep breath and nodded toward the mermaids out in the water. "You don't think that's what they've been trying to do to me, do you? Change me into a killer whale under that waterfall?"

"Maybe."

"Why isn't it working?" he asked.

Dad scrunched up his forehead. The time for denial was over. Magic was happening, and he couldn't say otherwise. He said to Carter, "Maybe because you're not of our people."

"Yes," I agreed. "Eddie from the docks at the reservation said men go missing each year in this area, all men from the reservation. He didn't mention tourists going missing. Do you think they're all being brought here and transformed?"

"I can't believe we're having this discussion," Dad said.

I had one more thought. "Juarez wasn't full-blood American Indian. He's Spanish too. Do you think that's why he got so sick? The magic wasn't strong enough for him?"

Dad put his hands out weakly. "I just don't know the answer to that, but you may have a point."

Water lapped up higher on the sandbar, beginning to lick at the slab of rock where we sat.

"The tide is going to rise," Carter said. "This cave gets very full. We'll have to get up to that shelf up there if we want to survive." He pointed to a cut out in the rock wall way above us. "It's very narrow and will be a tight fit for all three of us, but it's the only place high enough. I don't move as fast as I did, so we should start climbing. Especially before *he* comes."

"Who?" I asked.

"The rock monster. He comes every day. He can come any time, and he can be anywhere. Oh, crap!" He skittered backward as he pointed out at the water.

I looked to see the tops of the mermaid heads parting like they were letting something through. My breathing got shallow, and I began to tremble. The rock monster had to be the murderous warrior that had been turned into something made of stone. What power did it have? Why was Carter terrified of it? Dad rose to his feet and nudged me to get up as well. They both faced the wall behind us and began to climb.

The Red Cedar tree wreath flicked out of the water onto the rock slab right near my feet. I crouched down to reach for it.

"No, June! It's a trick!" Carter shouted.

A webbed hand snaked out of the water and grabbed me before I could back away. It yanked me forward, causing me to land hard on my chest, my armpit bruised by the edge of the rock. My arm was submerged in the water. Carter and Dad jumped down beside me and pulled at my legs. The mermaid was stronger than the both of them. Of course, Carter had barely any strength at all. She won the struggle, and my head went underwater.

But that was all. The mermaid didn't pull me the rest of the way. Instead, she put her hands to my face, almost as if she might kiss me, and then she smiled. I saw dimples in her cheeks.

Could it be possible? Finally, after all this time. My mermaid. The one I'd rescued was here to help me. At least I hoped she was here to help me.

Before I could send her any kind of message asking her purpose, she flooded my mind with dark images of a presence in these caves, a creature that could come out of the walls. It was strong, fierce, and angry. Her image showed the mermaids, male and female, cowering to him, living deep down in burrows beneath this cove. Hundreds of them, with children, hiding from the world and held captive by the fear this monster evoked in them.

She lifted my head up so I could gulp air and then brought my face down again. I stared into her midnight eyes, and she sent me another vision. It was hurried, like she knew there was precious little time. This was of the waterfall. Of the mermaids holding a man underneath it until his body elongated and his legs sealed together. His toes turned black and then grew into a tail. His head rounded and enlarged, his black hair smoothing out and becoming his skin. When he became too heavy for the mermaids to hold, they let go. The newly created orca sped away from them, aiming for the deeper waters of the Pacific Ocean. The laughter of the rock monster behind them shook the earth. Fish rose to the surface, easy for the mermaids to catch and eat.

My mermaid lifted my head again to get air. She rose her own face up out of the water now, only high enough to keep her neck gills under. Her glance moved from my face to the men behind me.

"Is that what you're trying to do to Carter?"

I knew she didn't understand my words.

"She's not looking at Carter, honey," my dad said. "She's looking at me."

Now the mermaid grabbed my head again and pulled it toward her until our foreheads touched, her skin cold and clammy against mine. I could see my reflection in her dark eyes, and my own eyes seemed to glow back at me. One more vision worked its way into my mind. Another killer whale. This one swimming toward a small boat filled with people. He was trying to outrace a pod of mermaids and mermen. They were fast, but the orca was faster. He swam around the boat, trying to guard it.

The mermaids worked as a team and swam fast and hard at the boat, creating enough of a wave to knock the boat over, and the people in the water.

But not the right ones.

The mermaid sent a clear image of my father climbing back onto the boat with Randy and my mother. It was my father they wanted, not Carter. The mermaids backed away from the boat, watching as I resurfaced and tread water. They scrambled about, deliberating what they should do.

Carter surfaced then. Without hesitation, several mermaids pounced on the boy and hauled him away. My mermaid lingered behind, watching me on the boat trying to wrench myself free of the other people and dive back into the water. She waited until she was sure I would not need saving and then swam away.

She let go of me and slipped back into the water, her eyes watching the walls of the cave warily. I turned around to face my dad. "They want you, Dad. You're pure blood. They were hunting you, and the killer whale was Juarez attempting to stop them. He was trying to prevent them from getting you."

"We've got to get out of here," Dad said. "Now."

"There's no way out," Carter said, headed for the rock wall again. "You have to go through the water to get out, and they'll stop you. There are too many of them. There's no other opening except a small hole up above where sometimes rain water trickles through. It's the only water I've had. The only food I've had is the occasional raw fish that has been tossed up to me." He grimaced. "We're stuck here."

"Your mother, Naomi, and Greig are right outside the cave," Dad reminded me. "If we don't come out soon, they'll get help. We'll be okay."

"The mers block anyone who tries to come in," Carter said.

"You don't know that," Dad snapped at him. His voice bounced along the walls, and Carter flinched.

I noticed that he didn't say 'mermaids'. The creatures weren't all female so mer*maids* wasn't the most accurate name for them. After spending the past few days trapped with them in this cave, he knew better than I did what they should be called. I decided to adopt his new word. "The mers moved aside for my friend. Maybe she can lead us out."

"She can't," Carter said, "or she'd have done it by now."

"When did you get so negative?"

Carter sparked. "When I got trapped in here for... how many days has it been?"

"This is the fifth day since you disappeared," I mumbled, ashamed of myself for barking at him.

An earthquake rumbled mysteriously from one side of the cave to the other. Carter shivered and said, "He's here. Come on. We have to get up."

He began scrambling up the rock wall. Dad saddled my bare foot with his hands, boosted me up, and followed right after me. Only, the boulder supporting him suddenly pushed out of the wall as if automated or on some kind of track. It carried my dad on it toward the water. I slipped, and Carter grabbed my arm, holding onto me until I got my footing again.

With a horrible cracking and groaning that reverberated around the cave, the boulder vibrated and grew. It stretched until it morphed into a giant man made completely of stone. Not quite a man, really. A troll. Its massive hands had my father by his upper arms and looked like they could crush them without effort. He dangled my father over the water. The mers gathered, hands grasping hungrily for his feet.

I tugged away from Carter's grasp, and he didn't have the strength to hold onto me. He shouted at me to stop, but I jumped to the rock slab below and skidded to the sandbar at the troll's feet.

"Jolon!" I shouted, recalling the name from the vision. "Jolon, please stop."

The monster turned its giant head to look at me splayed out at his feet. I could see a distinctly American Indian face with a high forehead, long sharp nose, and pronounced cheekbones. The eyes were as much stone as the rest of him, and that frightened me. Its top lip curled into a sneer at the sight of me, and its sharp teeth resembled the stalactites around us.

I struggled to speak as I scrambled to my feet. "Please stop. That's my father. He hasn't done anything to you. Don't take him." My head only reached as high as his broad chest. Had he been a large man when human, or had the magic spell increased his mass?

Jolon didn't acknowledge me at all. I was but a pesky beetle to him. As if my father were a bag of dirty laundry, the troll dropped him into the fugue of mers and melted back into the stony ground.

Dad fought against the mers as their hands and arms tugged at him. I don't think they were trying to drown him, and that was in his favor. He lunged toward the sandbar. I grabbed my dad's arms, trying to pull him free. He scrabbled to his feet to get away, kicking at arms and faces until they backed off.

"June, watch out!" Carter had jumped off the rock wall and was almost to us. He pointed behind me. I flipped around to find the troll peeling out of the stone wall on the far side of me and reaching for me. I somersaulted past my father to get away, and the troll sank back into the wall again. I wondered if it was too hard to walk with all that weight, or if it was unable to get too far from the stone.

The sandbar was thin and short, and every inch of the cave was made of rock. It was impossible to get far enough away from the stone without diving into the middle of the pool. The tremor rushing past happened again, and this time the troll came at me from the other side of the cave. He was faster this time, clamping a massive arm around my torso and pulling me to him so tight I lost my breath. My ribs felt smashed, and my nose bashed against his stony pectorals, until it lowered its face toward mine and studied my features intensely.

"You look like her," he growled. "Isu."

My heart was in my throat. This was the moment where I could be crushed to death, and I wasn't sure which response would prevent that from happening. I tried my first thought, hoping it might prompt him into conversation and away from destruction. "You speak?" It was a question. An invitation.

"Yes."

"Your name is Jolon? Is that right?"

"Yes. Once. Long ago."

From behind me, I heard Carter, his tone full of unease. "What's happening? June?"

I didn't answer him. I didn't want to change the monster's focus back to either of the men. "Is Isu the girl you loved?"

"Yes. You are my Isu."

My whole body was rigid with fear. His arm pressed perpendicular to my spine made me hesitate to say anything. If I said 'No, I'm not' would he snap me in half, then kill Carter and turn my father into a killer whale? If I said yes, what would he do to me?

"I...I..."

A loud splash caught my attention. From the corner of my eye, I saw a mermaid tail slap the water. I thought it might have been my mermaid friend trying to help me. I turned my head a fraction, attempting to get a better look. Her fingers came out of the water and pressed against her temples. A vision. Of course. I needed to share something I knew with this beast.

I didn't want to, but I closed my eyes. I brought up my hands as high as I could and placed them on both sides of his barrel-sized trunk. It startled me to feel him breathing. For some reason, I thought him merely animated, not actually alive. With all the concentration I could muster, I focused on my memories of the Red Cedar tree. I shared the face in the trunk, the branches that thrashed about like arms, the warm, mysterious room inside it where I'd been trapped.

Jolon loosened his grip on me a little. It was difficult to read his expression. He didn't have the fine lines around his eyes, mouth, or forehead that I took for granted on human faces. His stony face was difficult to interpret as anything but angry.

"What is this?" he asked. He put a hand on my forehead. Stopping me from doing more visions? Or holding the place where they were stored? Either way, it was unexpectedly gentle, feeling like someone laid a bag of smooth stones on my head to relieve a headache. Although I couldn't stop from thinking how one swift movement would have that giant hand over my nose and mouth, smothering me, or how easily he could collapse my skull by simply squeezing.

"Isu's brother," I told him. "He's alive like you, trapped forever in a tree."

"How?"

"I don't know," I said. "I just thought you might want to know."

The grip around my body tightened again and pulled me off my feet. He shouted, the sound so close to my ears it was deafening. "I do not! I

204

wanted him dead. I wanted Tuari dead! I want them all dead!" The cave rumbled.

From the corner of my eye, I saw Carter skitter on the sandbar to keep from falling into the water. I forced myself not to turn my head away from Jolon. His voice was rich and deep. It entranced me to some degree, because the mermaid had never spoken to me and the tree had only whispered fragments of thoughts. Most of my communication with the mythical world had been done through wordless visions. As terrifying as his words were, I wanted to keep him talking, to learn as much as I could from him.

"The waterfall gave Tuari life and freedom, and it imprisoned me here. Forever. He taunted me, swimming out to the ocean, beyond the horizon, for days, weeks, and months at a time. Always he returned to her, to feel her presence in the tears that endlessly fall. I tried blocking the water from flowing, but it always broke through to get to him."

A grin spread across his face of stone, revealing more of those sharp granite teeth. "She couldn't protect him from me. He was foolish, and I learned my strength. While he showered in the waterfall, I grabbed him and held him high up on the wall where his hands could touch the ceiling of the cave. He couldn't breathe, and I held him until he was no more at last."

I shuddered, understanding that I was in the clutches of a man who had poisoned one friend and suffocated another. My life was meaningless to him, and any moment he could end it.

"My mistake was that I thrust his lifeless body at the waterfall, proclaiming that I had won and the curse was at last broken. Isu's tears increased as Tuari's broken body passed through her water. With magic no one could expect, his body burst into a thousand tiny silver swimming creatures that dashed away."

I had wondered how the mers evolved from one man. This made sense, if anything about magic could make sense.

"June, what's he saying to you? Can you understand him?" That was my father. I refused to separate my attention from Jolon to acknowledge him, but I wondered what Carter and Dad were hearing instead of the words that sounded clear and English in my ears.

"I was left alone for ages," Jolon continued, ignoring the pesky sounds coming from my father.

He seemed to feel a need to tell me his story, and I let him. I imagined that in all the eons that had passed since he had become this monster there had been no one to talk to at all.

"My anger continued to grow and boil. One day a young warrior found his way into this cave. He reminded me of Tuari, young and cocky. He climbed out of his canoe, and I reached out to grab him. I was about to snap his neck when that waterfall..." He snarled, rock dust coming out of his nose like smoke. "She started pouring. Why does she have to cry all the time?"

I trembled inside his hold. His anger was intensifying with every word, and the words "snap his neck" ricocheted in my brain. He lowered his face so close to mine we could have kissed, or he could have bitten off my nose.

"*Why!*" The word echoed around the cave. "She made me like this and trapped us here together. Why can she not accept me and be happy? If she'd stop crying all the time, maybe we could..." His voice softened, and his eyes roamed all over my features. "You look so much like her."

"Do I? Her brother, the tree, said the same thing. He called me his sister. He wanted me to stay with him."

A corner of the troll's lips lifted into a wicked grin. "Perhaps you should have."

I took in a shaky breath. "What happened to the warrior? The one that you were going to snap..." I couldn't finish my question.

"I decided to drown him instead," he answered. "I held him under her tears. The longer I held him there, the more she cried. He couldn't breathe. He was dying. Then he began to change. I thought he would turn into a merman like Tuari, and I pulled him out of the water before that happened. It was too late. The transformation had begun. It was marvelous to watch the agony of his body twisting and contorting."

"He became a killer whale," I said.

"Yes, and it was glorious. Every warrior that made the mistake of entering this cave from that day since became mine to transform." His smile faded. He unwrapped his arm from my back but still held me firmly by the upper arm while he gestured at the water with his now free hand. "Until *they* ruined it. Tuari's spawn communicated with the killer whales and returned, full grown, and found ways to distract new warriors away from my lair."

"But they work for you," I said. "I thought they brought the men to you."

"They do now," he said. "A great wave came across the ocean. It was higher than the cliffs, and it drove all the mermaids into the lagoon and into my cave. I trapped the ones who dared to enter, and the ones who stayed outside begged for their release. I made them a deal, one warrior for each of their friends. Many of the people were killed by the great wave, and it took years, centuries, for the mermaids to bring me enough warriors to even the trade."

I heard Carter groaning somewhere behind me. I didn't dare look. My dad could tend to him.

"That exchange with the mermaids is over now. Why are they still serving you?"

"You did that," Jolon said. "*Man* did that. Man began poisoning them. Hunting them. Killing them. The mermaids no longer wanted to protect the men. They came to me, telling me of a great trap where many of them died. They are more than willing to help me now, and they bring me warriors of their own volition."

"No," I said, my heart clenching. "No, they don't understand. They aren't bringing you the men who trapped them. They're bringing innocent men. I stopped the men who trapped them."

"*You* did? A girl? You lie."

"It's true."

"Fine! Explain it to them yourself."

He swung me out over the water, holding me by my arm. It burned under his tight grip, and I feared it was about to break as he leaned me forward, face toward the water. The webbed hands reached for me, brushing my face and body eagerly. Before I could touch the water with my free hand and send even the smallest message to them, he jerked me back to my feet. I heard Carter and Dad shouting my name desperately.

"I'm okay," I cried back to them and immediately wished I hadn't.

Jolon looked over my head at them, his eyes hungry as they settled on Dad. "The fair one is not a warrior. He is not of true blood. The other one is old, but he will do."

207

"No!" I said, pounding my fists on his chest, something he probably couldn't even feel. "Please! No! Keep me instead. You said I look like Isu. I can be Isu for you. I'll stay here if you let them go!"

The troll cupped my chin and held my face up, inspecting my features again. "You look so much like her, it's true." He brought my face to his and pressed his hard lips to mine. The inside lining of my lips ground against my teeth. His face was so much larger than mine, that his lips covered my nose as well, and I couldn't breathe.

From behind me I heard Carter yelling something brave and heroic, some threat that he couldn't possibly follow through on.

The monster pulled back his face, but he was not smiling. The kiss, if that's what it could be called, brought him no joy. "You love that boy over there. You will leave me for him."

"No. I promise. Just let them go."

His hand still cupped my chin. He ran his gaze over my face, and I thought he would try to kiss me again. I braced myself for the sensation, but he merely ran his hard thumb across the skin under my eyes. "You look like Isu, but you have blue eyes. You are not full-blooded." All at once he pulled his hand away, my chin dropping so fast my neck popped. "You are not her. You cannot be her or replace her. She is a waterfall, and I will make her cry today!"

He dropped me and melted into the slab at my feet. I spun around. "Dad! Watch out! He's coming for you!"

What could my father do? He couldn't climb up the walls. He couldn't dive in the water. He was trapped, and if I didn't figure out something fast, my dad would be turned into a killer whale.

Chapter Eighteen

In a flash, the troll expelled himself from the ground behind my father, scooped him up, and flung him into the pool of waiting mermaids. I barely had time to shriek before the multitude of hands latched onto his body and submerged him. Had he even had time to take a breath? God, I hoped so. It was a long way to the cave opening. He'd drown before… Before what? Before they thrust him under that waterfall?

I spun away from the sight of the now dark and empty pool, wanting to attack the monster, beat on him with my fists, demanding him to spare my father. Only, Jolon was gone. He'd vanished as quickly as he'd appeared.

Carter saw my dismay and dashed to my side. He put his arms around me and spoke into my hair. "It's gone. It can go anywhere in the rocks and lining of the cave. It'll be there at the waterfall waiting for them."

"We have to go," I said. "We have to stop them."

"How?"

I lifted my face to look at his. His eyes were so tired and dull, his cheeks too hollow, his lips cracked and dry. He could never swim through that underwater cave opening. He touched my lips with his dry fingertip, and I flinched. Jolon's kiss had bruised them. "What were you saying to him? Do you know that you weren't speaking English? Your dad said he thought you might be speaking an ancient version of the language from this region."

"I didn't know I was doing that. It sounded English to me."

I had every intention of relating the whole conversation with Carter but not right then. My only concern at that moment was escape.

I pointed toward the ceiling of the cave. "What about that hole up there, where you said the rain water and the light come through? Could we make it bigger somehow? Crawl through?"

"No. It's too high up and too small."

I nodded resolutely. I squeezed his forearms as I told him, "You stay here. I'll swim for it. I swear I'll send help back for you." Before he could tell me not to, I ran and jumped into the water. The glacier cold water cut right through the wet suit and immediately chilled me. I'm sure my lips turned as blue as my new eyes. I treaded water and waved weakly at Carter.

He stood there, his shoulders hunched over, one hand on his hip. "Hey," he called to me. "I love you, you know."

I wanted desperately to believe this wasn't the last time I'd see him, but I had my doubts either of us would survive this day. I might drown on my own, or the mermaids might help me out with that. Jolon would come back and put an end to Carter now that he was no longer a lure for us.

With a forced smile, I said, "You know what? Tell me that sometime when we're back in Olympia snuggled on a couch, okay?"

"You can count on it."

I gulped in a breath and dove under the water. Again, my new eyesight allowed me to see well under the water and grasp how deep the hole went with other openings further down leading to a labyrinth of tunnels. I swam toward the entrance, but before I got to it a thick, silver tail wrapped around my legs, stopping me. I tried pushing it off and squeezing out of the grasp, but it had me as tight as an anaconda. The mermaid pulled me back away from the tunnel that would lead me out and toward the shore, dumping me once again on the sandbar. The tail slid back into the water, and a face appeared above the water line.

It was my friend.

"I have to give you a name one of these days," I said once I caught my breath. "I know you don't understand, but I'm trying to get out of this cave, not stay here." I pointed and gestured, but she showed no sign of comprehension. Instead, she did her own pointing and gesturing. She pointed at Carter and curled her fingers for him to come forward. She put her finger to her face and then toward the direction we needed to go. She was going to help us. At least, that's what I decided she was telling us.

"You're back quickly," Carter said, coming down to join me.

"Looks like you're coming with me after all."

"That's the way I prefer it. Remember, I said I didn't want to ever spend a day without you, and I've broken my promise."

A lump hardened in my throat. "You can make it up to me," I whispered. "Just survive this."

"I'll try."

We held hands and slid back into the water. His body went instantly rigid from the cold, and in seconds his breathing became very shallow. This was too dangerous. He wasn't going to survive. I gave him a concerned look, and he just raised his eyebrows at me in resignation and took a huge breath. Then he lowered his head completely under the water. I copied him.

My mermaid weaved her arm under his and around his back, getting a tight hold on him. She held me only by the hand. With the power of her tail, she thrust us forward so much faster than I could ever imagine swimming. It wasn't as lightning quick as I remember moving with the multitude of mermaids, but it was a phenomenal speed. Still, the tunnel was long, and my air was beginning to run out. It took tremendous concentration to keep from opening my mouth and taking in the water. I couldn't see much of Carter on the far side of the mermaid, only his arms and legs dangling limply below her. I felt her adjust her body to keep him tightly attached to her. I assumed he wasn't much more than a heavy rag doll to her at this point. I prayed that he also was still holding on to that last milligram of air in his lungs.

Finally, we burst through the tunnel opening and broke the surface. It was lighter in the cave now that the sun had come over to this side of the mountain. The small cave was frantic with commotion. The bulk of the noise and bustle came from over by the waterfall. I saw Jolon half in and half out of the wall right behind the waterfall, laughing wickedly as the mers held my father under the shower, their tails flapping. Dad hollered through his gurgling. On the far side of the opening, Mom stood pressed against the wall as tightly as she could, her face frozen in horror as she watched her husband tortured.

Beside me, Carter, lifeless on his back, balanced on the mermaid's arms.

Too many things to try to fix, and no time to do it. No *way* to do it. Why did I think I could be hero? I was just an eighteen-year-old girl who dropped out of high school. I didn't know how to save someone from drowning, or stop a mob of mercreatures, or defeat a man made of anger and stone. I didn't know how to prevent a waterfall of magical grief from changing my father into a killer whale. All of the emergencies swirled in my brain, and I felt an overwhelming desire to let myself sink with the despair of it all.

"June!"

My mother's voice. Her calling my name. So many times she'd shouted my name in frustration or impatience. So many times have I heard her say my name with disdain or bitterness. Not now, though. Now it rang out with a strange mix of desperation and hope. She and I were still alive, and we could accomplish something together.

"Mom! I'm okay! Help me!"

The water level in here had risen considerably in the time that had passed. The mass of all the bodies in it displaced it, too. Mom was higher up on the wall, more where Dad had been when he came in here the day before. I wondered for a split second why he wasn't trapped by Jolon then. He'd been like a mouse with a foot on the trap. The flattest place was right over the tunnel opening where there was a smooth but gentle slope. I pointed to it. "Can you get there? I'm going to bring Carter over. He's not breathing. Can you help him?"

Mom nodded and began moving along the wall. Her fingers were red, and I saw that she left bloody fingerprints behind her. She'd been holding onto that wall this whole time, waiting for us to re-emerge.

With the mermaid's help, we lifted Carter up onto the rock. He began to slip back into the water, but I climbed up enough to help settle him into place. Mom hugged me tightly when she got to me, and even though it felt so good, I couldn't allow that moment to last. I tore myself from her arms and jumped back into the water. I saw her get to her knees and immediately begin CPR on my boyfriend.

I wanted to watch to make sure it worked. Not a choice. Dad screamed in pain. I saw his back arch painfully and unnaturally then rubber-band back again. The metamorphosis was beginning. I had to convince the mers to stop. But how? I dove under the water and locked eyes on my mermaid friend. I touched my head, and she touched hers. Would it be enough?

Holding hands, she and I swam toward the mob. We each reached out with our free hands and touched the backs of the nearest ones. I took the lead and concentrated on my memories. I started with the memory of the mers escaping from the giant Affron aquarium, hoping to remind them that I was there and responsible for them being released. The mermaid under my hand turned sharply toward me and snarled, her face anything but peaceful or beautiful.

That memory wasn't going to work. From their perspective, I was in that room watching them trapped in the tank. I wasn't the one who opened it. I wasn't the one ushering them out. Their memories of me weren't as their rescuer at all. How could I show them otherwise? And I needed to not only win them over to help me but to see that Dad was a hero, too, one worth saving.

I backed away and peeked up at my mom. She was sitting back on her feet, Carter lying on his side on the far side of her. I noticed one of her hands was stroking his matted hair. I don't think she would be doing that if he were past saving. Okay. Good. One thing done.

"Mom!" I cried. "Is Naomi still up there?" I point to the cave's roof.

She shouted back, "Yes, I think so. I told Greig to get help, but she stayed."

I swam sideways, trying to squeeze past the throng of slapping tails and out of the cave opening. The afternoon sunlight blinded me, and I had to cup a hand over my eyes to see. Naomi was perched atop the waterfall, her face a mask of horror. I called her name several times before I caught her attention.

"You're alive! Oh! Oh! You're alive! What's happening?" The panic was clear.

"I need your help! Get as many rocks as you can and try to stop the flow of the waterfall. Can you do that?" She immediately began stuffing stones into the crevice from where waterfall spouted. The stream narrowed and then stopped. Naomi smiled at me, but the joy was short lived. A roar came from inside the cave, and then the rocks Naomi had so neatly positioned blasted out of the crevice like cannonballs. I ducked as they rocketed over my head, smashing into water of the inlet.

Naomi's eyes were wide, and I noticed her nursing one of her hands and bringing red knuckles to her lips. Her hand must have been resting near the stones before they exploded. I put up my hands to keep her calm. "Okay. Okay. That didn't work." I considered a different plan. To Naomi I redirected, "Do it again, but *not* with rocks! He can control those! Get wood! Tree branches! Sticks! Build a dam! Quick as you can!"

She jumped to her feet and began gathering up anything she could find. I let her work at that task and swam back to my mermaid. We were going to have to try this again. I pointed at my head then pointed at hers. I repeated it a couple times. My memory. Her memory. I hoped she understood what I was trying to say.

Once again, I concentrated. I went to my first memories of the mermaids, finding the three bodies writhing in the sand, covered with oil. I recalled approaching them cautiously, kneeling beside them, and just as I was about to touch one, her eyes opening.

I stopped my memory and looked at my mermaid friend, imploring her to understand. She closed her eyes, and there was a strange sensation of vertigo as the view of the memory switched directions.

Hazy glimpses fading in and out of the sand around my face, the water lapping against my tail, the bodies of her sisters beside me. Against the blackness of my closed eyelids, the wheezing of our breaths and the crunching sound of something approaching. Fear forcing my eyes open again, revealing a face right in front of hers, both terrified and concerned. I was looking at my own face through her eyes. My father's face came into view. The emotions running through this moment were not of alarm but of desperation. Could these humans help?

Her vision stopped. It was my turn again. I recalled holding her in my arms as my father shot the video explaining our discovery. I remembered him and me carrying the mermaids to the truck.

She recalled me wiping the oil away from her gills but still struggling to breathe. She shared the sensation of feeling safe in my arms and hopeful as my father and I carried her across the sand and up the hill.

Finally, I thought of the Marine Animal Rescue Center and the giant tank. I pushed this memory as hard as I could, the one where Carter and my father lifted my mermaid up and into the tank, saving her life. Her color returning to normal as she became able to breathe once more.

My mermaid's visions were again hazy. She had been struggling so close to death at this point. The shortest of glimpses revealed my father's face and Carter's face above her, their arms holding her carefully, tenderly. They gently lowered her into the water that was too warm, but still comfortable. And then, at last, a gasp to fill her gills and lungs. She was alive!

This whole time I had refused to weaken my concentration in order to see how or if the mers were accepting these visions. I turned my head toward them now. The mers as a group had settled down, and the water around us had stilled considerably. I lowered my face under the water to find all of their faces staring at us. The one I had laid my hand on rolled around and caressed my face. Others reached out to my mermaid friend and me, drawing us through their cluster, each one taking a turn to touch me and acknowledge that they understood now. Carter, my dad, and I were their rescuers, not their enemies.

I lifted my head for a breath and discovered they had brought me to my father. The waterfall had been blocked to all but a trickle, stopping the progress of my father's transformation. He was no longer screaming, but he was limp in their arms. The torture had worn him out.

Jolon broke away from the wall, reaching for my father's legs. "If you can't hold him, I will!"

The mers slid my father away in time, moving toward the center of the pool.

No, that won't work, I thought. Jolon could go anywhere in this cave. *There had to be a way to get away from him.*

To prove me right, Jolon blended back into the wall of the cave. A moment later I felt water pressure against my dangling feet. He was coming up from below. There was no time to linger and think it through.

I grabbed the hands of the two nearest mers, two male ones. I looked toward the cave opening and the lagoon beyond it and pushed them in that direction. They enveloped my father in their strong, silver arms and swam him out of the cave a breath before Jolon's massive arms came up to grab him. Furious, he lashed out toward me, but I was faster than him. I swam away and dove under the water.

Jolon was bigger than a real man, but he wasn't tall enough to touch the ground and have his face above the water. He must have launched himself from the ground to try to get my father. We'd have to be quick before he connected to rock again. I caught the eyes of several of the mermaids and pointed to Jolon's feet. The weight of the rock monster's body made him sink fast.

The mers clustered around his legs, lifting them up and tipping the troll over. Other mers swarmed around his arms and torso, pinning his arms to his sides before he could bat any of them away or get his hands on anything made of stone. This collection of silver arms, bodies and flapping tails pushed the heavy man of rock through the cave's entrance. The passage to the lagoon was narrow and pocked with jagged rocks, so some of the mers had to let go.

Jolon writhed against them, but the mers were strong and determined. They took him past my father, who was now recovering on a smooth, flat stone above the waterline. They got him past the rocks where I'd said my farewell to Juarez. I thought they might leave him in that deep pool where Juarez died, but they continued to carry him all the way past the sea stacks and the Fuca Pillar to the open sea. Then they let him go.

I wanted to swim out there and use my new magic eyes to see if he would merely sink to the bottom, reconnect to the earth and come back. Knowing how fast he could move through rock, I waited. People were shouting my name. Naomi, my parents, Carter. The mers were making celebratory squeals, sounding like joyful dolphins. Still, I waited, hoping they were right to cheer but afraid they weren't.

The waterfall gave Tuari life and freedom, and it imprisoned me here. Forever.

My legs were about to give out from all the treading water and swimming. I stroked over to the cliff outside of what was left of the waterfall where I could hold onto something. I continued to stare out at the ocean, and it became clear to me at last. Jolon wasn't coming back.

Naomi's voice broke through all the noise now that I was closer to her. "June, the waterfall is about to run out."

I glanced up at her and saw that despite all the craziness that had just occurred, she had a profound sadness on her face at the loss of her beloved waterfall. She was moving all the sticks and branches out of the way, but it didn't change the flow of water at all.

"It's Tuari," I called up to her. "His name wasn't Torren, like you think. It was Tuari, and she…" I put my fingers in the trickle of tears, and now the tears did not feel like ones of sadness. They were of joy and love. She was ready to be done mourning. "Her name is Isu."

"Isu," Naomi repeated, smiling. "I love that."

An idea came to me. "Hey. Do you have a water bottle?" She tossed down a bottle from her pack, and I poured out what was left in it. I stuck it under the trickle of waterfall that remained and filled it. As I capped the bottle, the trickle dwindled even further until it became nothing but drops and finally went dry.

"She's gone," I whispered.

Once more I looked out to sea, sure this time we were safe. To my even greater joy I saw the Coast Guard ship pulling into view. At the sight of the ship, the mercreatures sank below the water and disappeared. I dipped my body under the water to watch them swim away, but I couldn't see anything more than a few inches from my face. My magic vision was gone.

I got back up and leaned around the edge of the cave opening to see my mother and Carter sitting upright on that sloping ledge. I gave them a thumbs-up and pointed at the horizon. Mom gave me a thumbs-up back.

"Guess you've seen some magic now."

"More than enough for one lifetime," she shouted back. "I'm all done, thank you."

I put a hand to my heart and then opened it up toward Carter. He smiled. Oh, his beautiful smile! He grabbed my flying heart to bring into his body and nestle with his own.

Chapter Nineteen

The Coast Guard sent Dad and Carter in a helicopter straight to a hospital in Seattle. Mom, Naomi, and I were checked over at the station in Neah Bay and released that evening. After many thank yous and hugs to Naomi and Greig, and buying three copies of her novel, we drove through the night to get to Seattle. Mom paid for a cheap motel so we could get a quick nap and showers before heading over to the hospital.

Dad was signing release papers when we got to his room. Mom had a hot coffee and some donuts for him, which he took hungrily from her.

"There are going to be a lot of questions," Mom said as he devoured his food.

"I know," he said through a mouthful of donut. "The police have already been here, and I didn't give them very satisfactory answers as to what we were doing up there."

I piped in then, "Our story to the Coast Guard was pretty weak, too."

"I told them we were looking for more evidence about what might have killed that orca," Mom said. "We couldn't come up with anything brilliant to explain how we found Carter. We'll all need to put our heads together soon and come up with something that sounds logical."

"Yeah," I said. "Angry mermaids bent on revenge against mankind and ruled by a rock monster in a hidden underground cave probably won't fly."

A nurse came in and told Dad that he could get dressed and handed him his plastic bag of clothes. Mom took the bag and handed him some of the clean clothes we had in the car. We went into the corridor as Dad dressed, and I approached the nurses' station to ask about Carter and what room he was in. I told Mom I'd be right back and headed down the hall.

Carter's parents were in the room when I arrived. His mom was sitting in the guest chair, her purse in her lap while her fingers fidgeted with the strap. His father stood at the foot of the bed, his shoulders rounded and his hands on the metal railing. Carter's face was clean but covered with scratches and bruises. He still needed a shave, and his hair was still a nasty, tangled mess. His eyes were closed, and he slept peacefully. An I.V. bag, probably of saline and maybe some morphine or other painkiller, was attached to his arm.

I couldn't quite read the expression on Mr. Crowe's face. There was concern, but I still felt waves of anger and hatred coming toward me, like this was all my fault. "He hasn't woken since we got here," he told me.

"He was in a cave for five days and sleeping in a tiny hole in a wall. I imagine he's tired. Plus, the drugs." I pointed at the I.V. tentatively. I wasn't saying anything he didn't know.

Carter's mom looked at her husband and then cautiously to me before saying, "We thought he was dead. Everyone thought it. We had planned the funeral. It was supposed to be tomorrow. People are already arriving…"

She broke into sobs. Mr. Crowe lowered his head and shook it, out of ideas for how to comfort her.

I knelt beside her and slipped her hand between mine. "Well, now you can have a family reunion party instead. Won't that be nice? I bet you've been talking about doing that for years."

She gave me the sweetest, most grateful smile through her tears. Her mouth was so similar to Carter's, and they shared the same twinkling blue eyes. "I have. You know? I have talked about that with my mother and my sisters so many times." I handed her a tissue, and she dabbed at her eyes. "Thank you."

I wasn't sure if the gratitude was for the tissue, the comfort, the idea, or for finding her son. I accepted it regardless.

I stood up. "Will you let me know when he wakes up? My dad's being released, and they're going to want to head home, I'm sure."

I was almost out of the room, when Mr. Crowe's voice caught me. "Juniper, how did you know he was still alive?"

"I couldn't accept otherwise," I told him. "There was no reason to believe he was alive, and everyone told me I was wrong. I just *knew*."

219

Mrs. Crowe looked at her son as she said to me, "You two must share something very special."

All of the magic and mystery of the last half year flooded through me, and part of me wanted to share it with her so she could truly understand our connection. Instead, I said simply, "Yes, we do."

I joined my parents in the lobby, and they took me home.

* * * *

Carter was released the following day, and by then I had a brand new cell phone to use. Haley had come with my parents and me to the store to make sure Dad and I got the best possible ones, and she spent a lot of the afternoon downloading apps for me and teaching me how to use them. She reminded me constantly that the internet service at our house still sucked, and my parents had to do something about it. I reminded her that my dad didn't really earn any significant income at his job, and my mom had to win another case before we'd even have grocery money. She just sighed at me and plugged in the password to the Wi-Fi for her house.

I wasn't allowed to see Carter right away, because his mom took me up on my idea and held a big party for his family that had all come to town for the funeral. I wasn't invited. Carter tried to appease me by saying it was only family, no friends, but I still felt jilted after having saved his life and all.

"I know what you did for me," he reminded me during a Facetime session that morning before the party. "They do, too. They're just… my parents."

"Well, if you can sneak away at all, I'm going up to the tree around four this afternoon. I'd love it if you could be there."

* * * *

It was Saturday afternoon. My dad drove, Mom in the passenger seat, Haley and I in the back. We were all eager to see what would happen when we got there. I had called Uncle Nathan and Grandfather to come as well. Ronnie was still in casts and couldn't make the walk. I doubted that was the whole truth and figured he'd never go near the tree again after the beating he'd taken from it.

We all gathered around the tree as the sun lowered in the sky casting an amber glow to the forest. The red hue of the tree was vibrant in this light. I was grateful that the sky was clear of rainclouds so we could fully appreciate the glory of this moment. With everyone watching, I stepped up to the trunk of the tree and put my forehead and palms against it. I shared the memories of what had happened to his friends and his sister both in the past and present. The tree shuddered at the tale of the fight on the ledge and moaned at the news of his sister jumping to her death. Its branches sagged visibly as the story continued about the evil Jolon exacting his anger out on the unassuming warriors that had come into his trap and the terrible deal he'd made with the mers. By the time the story was done, I could feel the relief and sadness pouring out of the tree.

The bark of the trunk softened beneath my hands, and I felt myself sinking into it. I tried not to panic, although I feared it was gearing up to trap me inside again. If I was all that was left of the story, maybe he wanted to keep me always with him. Then I heard his voice.

Thank you.

The tree folded around my body like a soft pillow. It wasn't trapping me. It was hugging me the only way a massive tree could.

"I have something for you," I said, pressing my face sideways against the tree the same way I might if I were hugging my father. "Let me get it."

The tree relaxed its hold. Behind me, I heard a collective intake of breath from my family. I bet it was a little disconcerting to them to see me halfway disappear into a tree trunk.

I reached out a hand toward all of them. "The bottle."

Dad stepped forward, unscrewed the top, and handed me the water bottle. The smell of the salt water attacked my nose, and my heart began to race. All of the terror from that afternoon was still so fresh. I twisted around to see all their expectant faces. Uncle Nathan was rocking back and forth on his feet, and I worried he might fall over. Haley had her phone up, ready to catch a video if anything happened. Grandfather had a hand over his heart like it was some sacred moment, and Mom had her hands to her mouth as if stopping any doubts from bursting out.

"I don't know if this will work or what it will do," I warned them.

I tipped the bottle and poured it out along the base of the tree, walking slowly around the perimeter. I only got three quarters of the way around before the water ran out. If I thought the tree was radiant before, I was wrong. I could see the effects of the water immediately as the water sucked up through the rings and ever upward toward the crown. It was a drop compared to the amount of water a tree of this size needed to survive, and yet all the colors of the bark and the pine needles became so vibrant. The branches stiffened so that the birds up near the top squawked and flew away, disturbed by the motion.

I heard a rustling in the moss and mulch, and then my family began calling me. "June. Hurry. Come here."

I dashed around the tree to them, to find Amelia, my aunt, emerging from the tree in exactly the spot where I'd been standing moments before. She still wore her tight jeans and crop top T-shirt, just as I remembered her. Her hair was still in the braid I'd done for her up in the tree over a month ago. The smile on her face was broad and full of joy. She came completely free of the tree, stepped over a protruding root on the ground and walked toward all of us.

"You're all here," she said cheerily.

Nathan and my father stepped toward her. Nathan took her hand into his and rubbed his thumb along the back of it. "You're real."

"Of course I am, silly," she giggled.

Dad reached out a hand and ran it over her head, a motion he'd done to me many times in my life. That made her giggle more.

"Are you... Can you stay with us now?" Dad asked.

She looked back at the tree, used to needing permission from it, and then after a beat returned her attention to her brothers. "I'm not sure. He's gone." One would think she'd be elated, having earned her freedom after decades of being trapped, but instead she looked a little lost. A little helpless.

I came closer to her. "Amelia? Are you okay?"

She gave me a half smile. "Junie. I'm okay. I just..." She squinted up at the sky. "I can't get to the top of the tree anymore."

"I know," I said. "I'm sorry. I think that's my fault."

Nathan squeezed her hand. "But you have the ground now. You have us. You can come home with us. We'll take care of you."

My dad nodded. "Whatever you need."

I wondered what it would be like to have an aunt my age that had been trapped inside a tree for thirty years living in my house. How would she adapt? How could I help her adjust to the new world that had changed so much since she'd vanished?

"I'd like that, but..."

She took a step backward, taking her hand away from Nathan. Her hands searched behind her for the safety of the tree trunk.

"You'll be safe," Dad reassured her.

"We want you with us," Nathan added.

"But I don't belong here anymore."

She touched the tree, and it didn't do what she expected. She spun around and frantically ran her hands along the trunk. She pressed the balls of her bare feet against it. I think she was trying to get back inside, but the tree wasn't magic anymore. Now it was just a really old tree.

I went up to her and put an arm around her to calm her down. She collapsed into my side and began to cry. I held her and looked over her gently bobbing head at my father and uncle. Their faces were torn with grief and confusion.

"Why don't you want to be with us?" Nathan asked, his voice almost like a child's. "It's all I want. It's all I've ever wanted. You to come home."

She whispered into my ear so only I could hear her. "I can't come with them. Please tell them. I can't look at their faces. It hurts too much."

"Why?" I asked.

"I don't know," she whined. "But I feel it coming. It tingles."

"Please, Amelia," Nathan said. "Look at us."

Dad's voice cracked as he said, "Amelia. We love you. We want to see you."

I whispered to her. "Just give them one more moment. That's all."

Her eyes met mine. "It's all I have."

I helped her face them, and they stepped toward us so she wouldn't have to leave the comfort of the tree. She put a hand on each of their cheeks. Tears rolled down her face. "My little brothers. Be good, okay?" She turned sharply to me. "Oh, the tingles, Junie! They're so strong! So many tingles! They tickle!"

Then as if she were made of a billion stars, she twinkled bright and vanished into the night.

The forest was still without the tree spirit and the ghost that kept him company. The birds refused to chirp. The bugs refused to click. Even the wind refused to blow. We couldn't see the sun, as it had dipped far below the tree line, and it was getting dark.

Nathan turned on me. "This is your fault. You shouldn't have poured out that bottle."

"My fault? I just brought peace to a spirit that's been trapped in that tree for hundreds of years."

"I'll never see her again! At least when the spirit was in there, I had the chance to still see her or communicate with her through you." He pounded his fists on the trunk of the tree. "Now it's over."

Dad looked at me and his brother and then walked away. He was thinking the same thing but didn't want to say anything.

Mom was the one who spoke up. "You selfish men. How dare you blame June for this! You wanted to keep your sister trapped forever in a tree just so you could say hello once in a while? That is the most heartless thing I've ever heard. I'm ashamed of both of you, especially you, Peter!"

He acted shocked that she would say that to him, because he hadn't uttered a word.

"Oh, stop," she said to him. "I know you were thinking it." She came over and hugged me as tightly as she could. "Thanks to your daughter, Amelia's spirit is free. That tree was a prison. She can go on now to where she needs to be. It was the right thing to do."

"Thanks, Mom," I said weakly.

Haley piped up. "I agree with Mrs. Sawfeather. June is a hero."

I smiled at her for trying even though I knew her vote didn't matter. She looked back at her phone's screen to avoid eye contact with any of the adults.

Grandfather spoke slowly then. "I also agree with Natalie. Juniper saved Amelia from a terrible fate. My daughter can now go to the great beyond and join her mother. I have never been so..." He struggled for the right word and finally said, "...grateful."

I left my mother's arms to go hug my grandfather.

Dad and Nathan looked at each other for a long hard moment and then smiles broke across their faces. They began to laugh, Dad throwing back his head with some mixture of joy and relief. They came together in a big bear hug with lots of slapping on each other's backs. No words were said, but I knew as their laughter ebbed that they were going to be all right.

"I have an idea," I said. I pulled a box cutter out of my pocket. "I normally despise people who do this and seriously want to hurt them, but I brought this just in case." I handed the knife to my dad.

After getting nods of approval from Nathan and Grandfather, Dad began carving into the trunk of the tree. He wrote Amelia and carved a heart around it. When he was done, he handed the knife to me, brushed off his hands, and said to his brother, "You still promise not to cut down this tree?"

Nathan patted Dad's back and left his hand there as they took in the sight of the tree. "Never, Peter. Never." Then he asked me, "Did we ever determined how the murdered warrior became a tree in the first place?"

I glanced at Grandfather and he nodded at me to answer. "After talking it through with both Grandfather and Naomi, we decided that the prayer Isu's father made to the twin gods of the sun and moon transformed her brother, too. It explains why the myth says that the three warriors were granted wishes by the sun. It's also why I wondered if his sister's tears might help him."

Haley took a bunch of pictures of us around the heart, and then we all walked out of the forest. We stopped in our old pathetic protest campground and lit a small bonfire. As night came on, we sat around in the dirt listening to the three men tell all the stories they remembered about Amelia. Carter came to join us after a bit, and he brought some snacks and drinks from his reunion party with him. We all stayed late into the night laughing, singing, and happy to all be alive.

Chapter Twenty

I'd say things went back to normal come Monday morning, but they didn't. My parents got back to work on the water pollution case up in San Juan Strait. Haley continued at school. Carter and I returned to work at the pet store. Other things were different. We all had a restlessness that couldn't be cured. Without all the action, everything seemed dull. It affected Carter and me the most, and we leaned against the counter in the fish section of the store one afternoon after my shift talking about it. The darkness of that area of the store gave us the illusion of being more private than we were.

"I've missed too many classes to catch up," Carter was telling me.

"It was only one week."

"It's not high school, June. Missing one college class is like missing a whole week of high school."

"I'm sure your professors will understand…" He interrupted me with an exasperated sigh, and then I got it. "You don't want to go back, do you? Are you dropping out for good?"

"Not for good. Just for the rest of the semester. I need time to think."

"About what?"

"What I want to do with the rest of my life. I almost died in that cave. I should have. Now I just feel like I want to do more than I originally planned."

I intertwined my fingers with his. "You're already amazing. You were an intern at a marine rescue center your freshman year of college. Who does that?"

"I'm not doing it anymore. I want to find something else like that. Something more than selling goldfish to snotty kids who are just going to forget to feed them."

I laughed and leaned in to him, whispering, "I swear the Hennick family has been in this store at least once a week since I started."

"Oh, I know," he laughed. "I almost feel like we should have an official waiting period between buying fish. We could put up a sign right here." He spread his hands to display where the sign should be over the counter.

"Or maybe they should be required to show a picture of their existing tank to prove the conditions are inhabitable."

We were laughing too loud, because Paul gave us a cross look as he passed on the way to the back office.

"He's going to kick me out soon."

"I know."

We held hands again and looked at each other as we quieted again.

"I also know what you mean about doing something more. I've almost died a couple times, too."

He wrapped his arms around me and pulled me tight to him, his cheek against my forehead. "Whatever happens, I want to be with you."

"Every day," I said.

"Like I promised."

We kissed under the blue lights of the aquariums until Paul cleared his throat that it was enough already. I said goodbye to Carter and promised to call him later.

Haley continued to evolve in her new role as School Rebellion Leader. A couple weeks after the big rescue, she cut her hair short and got some magenta highlights. I was kind of surprised her mother let her do this until I saw that she had a streak of purple in her hair, too. Haley came home from school one afternoon bursting with so much news she almost launched herself out of her window and into mine. She and a bunch of her friends were going to host an Anti-Prom party, and they were petitioning to add more members to the Student Council for the following year. There was more, but I had a hard time keeping up with it all.

We had been working together a lot. With her help, I'd taken over Juarez's website. It started after I decided to go onto the forums and let everyone know that TruthBeKnown had been killed at sea when searching for evidence of the rock monsters and mermaids. I told them I had no idea if he ever found what he was looking for, but I really hoped he did. All the regulars popped on to say a nice word about him. Soon the questions began, wondering if the website would be shut down now that he was gone. Before I knew it, I was being nominated for the task of keeping ???SCIENCE OR FICTION??? going.

The usual voices that claimed I was a fake and phony chimed in, but the majority of the group voted that I was the best choice. Clearly, they didn't know about my ridiculously bad computer skills or the fact that I wasn't exactly that interested in writing blog posts about the possibility of mythical creatures in our world.

I told Carter and Haley what was happening, and they both were jazzed about the idea. Haley offered to help me give the website a new look and make the interface easy to change and add stuff. Together, we created a sharp-looking site, and I found some legitimate articles from news sites to quote in my initial welcome article. From that point on, we treated it like a creative writing assignment, taking turns writing stories. Even her new boyfriend, Leon, got on board. He was really good at writing the stories. I added some of my art, too, because I got back to sketching in the afternoons while I'd wait for Carter to get off work. Haley was already courting advertising offers.

Some of the old members left, saying it was just a fiction site now and they wanted to find a group that took them seriously, but we more than doubled that amount in new followers. It wound up being really fun and something I looked forward to doing each evening. We even held an online wake for Juarez one evening, and it was pretty special. Chuck Emory logged on for a bit to join in with some stories of his own from when they worked together at the news station.

Chuck convinced Channel 4 News to do a brief tribute to Juarez as well. They did a montage of some of his best stories. I have to admit I was a little disappointed they left out the mermaid story, being the last and probably biggest one he'd ever done for them. Although, when the montage ended, the handsome news anchor, who was known for going off script willy-nilly, said, "Lost at sea. Hmm. That really is too bad. For anyone else I'd be really sad right now, but somehow I feel like Juarez found what he was looking for."

The pretty female anchor nodded her head vacantly, saying, "I hope so, Doug. I hope so," while completely unaware of what her partner was referring to. "Coming up next, a donut shop is in the *hole*. Financially, that is. See what sweet new treat might bring them out of debt and how you can get one!"

I remember texting "thanks" to Chuck and him texting "sorry" back. I haven't heard from him since.

Now, while putting too much trust in the strength of her window screen, Haley whistled to pull me out of my thoughts. "Hey, you should come by school tomorrow. We're having a big assembly to welcome back Mr. Mains, and it would be neat if you could be there. You could even speak. I think people would like that."

"No one would like that."

Haley insisted, "I keep telling you, things are different at school ever since Mrs. Slater got fired for barring the doors on us the afternoon of the planned walk-out. Have I thanked you for warning us not to do it?"

"Like a million times," I said.

"Well, I'll thank you a million times more, because none of us did it. The press had been tipped off and were all there to see her barring the doors, which was against the fire codes. She was fired right then and there."

"I know, Haley," I said.

"And Nick and Regina got suspended for helping her."

"You've told me all of this."

"Regina is so pissed off," Haley said. "You know she stopped her college classes to come back just so she could be prom queen, and now she's ineligible. It's hilarious!"

"I'm laughing so hard inside my head right now."

"And Nick got pulled off the yearbook and isn't allowed to do his column anymore on the school's blog. So, see? If you come tomorrow, they can't do anything to you."

"It's not about them," I told her. "I'm just not interested. I'm glad for Mr. Mains and stuff, but I don't care anymore."

Haley made a pouty face. "I told everyone I'd convince you."

"Well, you can tell them I've made some other plans."

"Like what? Working at the pet store?"

Now it was my turn to be giddy, and giddy is not a word anyone ever used to describe me. "I'm going on a trip."

"No! Seriously? Your parents agreed to it? His parents agreed? Tell me no adults are going with you."

I shook my head and smiled proudly. "Just Carter and me."

"I can't believe it."

"He said you'd say that."

"His parents offered to pay for plane tickets to San Francisco, but neither of us is old enough to rent a car when we get there so we're driving the whole way."

"Are you going to be staying in the same hotel rooms?"

I had to hush her. "His parents gave him a credit card and reserved suite rooms at a couple hotels between here and Santa Cruz. They made us promise to sleep on opposite sides of the doors."

"Well? Are you?"

I giggled. Me. Yeah. I giggled. "I doubt it."

Haley lost her mind then with a thousand more questions and pieces of her own sage advice. After I got her to hush up already before my parents heard any of this and cancelled the whole thing, she said. "So, I guess this means Mr. and Mrs. Crowe are cool with you now."

I bit my lip and shrugged one shoulder. "I did save his life, so... there's that."

"But, I mean, the lawsuit your mom is doing against his dad's employer. That's still happening, right?"

"Oh, yeah," I said, my joking manner gone. "It's on. Mr. Crowe dropped any charges against my parents for Carter's disappearance after Carter insisted multiple times that it wasn't our fault. As for the other suit, Oceanside Construction is trying to settle. It might work because Mr. Crowe said he will personally oversee the construction sites and make sure the pollution is kept to a minimum."

"That's good, I guess." She cocked her head. "Will your mom be okay with that? She doesn't seem like a person to settle."

"She'll fight for more I'm sure," I agreed. "There is still poison in the water killing the orcas and the fish that they eat. She's going to want the company to make some kind of recompense for that."

She rolled her hand for me to continue, but she was yawning. This

230

wasn't nearly as interesting as the prospect of Carter and me sharing a bed.

"I came up with an idea to help. Thought of it at work, actually. I was going through the catalogs for ordering fish one morning when I was bored and came across a company that has a hatchery for salmon."

"People have salmon for pets?"

"Some people like to buy fresh salmon to keep in their own ponds for food," I said. "They get it from this company. Well, I mentioned it to my parents that maybe we could work with this company to increase the amount of healthy, non-toxic salmon for the orcas of Puget Sound and the San Juan Strait, funding it with money from Oceanside Construction. Dad looked into it and said it was a viable plan. And would you believe this?"

"What?" Bigger yawn.

"Mom let *me* present it at a meeting between her and the board of Oceanside Construction. She didn't interrupt me once."

"Wait! You did a presentation? When?"

"Last week."

"Did you use a PowerPoint or anything? I could have helped with that."

"I can make a PowerPoint," I said. "I'm not that lame on computers."

"Yes, you are."

"I think you're missing the point here, Haley."

"I'm not! I swear I'm not." She put a hand up against the screen, and I copied her. "Your mom respects you now, and I say it's about freaking time."

Almost on cue, I heard my mother shouting my name from the hallway. "Close that window and go to bed! It's freezing outside, and I can feel the draft out here! You want to be sick for the whole trip?"

We both laughed.

"Yep. Loads of respect," I said. Haley rolled her eyes.

"But no, seriously, what are you going to pack? What are you going to sleep in?"

The questions continued a little while longer until I told her I really did need to go to bed. Carter was picking me up early in the morning.

* * * *

Six days later I stood next to Carter, my hands pressed against the cool glass of a giant aquarium, with a mermaid waving at me from the other side. A troop of Girl Scouts tittered away, pointing and waving, their troop leaders snapping pictures that wouldn't show up later because they forgot to turn off their flashes. I marveled at the mermaid's tail and how agile it was despite being made of silicone. The girl could really move in it, although I wished she wouldn't bend her knees so much. Real mermaids didn't have knees. Her shell top was ornate but modest because she worked in front of children. Her long, blonde hair flowed beautifully around her, and she seemed to know exactly how to turn her head to get her hair up and spiraling perfectly. She could also go a really long time without breathing. It was impressive.

Carter snapped a picture of me with her in the background. He did not use a flash. I grabbed my phone back from him and looked at the picture as we walked away, his arm around my shoulder. I didn't delete it, even though I hated how I looked, and instead zipped it off to Haley who would get a big kick out of it.

We were way overdressed for the Monterey Aquarium. I wore a dress and pumps. My hair was clipped back behind my ears, and I wore makeup for only the second time of the whole trip. The first time was when we met with the Dean of Marine Biology at U. C. Santa Cruz three days earlier. Deepak had helped set it up for us, and it went pretty well. We got lots of helpful information to think about. Carter wore a nice white shirt with a blue tie, slacks, and shiny shoes. His curly hair had been trimmed a bit before the trip, and he had it as tamed as he could get it.

"You ready to tell her?" Carter asked.

I grimaced. "I would really-really love not to." I handed him back his phone. "How about your parents first?"

"Nah, they're pushovers," he said, pocketing his phone. "We've got to do the hard stuff first."

"Let's go see one more exhibit. The otters—"

"We just saw a *real-life* mermaid," Carter told me. He threw up his arms dramatically. "There is nothing else here worth seeing after that."

"*Real* mermaid." I looked down my nose at him, and he laughed.

"The world will never know, will they?"

"Not if I can help it."

I took a deep breath and let it out. Taking Carter's hand, I led him over to a bench away from all the tourist noise. I called my mom's cell.

"Hold on," she said, her face popping up on the screen. "Let me get your dad." The world disappeared, and all I saw were the blue and white pinstripes of her suit pants. Several seconds later, half of each of their faces appeared on the screen. Mom beamed. "Haley taught us how to balance the phone on a picture display frame."

"Nice. You look good."

"You look great!" Dad said. "Something special happening today?"

I hesitated and looked at Carter. He tapped the top of the phone for me to go on, no support at all. That's not true exactly. He had his other hand pressed against the small of my back, like a man leading a woman through a ballroom dance.

"Remember how I said we were going to stop at the Monterey Aquarium. Well, we're here and—"

"Oh, I love that place," Dad said. "Did you say hi to Ralph Henderson like I told you?

"We did, actually," I said. "We had a… meeting with him."

"A meeting?" That was mom. "About what?"

I said it slowly. "Jobs."

Mom repeated the word just as slowly, as if trying to make sense of it. "Jobs?"

"Yeah." I tread cautiously. "Remember how we told you the other night that we had to live in California a year to establish residency and reduce the tuition at Santa Cruz? You know, because the scholarship won't cover everything."

"Yes." That was not a pleasant sounding yes. It was a warning that a rant was coming.

"I'm trying to save you money."

No response.

"Carter and I talked to Mr. Henderson today, and based on our experience and the copies of the letters of reference we brought for the college, he offered us jobs here at the aquarium."

233

My parents remained silent. The fuse burned.

"It's great see," I told them. "We'll stay here for a year, with jobs, and work on finding some more scholarships in the meantime."

"What kind of jobs?" Mom asked smoothly. "What are you doing?"

Carter popped his head in front of me. "I'm going to be working as an assistant with rehabilitation."

"That's great," Dad said, not as much enthusiasm as he would normally show, but I could see it in his eyes. "And you, June?"

"Oh, well, I'm going to start out by leading tours and stuff," I said. "They said I might work into handling the animals in a few months."

Mom must've pushed Dad aside, because only her face was on the screen now. "I thought after everything that happened you would reconsider coming to work with me. Plus, I'm doing an appeal to get you re-accepted to school here. I'm positive it'll happen. Maybe not by fall, but definitely by spring. I assumed when you were told how expensive it would be to go to school down there, you'd change your mind about the whole thing."

I looked at Carter, ran a finger down his cheek, and touched his lips before winking and walking away from him. To my mom I said, "This is what I want. It's what I've always wanted. You know this."

"I know, but…"

"Mom, do you trust me?"

"I do, but…"

Dad stuck his face in. "Where are you going to live?"

"Deepak has some friends up here that have a house, and there's room for both of us—"

"A co-op? Seriously?" Mom said, disgusted.

Dad smacked her forehead playfully. "What? Like we didn't live in one once upon a time?"

"It was awful," she said. "No privacy at all."

Dad raised an eyebrow at her. "And that's a *good* thing."

I laughed at them, and they started laughing, too. Seeing me happy, Carter came over and put his chin on my shoulder.

"We'll be home in a week or so to start packing," I told her.

"A week? Why so long?"

I felt heat rise to my face. "Uh, well, see, I heard there is a Chumash legend involving an island near here. It's about how the Earth Mother Hutash created a rainbow bridge so her people could cross to the mainland. The people were told to look straight ahead and they would be safe, but some were afraid. They looked down and then they fell. Hutash didn't want them to drown, so she turned them into dolphins."

Dad was nodding, the little file keeper in his head putting his hands on the right folder. "I've heard of that one."

"We were thinking about going to see the island and poke around a bit before we come home."

"Oh, June," Mom whined.

Carter piped up. "Dolphins aren't as scary as killer whales."

I smacked him for them.

After I got off the phone, I hugged him instead. He kissed me on the forehead and said, "I love you, you know."

It wasn't the first time he'd said it since our big adventure up north, but every time felt new and real and wonderful.

"I know. I love you too."

Then he nodded back at the mermaid still in the big aquarium. "So, how can we get you her job? I'd love to see you in that costume."

"I only swim in my dreams," I told him.

"We'll see about that."

We walked out of the aquarium arm in arm, ready for our new lives to begin.

Acknowledgements

I hope you enjoyed this adventure with Juniper. I had a great time writing it. I felt so fortunate that each time I found a hole in my plot I discovered another wonderful piece of American Indian mythology to fill it and make the story better. Honest to goodness, it was pure luck. Even in the final edit, I stumbled upon one more bit of lore that fixed a scene that was troubling me. As with the previous books, I used authentic legends and massaged them to work with my story. There are many different tribal nations, and the mythology is different from region to region. I focused on legends from the Pacific Northwest, and I even pulled the 'Thunderbird and Killer Whale' story specifically from the Makah people.

There is a Makah reservation at the northwestern point of the continuous United States. I am grateful that they maintain a thorough website with photos and tourist information. I am also in debt to the dozens of bloggers who posted pictures and anecdotes about their vacations to Cape Flannery, the Fuca Pillar, and the Strait de San Juan so that I could get a better idea in my head of what those places look like. I dream someday of visiting that area in person and have started saving my nickels.

As always, I'm thankful to my publishers Nancy Schumacher and Caroline Andrus at Fire and Ice Young Adult Books. Their support and flexibility with my ideas is wonderful, and I love the team feeling we've established amongst all the Melange Books/Satin Romance/F&I authors. Caroline created a new look for the Juniper Sawfeather books that is simply magical. I also want to thank Larriane Wills for editing *Echo of the Cliffs*.

I've made so many author friends over the past few years since *Cry of the Sea* came out. I particularly want to acknowledge three groups I'm part of: The Fellowship of Fantasy, Clean Indie Reads, and SCBWI Midsouth. A special shout out to Rebecca Flansburg and the Multicultural Children's Book Day event and group for championing my books. I've been an author sponsor with them for two years, and they have been amazing to work with. There are also so many wonderful reviewers and bloggers that have helped me feel confident about finishing this book and completing the series.

In my personal life, I want to share a special thank you to Jeni Richard, Maria Olowoyo, and my stepdaughter McKenna Driver, who seem to love Juniper and Carter as much as I do and remind me that people do care what happens to them and are eager for their story to continue. Also, thank you to my family for understanding my need to dedicate so many weekends and evenings to this writing career.

Juniper Sawfeather has fought against oil spills, logging of Old Growth trees, and now construction run-off pollution – all real and troublesome environmental issues. If you are motivated by her to get involved in helping protect our environment, I've listed some great organizations you can support below. On your own, I urge you to be aware of your environmental footprint. Please recycle and reuse. Throw your trash in garbage cans when visiting the ocean or forest or any natural area. Leave nature as you found it.

This is my third and final planned book for the Juniper Sawfeather Novels. But don't be sad, I have written a prequel called "Beneath the Wildflowers" (available for free), and I'm working on a Christmas story involving these characters for a holiday-themed anthology. If you visit my website or follow me on social media, you can keep up with those stories and my other projects. And who knows? Maybe if this series ever catches a good tail wind, I just might continue with June's adventures. If you'd like to see that happen, you can help by spreading the word about these books to your friends. Thank you for reading.

Resources for young environmentalists:

http://oceana.org/ is a group that I follow on Twitter that does great work for ocean conservation.

http://www.oceanconservancy.org/ is another group I follow that is fighting ocean pollution.

https://www.arborday.org/ is a foundation dedicated to planting trees and reseeding.

http://www.oldgrowthforest.net/books a group dedicated to protecting Old Growth trees with opportunities for volunteering and fundraising.

Adopt a dolphin at
http://www.oceanconservation.org/involved/adopt.htm

Help killer whales at http://www.orcaconservancy.org/

Because you're mermaid fans:
www.savethemermaids.org is a program that does hands-on work fighting ocean pollution. These lovely ladies go to schools as mermaids to educate children, they do fundraisers, and they organize beach clean-up days.

www.mermaidsforchange.com
 This group, as well as www.projectmermaids.com, organize mermaid photo shoots. It's not cheap, but you can arrange to have gorgeous pictures of yourself as a mermaid, and proceeds from the photoshoot go to helping with ocean preservation.

About the Author

D. G. Driver sold her first story in 1995 and has been writing ever since. *Echo of the Cliffs* is Driver's fourth book with Fire and Ice. Her other books are *Cry of the Sea, Whisper of the Woods,* and *Passing Notes*. In addition, she has a short story in *Kick Ass Girls of Fire and Ice YA Books*, and in the Satin Romance anthology *Second Chance for Love*. She is a member of SCBWI Midsouth and lives in Nashville with her family. Please follow her on Twitter, Instagram or Facebook. And if you really want to help make her writing career blossom, please consider leaving a review on Amazon or Goodreads.

Author Contacts
www.dgdriver.com
blog: www.dgdriver.com/write-and-rewrite-blog
www.facebook.com/donnagdriver
www.twitter.com/DGDriverAuthor
www.instagram.com/d_g_driver#
www.goodreads.com/author/show/7867013.D_G_Driver
www.d-g-driver.tumblr.com
www.wattpad.com/user/DGDriver
www.pinterest.com/dgdriver

www.ingramcontent.com/pod-product-compliance
Lightning Source LLC
Chambersburg PA
CBHW050513260626
47157CB00004B/1304